Tales On The Yellow Brick Road 2023

YBR Publishing, LLC

YBR PUBLISHING, LLC
Ridgeland, South Carolina

Jack Gannon – Co-Founder, Production Manager
Cyndi Williams-Barnier – Co-Founder, Production Editor
Bill Barnier – Senior Editor, Manager
Loreen Ridge-Husum – Art Director

ISBN-13: 979-8-9852082-6-9

"Short stories are tiny windows into other worlds and other minds and other dreams."

~Neil Gaiman

TABLE OF CONTENTS

REVIEWS

By Liz Konkel for Readers' Favorite, LLC
5-Star Award

Tales on the Yellow Brick Road 2023 is a collection of stories and poems that pays tribute to L. Frank Baum and his famous work, The Wizard of Oz. This collection features works from authors who love this world and have expanded it with stories such as Ron Baxley Jr.'s A Juicy Rags to Rich-Oz Story, James W. Krych's The Flight to Oz, and Scott Blanke's The Oz Almost Coven. These stories are wonderfully paired with poems from the likes of Jack Gannon, JC Sulzenko, and Frank W. Howard Jr. that are humorous, charming, and lighthearted. The collection features excerpts and short stories with the same quirky and delightful tone of the Oz-centric stories from authors such as Cyndi Williams-Barnier, John T. Wayne, and Jennifer Burns.

The heart of the collection stems from a genuine love for the tradition created by Baum and carried on by authors such as Ron Baxley Jr. who is a notable Oz universe author, and Frank Blanke who had a connection to the saga from childhood. A Juicy Rags to Rich-Oz Story from Baxley explores several elements from the original series, expanding the world. The story is written using the same style as Baum with delightful phrases. Poems are featured throughout such as a Christmas tale about a white-haloed fur angel and Ode to Birdbath, which is a humorous and creative observation of a birdbath. Both are feel-good poems that have uplifting tones and feature curious subjects. The poems fit the style and ethos presented in the short stories and excerpts perfectly.

Other stories in the collection include Xcalibur and the Knowledragon, which features delightful writing such as a bespectacled and shabby-chic-attired teacher. The Gardener revolves around a special garden and the important relationship associated with it, and Mother's Coffin focuses on the idea of accepting impending death through the story of a mother picking out her coffin and making arrangements for her funeral. Each one is different and there will be something in the collection for everyone. Tales on the Yellow Brick Road 2023 is a collection for those that love The Wizard of Oz and those that enjoy whacky, humorous, and lighthearted stories, poems, and excerpts.

By Helen Huini for Readers' Favorite, LLC
4-Star Award

Tales on the Yellow Brick Road 2023 by YBR Publishing is an anthology of stories and poems. Each story has a different cast, with characters from different backgrounds and orientations. For example, in A Juicy Rags to "Rich-Oz" Story, Margerie and Buttery escaped being held hostage by Mrs. Yoop, who had enslaved them. Princess Ozma uses magic in this narrative to prevent Mrs. Yoop from enslaving anyone again. In The Gardener, Israel's scientists have recreated the Garden of Eden on the moon, working on producing safe food for human consumption. The Ode to Birdbath is a poem (by Jack Gannon that) details how his cat and dog were his only companions while he was sick.

Tales on the Yellow Brick Road 2023 by YBR Publishing features genres set in different settings, some fictional and others existing in the real world. This gave me a clear perspective of the time and space in which the events occurred. The characters have different traits and abilities, which suit their roles in the various stories where they feature. For example, through Princess Ozma, Ron Baxley, Jr. showed how magic could be used to do good and stop people like Mrs. Yoop, who wanted to manipulate others using their magic. I also appreciated the inclusion of images in The Flight to Oz, which complemented the vivid descriptions of the Sirenae Iustinianae Milites and enabled me to grasp its powerful abilities. I recommend this book to readers who enjoy short fiction genres that spark their imaginations.

PREFACE

By Jack Gannon
Co-Founder, YBR Publishing LLC

A long time ago in a high school not far from where I now live, my co-author and high school best friend, Cyndi Williams-Barnier, and I attended classes together and talked about writing a book as a team and becoming rich and famous. Well, that didn't end up happening until 2011 (writing-wise, and not rich or famous!) when we reunited after 32 years living in the same town yet never seeing each other! We began writing our first novel after both our retirements began. That book became the 5-star award-winning novel "2s And 3s".

Before we reunited in 2011, however, we were both writing short stories and poems for ourselves just to practice our writing skills. After our first two books were published, we talked about those stories we wrote during the decades between and decided to publish them as an anthology to establish them as copyrighted material. That book was called "Tales On The Yellow Brick Road", published nearly two years before we founded YBR (Yellow Brick Road) Publishing in 2016.

In the seven years since establishing YBR, we have published authors from the South Carolina Lowcountry and beyond, with twenty-two 5-star awards for the novels, poetry, children's books, and graphic novels we've produced for them; this book is now our twenty-third 5-star award winner!

But knowing there are still more writers out there not knowing how to get their short stories and poems published, I suggested dusting off the original "TALES" and opening it for both our established YBR authors and those not. The result is the book in your hands now, "TALES ON THE YELLOW BRICK ROAD 2023". Each author is introduced before his/her stories/poems. We hope you enjoy this exploration of the terrific literary talent within these pages…

ACKNOWLEDGEMENTS

We thank all the authors who submitted their works for this year's "TALES ON THE YELLOW BRICK ROAD" anthology. It is our greatest honor to bring their new works to print for all their collective readers and introduce them to their new fellow authors. May your own journeys continue brightly on the Yellow Brick Road!

Ron Baxley, Jr.

Photo: Jerry Morris

Ron Baxley, Jr., of Barnwell, South Carolina, is a prolific award-winning fantasy and "Oz universe" author and has been published for 31 years. An experienced former educator, Ron, who is a current caregiver for a relative, also works as a freelancer for multiple newspapers in S.C. and Georgia. Additionally, he also works as a travel specialist and as a full-time author. Also, for 13 years, he has been invited as an author to and has attended Oz festivals throughout the country, as well as a guest author at various conventions. During much of that time, Ron's Pembroke Welsh Corgi, Ziggy, was able to travel with him to events. In fact, Ziggy, who was adopted from a shelter at one year old, will be 11 this December and serves as Ron's emotional support dog. Also, in whole or in part, the zig-zagging Ziggy has inspired many of Ron's books. By the way, Ron, who has strong faith in God, does his best to be BOTH a good man and a good wizard. He is, of course, not a bad witch; if he were, he *would be* caught dead in the rain!

Ron has published many Oz novels dating back to the First Edition of "The Talking City of Oz" in 1999. He joined YBR Publishing as an author in 2017 and saw his Oz-themed novel, "O.Z. Diggs Himself Out", published in March 2018, which became the first of his interconnected Oz-universe books exclusive to YBR. His books with YBR in chronological order are: the children's book "Goldey Goosey of Oz"; the graphic novel "Ziggy Zig-Zags the Light and Dark Fantastic"; and the novels "O.Z. Diggs Himself Out" and "O.Z. Doesn't Diggs G.C.C. at Emerald City". The sequel graphic novel "Ziggy Zig-Zags the Light: The Ice Queen Hateth" is projected for 2024, and the next "O.Z. Diggs VII" novel for 2024.

His autographed YBR Oz-universe books are available on the YBR Publishing website store page.

A JUICY RAGS TO "RICH-OZ" STORY

(This story chronologically takes place after all the original L. Frank Baum Oz books and before "GOLDEY GOOSEY OF OZ", by Ron Baxley, Jr.)

A Munchkin lady's soiled blue clothing was in tatters, as was her small daughter's. They rushed into the Emerald City past the Guardian at the Gate and just by the glistening, glittering palace and several modest homes. The bells on these Munchkins' hats had been cut off, not even leaving the strings, and the Munchkin mother and daughter were both gasping for air from rushing. The Munchkin mother was named Margerie, and her daughter was Buttery. Their faces were filthy, and Buttery carried a life-sized doll made of rags. The doll had a face sewn into a permanent smile from a flat washrag; a torso, arms, and legs made from rolled rags; and a spine made from a measuring stick. Also, the rags of the doll looked as if they had been dragged in and rolled in the dirt.

Buttery simply called what she always thought was a male doll, "Rags". Where she and her mother had been living away from the Munchkin Country, it had been her only friend besides her mother. Rags, the doll, had been made by her mother from gigantic rags to be the size of a Munchkin child. Not only were the rags gigantic to the Munchkins but would be enormous to those of average size. The rags came from a place where that was the norm.

Inside the Emerald City, Margerie, smelling the sickly-sweet smell of her own sweat and that of her daughter's, pulled Buttery close to the Forbidden Fountain.

Margerie knew better than to drink from the Forbidden Fountain but also thought if she were careful, they could wash their face and arms in it. But what to do about that dirty rag doll?

Holding Buttery's hand and leading her along, Margerie walked to and knocked at a servant's entrance of the palace in the Emerald City; Jellia Jamb answered the door. Margerie quickly greeted Jellia and asked for some washing powder for the doll, some soap, and separate washrags, and mentioned wanting to wash her hands and face in the fountain. Jellia took pity on the mother and the young daughter. But she still did not want to steer them wrong.

Jellia said, adjusting her maid's uniform, "Oh, you better not use that water. I know drinking it causes memory loss. Bathing in it may not be good, either. I see no harm in washing something in it, though. Maybe use a stick to pull it out."

Margerie pulled a stick off a nearby tree from the courtyard where multi-colored flowers were planted in rows. She noticed just a few emeralds had been plucked from one of the buildings seven feet up from the ground but did not think much of it. It did not look like a Nome plundering.

Jellia Jamb said, before going back into the palace, "Are you both okay? You look disheveled."

Margerie nodded, replying, "I may need to explain everything to Princess Ozma eventually."

Buttery interrupted, "Like about the green monkey—"

Margerie shot her a "not-now" look and said, "For right now, I just want to get my daughter and me cleaned up."

"I don't usually like bath day," said Buttery suddenly, whose hair was the color of very yellow butter, "But I will make an exception this time! Rags will, too!"

"Please stop interrupting Mommy," said Margerie referring to herself in the third person, and Buttery said, "Yes, ma'am," while looking at her feet. Her mother hugged her, showing she did not mean to be so cross with her. It had been a long day and week and then some.

Jellia Jamb, feeling sorry for the pair, said she would find something for the mother and daughter to wash with as well as some washing powder for Rags. She said, "I am sure Princess Ozma will have an audience with you as you look like you're in such peril, but I just wanted to let you know Her Majesty is meeting with Muziker, the Crooked Magician Dr. Pipt, his wife Margolotte, Scarecrow, Tin Woodman, Cowardly Lion, O.Z.

Diggs, and Glinda about a matter of great importance. It seems that Scraps, the Patchwork Girl, has been missing for several days!" (Dorothy was helping assist her elderly Aunt Em and Uncle Henry who she had moved from Kansas in the Out World years ago to come live in the Emerald City; though they had not aged, they were seniors when they came to Oz and needed a good bit of assistance.)

Margerie opened her mouth as if to say something but then decided to wait so that she could tell Princess Ozma and the others. She said, "I will wait if I have to, and I definitely need to get washed up and get us all presentable before we go in."

Jellia nodded and said, "I understand. I will hurry and get you what you need."

While Jellia was procuring the items they needed, Margerie took a long piece of blue string out of her pocket. On it was a hook that she used to keep up with the string itself. She removed the hook from her pants pocket.

She tied the string with the hook to the stick. The string was a long-ago remnant from an under-armor uniform a Munchkin ancestor of hers had worn in service to King Pastoria and was the last remnant of it. The string was just the length of a short pair of uniform pants. Indeed, the uniform it came from was one of the smallest in King Pastoria's army of knights, and Margerie's ancestor was the smallest, shortest Munchkin ever on record. And she knew that was saying something!

Jellia, being careful not to spill any water on her black dress, came back with two large basins of water with pitchers already in them, soap, new rags, and towels balanced on a huge tray with handles. There was a metal canister off to the side that held what appeared to be washing powder. She never dropped everything, even with it being stacked up so high.

Margerie helped her unload everything, and she and her daughter set to quickly taking cat baths using all they had been brought, making the basins of water eventually appear brown and muddy. She knew they could not wash the doll, Rags, in those basins. Even if they were empty and had fresh water in them, they would not be big enough. She hated to ask if Jellia had one of those wash-bucket contraptions with a ringer. Anyway, she had planned to use the fountain regardless.

Margerie said, "We just need to wash Rags, my daughter's rag friend, and then we will join you. Thank you."

"You are welcome," Jellia said, gathering everything they had used save for the so-called tin of washing powder. She then turned on one black heel and went back in the servant door, shutting it behind her. Margerie took her daughter by the hand back to the Forbidden Fountain along with the stick, string, and hook, the metallic cylinder of washing powder, and Rags the male ragdoll.

From the throne room window, near the throne, there was a distant view of the Forbidden Fountain and the visitors, but they had not been seen from this vantage point yet. Jellia Jamb had not wished to interrupt and draw attention to the Munchkin woman and her little daughter. In addition, the assembled party in the Throne Room had been looking at the Magic Picture in a place to which it had been moved so that the gathered party could try to locate Scraps with it. However, the Magic Picture suddenly showed them Margerie and her daughter approaching the Forbidden Fountain with Rags and the metallic container she thought contained washing powder. Imagine Princess Ozma and her party's surprise when they rushed to and then glanced out the window to see Margerie washing Rags in the Forbidden Fountain with the last bit of what she did not know was Powder of Life. Jellia Jamb had just absent-mindedly grabbed it from a shelf, thinking it was a washing powder tin, and had unknowingly given it to the visitors earlier. The glint and appearance of the metallic cylinder Margerie held in the distance was a dead—or in this case, alive—give-away.

Margerie had Rags on the end of the blue string affixed on a hook on a stick and had submerged him in the waters of the Forbidden Fountain with the powder.

She started to read the words on the metal container as she stirred the rags of the bound-together rag-doll Rags with her stick, and the blue string became entwined with the rags as she did so.

Margerie yelled, as the instructions dictated, "Weaugh! Teaugh! Strange words to be on a container of washing powder. And such strange body movements to do, too." She had followed the instructions, but she had not read the last word and followed the rest of the instructions to complete the spell yet.

Princess Ozma and the others at the palace window could hear the magic words very faintly after their attention had been called to Margerie and Buttery approaching the Forbidden Fountain with the Powder of Life. Their attention had been called to the Munchkin visitor washing Rags, with what was now a Powder of Life slurry, in the famed fountain.

"No! Wait! If you bring something to life in there, it won't have a memory!" screamed Princess Ozma through the open palace window, her white silk shirt billowing in the wind, but could not be heard by Margerie. Princess Ozma once had direct experience, when she was magically converted into the boy Tip, with bringing non-meat creatures to life with the powder. Also, she had once taken away the memory of the former Nome King Ruggedo with the waters of the Forbidden Fountain. Now, she, with the vigor of an older youth, had stuck her head so far out of the window that her crown with its dried poppies on the side had almost fallen out as she grasped the windowsill to warn the Munchkin woman and her daughter. She was almost certain bringing something to life in that memory-erasing water would take away the new creation's memory.

Just behind Princess Ozma, Glinda also yelled, adjusting her tall, red hat, "And even our magic may not be able to bring its memory back!" She and the others, if they turned back from the window, could see everything in the Magic Picture in real time and magnified. Dr. Pipt, the powder's inventor, hunched his way through the two royals and yelled out, "Don't play hard and fast with Power of Life… it can have repercussions!" Princess Ozma, sensing the urgency, magicked everybody with her silver wand down to where Margerie was.

Right after Muziker was magically teleported by Princess Ozma with the others, he "oompa-pa-paed" to himself with all sorts of thoughts of note in his head. One such thought was that the Crooked Magician Dr. Pipt had just said he wished he had a jar of his poesy potion he used for Scraps because that might "jar" the ragman's memories. The matronly Margolotte said that they had not brought any of Dr. Pipt's potions he was no longer using (she was careful to say that in front of Princess Ozma because of the ban on magic). However, Musiker could be more brazen – right down to his brass instruments (perhaps more brass-en).

Musiker pulled out a "Musi-Cali-tea" potion from his pocket. He had Ozma, who could make and approve magic, make it from some sweet orange juice Jeb went back to recover from California and some tea from Oz, and some other magical ingredients. Musiker himself had been having problems with memory, and Princess Ozma approved of making it for him. It gave one more musical memory. It enhanced memories of music heard in the past and other memories tied to those musical memories. He had hoped that it might help trigger some memory of where Scraps was last but decided to use it quickly here.

"I oompa-pa heard pa-pa that oompa-pa-pa," Musiker said as his musical instrument innards carried on, "music oompa-pa brings back memories!"

Just right before Margerie could not stop herself from saying the last word, "Peaugh!", Musiker poured some of the Musi-Cali-tea into the Forbidden Fountain with Rags, the male ragdoll, the blue string of Margerie's ancestor that was entwined with the rags of the ragdoll at this point, and the Powder of Life slurry in the fountain.

Margerie then fished the slightly orange-stained but still clean and alive Rags out of the fountain.

She pulled the hook off quickly and Rags unexpectedly said, "So nice of you to help a knight of the realm. Sir Michaelo Rags, at your service."

And Margerie screamed while Buttery laughed. Margerie said, "Sir Michaelo was my ancestor." She thought for a minute. "I put in the string from my ancestor, and it must have become part of the creature's memory!... Say…where did all of you come from?" She was distracted by present events and had not seen the others from the Palace, including visitors, appear magically beside her. She had been so focused on her stirring that she had not seen the Musiker add the potion.

Musiker did his "oompas" again and explained that the potion he added helped with the memory as well.

"Well, thank goodness the creature's mind was not wiped out. I still see he kept the rags part of his old name, though," Princess Ozma said, leaning forward on her O-and-Z staff and peering at the creature with her large, innocent eyes.

Adjusting her tall red crown which indicated her Quadling Country sovereignty, Glinda said, "It's a good thing that string the Munchkin mother mentioned was placed in as was the potion. Again, I do not even think our magic could have restored an almost non-existent memory in a Powder of Life non-meat creature."

Sir Michaelo Rags suddenly bowed, his rag body looking even more saggy, and said,

> *As a knight of the realm,*
> *I have served the crown,*
> *and everyone within it.*
> *I hope you all know,*
> *as knowing you will grow.*
> *That I will be there for you*
> *Nearly every minute."*

Sir Michaelo Rags thought for a minute and asked, "Now who am I again?" The members of the party present wrinkled and contorted their faces with fear. They had hoped the fountain would not do this, especially with the extra ingredients. Sir Michaelo thought hard for a minute, wringing out his wash-rag brain. Some of the soaked-in Musi-Cali-tea potion was in there. The blue uniform string was in the very fiber of his being now too, and it helped as well. Through his inner-inner ears, the concert hall of his mind, he heard the triumphant trumpets of the knights' procession. This triggered his memory.

"I hear the military trumpets in my mind as if they are right here…I know just who I am…Sir Michaelo Rags…at your service," he repeated as before. It was a good thing his memory was aided by the Musi-Cali-tea potion. The uniform string helped him remember being a knight, too.

Scarecrow, who had been transported with the others, said as he pointed to his stuffed head, "If only I had thought sooner to throw one of the needles from my mind in. That would have made him extra sharp."

O.Z. Diggs, the Wizard, had once put needles and bran in there to make him "very sharp" and give him a "brand" new brain. O.Z. Diggs, who was in the present company, said, "That was right on point." (On a later adventure, Scarecrow even had some cash stuffed mostly into his torso, and it ended up partially in his head. However, Ozians seldom had money on their minds.)

"Yes, but he is feeling that music in his heart, and that is bringing back his memory," Nick Chopper, the Tin Woodman added, pointing to his own nickel-plated breast. His nickel plating had been later added in his adventures to prevent rusting. He thought and knew that Sir Michaelo Rags need not worry about rusting as he did not have any armor of any kind. The Tin Woodman wondered if they might need armor for the new knight but did not say anything at this point. He rather felt sorry for the saggy creature and his memory problem and was focusing on how he had recovered from that.

The Cowardly Lion next said, "He remembered his bravery as a soldier." He pantomimed being in a salute.

"And I may need his help as a soldier," Margerie added, "Mrs. Yoop, the green monkey who was once a giant or Yookoohoo we heard tell of, has kidnapped Scraps and even stole a few emeralds as well from what I could see recently. She is still back in her castle in the remote valley of the Yookoohoos in Gillikin Country."

Princess Ozma, thinking of the missing patchwork girl, said, "Well, that explains it."

Margerie said, "Years before kidnapping Scraps, she also kidnapped my daughter and me and made us do all her housework and other work for her. We were basically her slaves until I could not take it any longer and ran south with my daughter to the Emerald City to freedom. You may wonder why my husband did not search for me. My husband was destroyed by the Wicked Witch of the East before she was herself destroyed!"

Princess Ozma said, "I am so sorry for that great loss of long ago and for everything you have been through."

Princess Ozma thought back to when she transformed Mrs. Yoop, the giantess or Yookoohoo, into the green monkey and thought that would be enough to keep her at bay. Some felt sorry for her and were worried she would not be able to survive. However, Mrs. Yoop found ways to survive but at the expense of others.

Princess Ozma said, "I am so sorry you had to endure this, and we will do all we can to help you. You mentioned Mrs. Yoop stealing emeralds. Do you know what those are going to be used for?"

Margerie said, "No…all I know is that Mrs. Yoop is forcing Scraps to make up verses or poems about different kinds of animals from A to Z while she works at her table. Her back is always turned, and we can never see what she is working on. We think we hear an extra voice in there but never see anybody but Mrs. Yoop and Scraps."

"It's a tiny, scary voice," added Buttery and sort of hid near her mother's skirt.

While they had been talking, though having a walking stick for a back, his limbs were made of rolled washrags, so Sir Michaelo began to sag even worse.

"He needs something to hold him up more," O.Z. Diggs said, "And I have always had a knack for gifts. I remember in an old hallway of the palace there were suits of armor – one of them very, very small. I think it would be the perfect fit for Sir Michaelo Rags."

Princess Ozma said, "I remember seeing that, too, during my time in the palace."

"I was thinking earlier that a rust-proof suit of armor might be just the ticket for the gentleman, but we were so focused on his memory that I did not say anything," the Tin Woodman added. The rest nodded.

Suddenly, O.Z. Diggs used a staff to transport to the hall and back with the retrieved short armor.

The nipple areas of the small suit of armor's breastplate were studded with an aquamarine stone on the left for the Munchkin Country and, over the heart, an emerald to show loyalty to the Emerald City. In the middle was a ruby in the shape of a heart to show the love between the two areas. The armor itself was made of silver and even came with a silver sword and shield. It also had a visor that one could peep out of but not have one's face completely seen. Margerie could never prove it without lots of archival research, but with it being the smallest of all of the suits of armor, she felt sure this was her ancestor's original suit.

Glinda saw the red heart and said, "The red of Quadling Country…we are a country with great love!"

When they had placed the armor on Sir Rags, he seemed all the more eager to go on the quest and stood more erect, "I heard what each of you hath said about this damsel in distress. I shall venture forth to rescue her!"

Princess Ozma suddenly decided and decreed, "The Munchkin mother and her daughter will stay here in the Emerald City until we can find somebody in the Munchkin Country to take them in. Also, I felt as if I advised my friends incorrectly when it came to Mrs. Yoop. A good leader recognizes when she has made mistakes. I am going to transport Sir Rags with me and use his brave brawn and my magic to get Scraps back!"

Many had expected three of the famous four to go or those who had gone on previous quests to venture forth (Dorothy was busy). But Princess Ozma was adamant that she, herself, the Sovereign of Oz, would go.

"Glinda of the Quadling Country will rule in my absence," continued Princess Ozma, "And it will not take long. I am not some helpless little princess. I am an older young lady, and I take care of my mistakes!"

Just then, the party heard a bunch of boings, thumps, and some squeaky, springy noises.

"I didn't think Rags was that springy," said Scarecrow of the ragman, "But, no…it's not him making those noises. He's just standing still."

Bouncing into the courtyard after he had bounced over the head of the Guardian of the Gate with a pogo stick came Kaliko. He was a former steward of Ruggedo but now a long-time ruler of the Nome Kingdom. Also, he never really grew a beard either and that made him stand out. Kaliko had a skinnier body than the rest of the Nomes, and his pointy-shoed feet now rested in silver stirrups on the pogo-stick. Most of the party stood with their mouths agape at Kaliko on the pogo-stick.

Scarecrow said, "We know we have little reason to fear you, but what in Oz is that contraption?"

Kaliko said, "It is a magic pog-Oz stick. I have traveled on it from the Nome Country to here. It can even bound over the Deadly Desert and leap over mountaintops!"

The party admired its construction briefly, as more pressing matters were at hand. It had a coil or spring of soft gold, a cylinder of silver as well as the aforementioned strong, silver stirrups, and marble handlebars. "I used this briefly while answering to Ruggedo when I had to be his steward," said Kaliko, looking downward at the pog-Oz stick with his pointy nose pointed in its direction.

Kaliko bounced closer to Princess Ozma, but just in case something was amiss, despite the trust most did have for Kaliko in recent years, Cowardly Lion got closer to the princess as did Rags. The Tin Woodman and Scarecrow did as well. The others were still a little dumbfounded at the amazing, magic gadget. The ones who had gathered closer to the princess chuckled a bit despite themselves when they heard the boings and springy noises from the pog-Oz stick as Kaliko got closer. Most supposed it could be a weapon of sorts as one could bounce on another individual with it because it could magically go higher than any pogo stick. But if a weapon, it was a very silly weapon, and most felt they could find ways to knock Kaliko out of the sky if they had to. The Cowardly Lion knew he could leap bravely and swipe him down, and the Tin Woodman knew he could hurl his ax at the Nome. Also, the Scarecrow affirmed he could throw himself to the ground and make the ground uneven with his lumpiness to cause the pog-Oz stick to turn over when it hit the earth with Kaliko. Even Rags, at this point, remembered he could raise his long sword high enough at its tip to reach the Nome on the pog-Oz stick. What mighty, imaginary conquest arises out of such trivial things. However, Kaliko had no bad intention for his pog-Oz stick. It was merely magical transportation.

Kaliko got off the pog-Oz stick where it had landed before Princess Ozma. He said, "Mrs. Yoop has found somebody secretly performing dark arts to finish her magic apron. As you know, Mrs. Yoop's magic apron can cause objects to move."

The party all stared at him intently while he spoke.

Scarecrow pondered with his hand on his stuffed head like The Thinker and predicted, "I bet she has used some sort of projectile or a land vehicle or made some sort of flying machine and is using the magic apron on it to make it move!"

Kaliko said, raising a skinny arm with a pointy right index finger toward Scarecrow, "Yes, all of the Nomes have heard for years how clever you are, Scarecrow. But can you guess what she is making move?"

Guesses were everything from a large wooden horse on a string (no, there would be no Trojan horse here) to a wooden bird to a version of Princess Ozma's red wagon. None of the guesses were correct. Kaliko picked up his pog-Oz stick and flapped it about a bit as if playing charades. The gold and silver of it glinted in the gathered party's eyes.

Cowardly Lion then said in a bolder voice than usual, "I bet I can guess. It's something that used to scare me before a transformation occurred… I used to have nightmares about the winged monkeys before they were free and no longer under the influence of the Wicked Witch of the West! They are winged monkey wings!"

"That is correct," said Kaliko, "Only, they are not natural, and she or somebody has fashioned a set of wooden wings with supplemental feathers for her like a small airplane or glider or both… some of them have flown close to my kingdom from the Out World."

Princess Ozma asked, "But why has she done this?"

Kaliko explained, "For quick escapes! She was stealing bunches of every kind of gem from my kingdom in a sack. My Nomes saw her, the green monkey in the apron, flying away on wooden wings she was commanding to move up and down. They said they thought they heard her trying to use a squeaky voice to disguise herself further, too."

Margerie said, "So now she has other gems other than the ones from the Emerald City. But we don't know what she is using them for."

"I aim to find out," said Princess Ozma, "And, King Kaliko, I will make sure the jewels are returned to your kingdom."

Kaliko, who was more generous than the previous Nome ruler said, "If you find them, you may have half of them as a reward for your trouble."

Princess Ozma said, "That is most generous of you. Thank you. I will have the other half magicked to you immediately. I am confident we will be able to retrieve them."

Kaliko did a slight bow that one royal would do to another, got back on his magic pog-Oz stick, and bounded away with a BOING, way above the distant gate, and a bit into Winkie Country. He would make excellent time bouncing over great distances with the magic contraption and would be well-settled back into the Nome Kingdom by the time Princess Ozma finished her quest.

"We must really get going," said Princess Ozma, "The situation with Scraps is urgent. I am not so worried about the emeralds or jewels. A person we love is in peril!"

On Sir Michaelo Rags and herself, Princess Ozma started to use her silver wand when Glinda stopped her. "No, wait," she said. "The Good Witch of the North, Locasta, sometimes does spells of protection by kissing the forehead. I can do one by kissing the heart," said Glinda.

She kissed the ruby heart on Sir Michaelo Rag's suit of armor, and it glowed a bright red. He glowed the red associated with love, even having a slight blush to his rags. The aquamarine stone of the Munchkin Country and the Emerald in the armor temporarily glowed as well and did not stop glowing until the ruby heart in the middle stopped. Sir Michaelo's face cloth blushed even further.

"It reminds me of when my foot went down a small drain in the Fountain just as I was created," said Sir Michaelo, thinking hard, "Only, this time, I feel flushed all over." He laughed a hearty, soggy laugh.

Buttery laughed and gave him a hug after that joke. Her mother hugged him goodbye as well. The others all gave their goodbyes, and Princess Ozma, using her silver wand, then whisked Sir Michaelo Rags and herself straight into the inner chamber of the castle of Mrs. Yoop, who had been the green monkey for quite some time and was still in that form.

They had a front vision of the green monkey sitting in a highchair in what had always been a giant-sized chair at a gigantic table. The walls behind her were jagged granite stone with sloppy mortar between them.

Scraps was chained to that stony wall behind Mrs. Yoop and was just saying as Princess Ozma and Sir Rags magically transported in, "Zebras are like striped horses, with patterns of black and white. They make all sorts of hee-haw noises which annoy some but cause delight."

They had not arrived a moment too soon because Scraps was on the z in the a-z listing of animals for which she was doing verses.

Just below the dress the green monkey, Mrs. Yoop, was wearing, and just below the magic apron, on her right knee was a horrible, contorted face with little arms and legs. Princess Ozma and her companion could see them from their vantage point. They could also see that the bells of Mrs. Yoop's former Munchkin slaves had been smashed with a hammer and littered the floor with their cut strings. The tinkling noise had annoyed Mrs. Yoop, and it was this, and other violent actions, which had made Margerie and Buttery flee. Without Margerie (and in smaller ways, Buttery) there to clean, the floor had become squalid, and the table was littered with vines from wild berries. What Princess Ozma and Sir Rags could not turn their attention away from, however, was Mrs. Yoop's right knee. Again, her right knee had an alive little face on it with arms!

Mrs. Yoop said without turning, "Let me introduce you, Princess Ozma, to my second cousin, never removed! There's a secret to the Yookoohoos you never knew. We starts off as small tumors on another giant and pops off and grows. Guess you never thought whys my husband and me never had a child."

"But I turned you into a green monkey—"

"So, you did", said Mrs. Yoop, "But this grew later…and it isn't part of the enchantment. And it's still a Yookoohoo! And it still has its abilities with magic!"

Sir Michaelo Rags said, "Why…I think I can still remember that part of me basically grew from rags, though I know that I am a knight errant as well."

The mini-Yookoohoo on the green monkey knee, a flesh-colored deformed face with little arms was using magic with a needle-sized wand to make a diamond into a diamond zebra with black stripes. The miniature wand was forming the diamond into a translucent non-talking mini-zebra. Bunches of other alphabet-letter-based animals made of jewels were in the chamber and were making a din of noises comparable to the Ark's inner chamber.

Mrs. Yoop picked up the bucking diamond zebra from her second cousin-never removed.

The Yookoohoo's knee, in this case, the cousin growth on her second knee, said, "Careful... it's very IN-delicate because it's diamond and alive! It will buck you!"

Mrs. Yoop said, grasping the zebra tightly, "I will... I will, cuz...Now back to you, Ozma...I needed Scraps, who is good with descriptions, to describe these creatures to me, creatures she had seen in her travels. We have apes. Baboons. Cockatoos! You get the picture! I needed the magic of my cousin to help bring them to life. Soon, hundreds of these unstoppable, jewel animals will attack the Emerald City!"

A cacophony of animal noises combined with the tinkling sound of moveable gems could be heard throughout the chamber. The dissonance reverberated along its stony walls.

Scraps said, bouncing a little with her stuffed patchwork body moving to and fro as best it could with her being bound, "You evil creature. In Emerald City, you'll never feature. You think that you will always win... when all you ever do is sin."

Mrs. Yoop opened her green monkey mouth widely and shouted, "Quiet, you! You've served your purpose!"

Scraps the rag doll, who did not always rhyme, said with her yarn hair flinging to and fro in explanation and her patchy face looking downcast and almost as saggy as Rags', "I am sorry, Princess Ozma, for the longest time I tried to resist her, but she kept asking for verses about the animals, and you know how much I like verses!"

Princess Ozma said, "I do understand."

Mrs. Yoop started muttering, via the power of the new magic apron her cousin made for her, for her wooden wings, wings she had lined with feather duster feathers, to fly during this discussion. She indeed looked like a green flying monkey coming toward Princess Ozma. She had used these, on command, to move from the newly formed magic apron and travel over great distances to steal her former Munchkin slaves and the jewels she wanted.

Sir Michaelo Rags looked at Mrs. Yoop flying toward Princess Ozma and him with the wooden wings, an occasional feather disengaging and fluttering down. He said, scratching his silver-armored head, "Now, what was I supposed to be doing again?" Sir Rags thought for a minute. Mrs. Yoop was almost upon Princess Ozma and him.

He squeezed his head-rag in thought and the deep-down potion did its work. That memory of a military march entered his head. The navy-blue uniform string in the very fiber of his being contorted to and fro in his head like a navy neuron and reminded him of his military past, too. The potion filled the synaptic gaps.

At that moment, just as Mrs. Yoop was upon him, Sir Michaelo Rags remembered who he was and swung his silver sword and had a direct hit with her faux wood wings. She hit the ground.

Mrs. Yoop said, "I have always…'knee-ded' you, cousin! Help!"

The cousin on Mrs. Yoop's knee said, "Let's see how you do with a little magic!"

One of her deformed little arms pointed her wand toward Sir Michaelo Rags. A beam of sickly green energy came from the wand but struck the red jewel heart of Sir Michaelo Rags' armor. The heart glowed red. The entire armor glowed from the love Glinda had bestowed upon it and the protective spell. The sickly green energy went back to the knee and blasted her.

"Grrrrr!!! Curses!" yelled the knee. Not only did the flesh-colored knee creature on the green monkey look pinkish, but it had a minor char now. A slight burning smell entered the air.

Sir Michaelo Rags thought for a moment, 'Now, what should I be doing? What does a knight do when there is a damsel in distress?' He thought and thought and that deep-down Musi-Cali-tea potion in his washrag-sculpted head did its work. His blue uniform thread contorted. He remembered some heroic music from long ago. Sir Michaelo jaunted over and freed Scraps, the Patchwork Girl, from her chains.

She hugged him, her patches moving to and fro, and said, "I am close friends with the Scarecrow, you know, for he and I are both alike. Yet I have found kinship with you, a cloth creature, too, who Ozma did send. And now I think of you as a good friend."

Sir Michaelo Rags, with his silvery armor, gave her quite a tight yet platonic hug but did not squeeze any stuffing out of Scraps.

Princess Ozma thought for a moment and said, "I think I should help with the birth of the new creature."

"What do you mean?" asked Mrs. Yoop. The earlier confidence in her voice was waning.

"And as you like to have Out World-style animals around you who cannot talk, perhaps I should make you the same so that you truly cannot collaborate with anything evil ever again," replied Princess Ozma, pushing her poppies on her crown back and rolling up her silk sleeves.

Princess Ozma shot a beam of white light from her silver wand to Mrs. Yoop's knee, and the second cousin never removed was now removed, a second cousin once removed, and started to grow incredibly. Princess Ozma then shrunk the giant down almost to green monkey size; only, it was a little larger than what she had made Mrs. Yoop years ago.

"You thought you were going to make an ape of me…and you are no innocent…you've just been hanging around quietly on a knee for many years and just look nascent. Well, now I am going to make an ape of you!"

And Princess Ozma turned the second cousin Yookoohoo once removed into a non-talking ape.

Mrs. Yoop screamed, "How dare you! I thought you were the type to leave us to our own devices."

"Try this device on for size," said Princess Ozma. She shot another beam of white light from her silver wand to Mrs. Yoop and took away her voice.

Mrs. Yoop screamed in a monkey rant toward the princess. Her cousin (who they eventually figured out was named

Noop) started screaming in ape-speak toward the rescue party as well.

"And just so you will not feel the need to try to enslave anybody again to help you with anything. I am turning your broken wooden wings with the feather duster feathers into magic dusters." Princess Ozma did this with her wand. "Now you will not have the excuse, which was not a good one, by the way, to have to enslave somebody to clean for you," Princess Ozma added with a firm nod of her youthful head.

Mrs. Yoop, the green monkey, and her green ape cousin made all sorts of primate screams.

Princess Ozma said, "One more thing: few of my subjects were so concerned when I took away your magic (well, now your cousin's magic is, too, but that is neither here nor there) they were concerned that you might not have a way to get food. Well, obviously, you have, but not being able to get food may have been another reason in your twisted mind you needed to kidnap somebody to get it for you as well as do the cleaning. Specifically, a mother and daughter who are now safe in my kingdom."

Another cacophony of primate noises ensued.

Princess Ozma shot a beam from her silver wand into the courtyard and suddenly fruit trees grew there. She also grew bananas, apples, and oranges. She also added nut trees to give them some protein.

"Now, you are all out of excuses. All you will have to do is harvest these fruits and nuts, lazy ones, and I will be back to check that you have not somehow, even without your voices and without your magic, enslaved anybody to pick them for you," Princess Ozma added.

The primates were silenced, and Princess Ozma said, "Just one more thing to do. To take away your plan for vengeance." She used her silver wand to turn half of the Nomes' jewels back into regular jewels and transport them to the Nome Kingdom.

She then used her wand to turn the emerald jewel animals, of the half she was allowed to keep, back into the typical jewels of her home city just as they had been turned into green turtles with the shells being the most emerald-like. She asked Sir Michaelo Rags and Scraps to collect the emeralds for the palace itself. The rest of the jeweled animals, from amethyst apes to diamond zig-zag covered zebras, became a new group of protectors for the Emerald City.

She transported everybody who was good back to the Throne Room of the Palace of the Emerald City where Jellia Jamb had already set up a long table with green punch and refreshments in celebration of a triumphant return. All the people and non-meat creatures who had joined her before, and more, were there for the celebration.

Princess Ozma, for one of the few times in Oz, was the one to tell about an adventure where the former adventurers were allowed to rest for once. Sir Michaelo Rags got his rag feet wet in a first adventure, and he was sure there would be more in Oz. He served as a true knight to Princess Ozma from then on (alongside who were other knights of the realm), sworn to protect her and keep the love and honor of Oz alive. His relatives through a long line, Margerie and Buttery, were going to go live with a kindly widowed lady in the Munchkin Country and would gladly help her in return for room and board. There was a difference between cleaning and cooking for somebody by choice or cleaning for somebody via enslavement.

The bejeweled or jewel-based animals were allowed to be around the palace to help guard it and alert Princess Ozma of any potential attacks in the future. Princess Ozma's new knight, Sir Rags, looked after them as well.

Finally, as money and jewels have no real value in the fairy country of Oz yet with jewels still being considered riches by many (especially in the Out World), this truly was a Rags to riches story…

**Excerpt from
"O.Z. Diggs the Fifth Estate in Gillikin Country":
Book Three of the O.Z. Diggs VII Series**

(This excerpt takes place after all the current and future ZIGGY ZIG-ZAGS graphic novels, as well as after the first two O.Z. DIGGS VII novels.)

EPIGRAPHS

1. The purpose of the press is to tell the truth and to raise Hell. (Chicago Tribune, 1861)
2. The job of a newspaper is to afflict the comfortable and comfort the afflicted. (Paraphrase from Peter Finley Dunne, Chicago Evening Post, 1893)

PROLOGUE
The Kind Kalidah of Oz

My father was once a Hissy-fit-story-ian for the Court of Princess Ozma, which was quite the accomplishment for a part-tiger and part-bear creature. Oh, my!

Under orders of the Princess, my father's group threw hissy fits when something was not right to them about Ozian history or what would become Ozian history.

My father, a kalidah, even wore green prescription spectacles on his brown, animal eyes, making him look somewhat like the Cowardly Lion did when he wore green spectacles (as the rest of the Famous Four did when they first entered the Emerald City). It was said that Hissy-fit-storians went through like looking through green tinted glasses, only wanting to see things from the perspective of the capital Emerald City.

Father became a scholar when he and another kalidah who rebelled and continued to give Ozians a hard time with a gang of punk kalidahs were hanging around a gorge in Munchkin Country when they should not have been. Ignoring advice from his parents never to follow bad examples of peers, the kind kalidah's father listened to the punky kalidah who told him they should have some fun and chase Dorothy and her friends during her first adventure. The Cowardly Lion confronted them, and they ran. But eventually, the Tin Woodman chopped down a tree that had allowed Dorothy, the Scarecrow, and the Cowardly Lion to cross the gorge but had eventually chopped it to make the kalidahs fall in the gorge. Some presumed they were dead, but nothing seldom if ever dies in Oz.

Father Kalidah told me when he told this story that he harbored no ill will against the Tin Woodman.

"Well, I did at first. He made me gggggrowl something fierce. But then when we made the discovery we did after our fall, it was easier to forgive him," Father Kalidah often explained to me. I can retell the events as he told me; I have been told that often.

Deep in a cave at the bottom of the gorge, Father Kalidah and his punk friend found something magnificent. There were stone tablets of all sorts of information about Oz and the formation of it by Lurline, Fairy Creator of Oz, and how she had intended the animals to be just about equal to humans. She wanted the humans to rule but wanted the animals to be respected and treated as well. Father Kalidah studied these many tablets, but his friend eventually wandered off, unenlightened.

What Father Kalidah had discovered was the Library of Apex-land-right-here. The apex of that hill in Munchkin Country marked the spot. And if you landed in the right spot just outside the jagged rocks as Father K. and his friend actually had, you could discover it.

Father K. loved to read so much and found that he often had to hold tablets very close to his face. Therefore, he eventually got prescription spectacles.

Anyway, the spectacles were the green lensed glasses O.Z. Diggs VII's ancestor, the original Wizard of Oz, had given out to people as they entered his mostly white yet emerald-covered city that he ruled for some time. They were G-R-R-R-eeen! (What'd you think I would say?)

Anyway, Dad grew tired of making a public fit when Ozians basically created their own stories in life by doing things that Glinda objected to with the Book of Records (and sometimes Princess Ozma did with the Magic Picture). (After all, Father had become more well-acquainted with ancient/classic Ozian history than many of them had.) He and his team would go in and stop people from trying different things or going on certain quests. They especially did this when magic was involved and when Princess Ozma did not want this to become a part of Ozian history.

How did I know about all of this? I read a lot like my father. My mother has always been an avid reader and taught me at home while being a cave-maker. We are not your typical kalidahs – many of which were wild beasts or were shown to be wild beasts.

Dad became a tutor to Munchkins who needed further help with the complicated, highly literate and magical (in the imparting, not the teaching) lessons of Locasta the First, who kept a little schoolhouse in the Southeast corner of Gillikin Country close to the Munchkin Country where Munchkin children could be magically transported. He was not allowed to be a teacher because only females of any species were allowed to be teachers in Oz. The college, however, was headed by a male insect, H.M. Wogglebug, T.E. He taught his students through a kind of information osmosis, learning through ingesting information pills.

What made Dad quit being a Hissy-fit-story-ian was that he found out that kalidahs were once a part of the Phantfasms and that, though stories of kind kalidahs had circulated, Phantfasms were still seen as evil hybrids of different animals. This kind of information was still being spread through the information pills students would ingest at Wogglebug College.

Our particular hybrid form of Phantfasms, kalidahs, were ostracized from their volcano location and, by being carried by flying versions of the original hybrids, scattered throughout Oz. Daddy wanted to go on a quest to find our people's origins and see if the ones we came from could be rehabilitated. Daddy was a rolling stone. Wherever he laid his fur was his cave home. But he hasn't died and has not left us alone. He had grrrrrr-and plans, and those Hissy-fit-stor-ians have had different ones. Grrrrrrrrrrrr! It makes me have a fit of a different kind.

But unlike with the Nomes who the current administration still trusted in some ways despite everything they had done, the phantfasms were labeled as evil and unredeemable. Daddy was going on a quest to go see them and see what he could do and was stopped by a group of sniveling humans and a few critters with whom he worked – the Hissy-fit-storians of Oz. That was when he resigned. That's grrrrr-atitude for you.

But now, in the dead of night, with no one watching in the Magic Picture and the Book of Records and with secret letters sent to the Scarecrow and Tin Woodman (flown to them by the Ork of Oz who gathered O.Z. Diggs the First's balloon basket to fly us all in), I have gathered enough Scarecrow sense and Tin Woodman empathy and comradery. I have gathered this with the unusual Ork to go on the quest my father was not allowed to and help the persecuted group (O.Z. Diggs VII has been contending with helping his adopted son Marteen with some persecution of his own and wrote back that he would gladly help from a distance with magic as would his father and ancestor but could not go on the quest directly). Grrrrr… But good enough for me.

Before I contacted the men of straw and tin and the zany bird (and even the eccentric wizard who could not make it), though, for weeks before the quest, I have tended to some large, blue eggs. These are very special eggs and are not chicken eggs (after all, we are not going to battle against the Nomes). I have protected them in the Scarecrow's pulled-out straw in a hollow cavity inside the Tin Woodman. When I am sure I am not being spied upon again, I will reveal what they are. May the Fairy Queen Lurline guide us all in our quest and send help from the Diggs men when needed! Grrrrrrrrr-gariousness is needed!

Chapter 1
The Marquis… DUH… Said Good Leadership
O.Z. Diggs VII

Marteen, the young marquis of Gillikin Country in Oz, had managed during the past few months to gather together some knights and knight-ettes and place them at the Ground Table. The Ground Table (isn't the name delicious?) is a place in the main castle chamber floor where my aforementioned adopted son invites these Gillikin leaders, male and female, from the mostly purple country to share in the power of his red and blue place of leadership. He has red and blue mats placed on the cobble-stone floor, so they do not get their armor too dirty. This is unprecedented in Oz, but Marteen does not like purple because of its connection to the former and now deceased Wicked Witch of the North who was his mother (Like poor dear Sybil in the Out World, it truly could have him screaming, "The purple! The people! The purple! What a mess.)

Marteen has the humble and jovial blue of Munchkin Country (humble and rustic as dungarees) mixed with the loving and passionate (even in battle) red of the Quadling Country as his colors. When people ask, he just says he has split the usual Gillikin color in half. After all, red and blue make purple.

Months ago, Marteen, towering over me via a final growth spurt, explained to me the reasons for the cool and hot color mats on the floor, flinging his dark, long hair back, "I once saw a hippie instructor and she who called herself my mother's college teach this way – everyone in a circle on the floor. It made people more equal. My mother, the Dean, hated it." Not only was Marteen's mother a now deceased wicked witch, but she was also the dean at a college. Marteen's birdsong that he as an enchanted human always spoke through was translated by a special device from a previous adventure.

"Besides," he said now, repeating this to the gathered and clanging in his half red and half blue armor in front of some of these leaders and me, "It gives me a chance to do a parody song.

My adopted father loves puns… I love parodies! … We're knights of the ground table…" His voice reverberated around the rocky castle chamber which had been magically chiseled out of a mountain.

And he started to sing his own variation of a certain British comedy troupes' song. It started as bird whistling and then, through the translator, became more like human lyrics. I feigned needing Marteen to do some errands and took him aside out of earshot of the knights and knight-ettes. In fact, we walked to a foyer away from the echoing chamber, my audibly stating, "I need you to do a knight errand." Pun intended again!

My knight errant, Marteen, said, "Good… what is it those college students said…Dad joke." He ran his fingers through his now mowed lawn of dark hair, just as short as that on some prestigious golf courses in the Out World, just a couple of inches above being an Out Worldian crew-cut and clucked his tongue as I pulled him to the side.

I flung my long locks of hair back. -Hippie-hair Dad meets 50s-hair son – a role reversal. -90s grunge or hard rock Dad meets 80s yuppie son perhaps works as well. But not with the personalities.

"They are not going to understand anything related to Camelot or even pop culture related to Camelot unless you teach them," I whispered upon arrival, "They're Ozian and not familiar with the Out World."

Marteen looked forlorn, so I muttered in hushed tones, "Besides… that parody makes this a silly place." He got the reference and laughed. He then returned to the chamber and those who awaited him.

Marteen, who was a military leader of a different sort in his not-so-distant past, had been working with the knights and knight-ettes to train a blue and red guard militia in case any future Nome leaders decided to attack Gillikin Country from their strategic position at the Northwest corner of Oz across the Deadly Desert. He also wanted them trained in how to find Nome tunnels and fill them in. Finally, he also wanted me to train the militia to send magic missiles – just bursts of powerful light – toward the Nome Kingdom should they ever attack.

Marteen's castle made the fourth estate in Gillikin Country. Mombi's was the third. His mother's had been the second, and his grandparents' had been the first.

There is another type of estate, too, which I shall mention momentarily. The other four estates which go along with it in the Out World are different too, but I am not going to go into all of those.

Next, as news of Marteen's plans made their way to the Emerald City, I soon received a message via extrasensory communication or Emergency Telepathic Service/ETS from Princess Ozma.

"H.M. Wogglebug, T.E. has informed me that Marquis Marteen is starting battle preparations for the remaining Nomes, though they have done nothing wrong. He says this starts a bad precedent," she said.

I replied through my thoughts, stroking a long gray beard I had only within the past year been able to get used to, but the dyed colors had gone out of temporarily and very recently, "We are constantly working to fill in their tunnels which they continue to make from the Nome Country to the Emerald City. There is even an older one that we almost have completely filled. They do not always attack, no. But Marteen wants to be ready."

Princess Ozma slightly whined but more out of concern, "And what of this army of males and females that he has? We do not usually have female soldiers – especially from the Emerald City, for example."

I replied, "I would have thought you would have been all for a progressive army. After all, you have never really condemned the historic all-female General Jinjur army, and they did not really have much purpose other than to give men a taste of their own misogyny."

"Well, we will be keeping an eye on everything through the Magic Picture and Book of Records. Do not forget who is in charge in Oz," Princess Ozma said tersely in my mind.

I said that I would not, but this brings up the fifth estate idea I had. The Fifth Estate in the Out World is the newspaper business. I worked as a reporter for many years in N.C. in the U.S. and did not like the one-sided way that H.M. Wogglebug, T.E. and his academics and now Princess Ozma were just being careful about the future threat of the Nomes. It was as if being cautious was too much and offensive.

When I was a reporter, I did try to fight for those who were not getting attention in the nineties to the new millennium, people such as gay people and some minorities. We and others gave plenty of attention to those groups. I tried to help gay people where I could because I was gay, and I did my best to empathize with minority groups, though my Scots-Irish, Irish, and Jewish lineage were not seen as a minority when combined. I remembered what it was like to be a boy in a little North Carolina town and being bullied for being gay – particularly in high school. I went through the stages of trying to hide it. Now, I am comfortable just having platonic affection toward guys. But I do not ever hate myself for loving fellows. I just do not engage in all of the physical activity I used to with them. Anyway, as we have progressed two decades into the millennium, it seems like the focus in Out World U.S. newspapers is on sub-groups of gays, trans-gendered individuals and drag queens, and on the rights of certain other groups. But people forget there has been a big media push for these groups dating back at least the 90s and civil rights fights for all of them dating back to the late 60s and early 70s. As I have become older, I think there are too many sub-groups or sub-sub-groups fighting for bigger pieces of pie under other groups.

Anyway, I have not only had these experiences with groups in the media, but with newspaper work in general. Back in a small city newspaper in N.C., I worked with a truly senior reporter named Lyle Listley. Lyle Listley wore a newsboy cap with a nice suit and covered courts and County Council. Through the years, his brogue seemed more pronounced and his bass voice more booming in the newsroom's bullpen. We were all there together in an open space, and I could still see him rattling a print-out with some condemning evidence and could still hear him saying, "I got that paperwork… I got the proof right here. You better talk!" A few times, he even bluffed!

At this same place was a short-haired woman who was like a geekier version of Lois Lane but with Clark Kent's glasses. She could do the hard news and investigative journalism with the best of them, but she preferred features and food stories. Unlike me, she did not have as much of a pronounced paunch and was quite thin except for just a small gut which showed her appreciation of fine rare steaks, cheeses, and other items from local restaurants. Like me, she loved fantasy, horror, and science fiction. She wrote "Dark Shadows" fan-fic (some of which would be called slash fic now), and it made even me blush (the things she would do with Barnabas and Willy Loomis!) She and I grew to be great friends, and we would go on tacky light runs to view lights during Christmas, and she threw the best Halloween parties. She lived in Greenyville, in the old mill-town part, and commuted to a suburban paper near Boone, North Carolina. Anyway, she said what she liked most about features in that people revealed sides of themselves they might not otherwise when sharing their creative work, woodwork, or whatever it was they were discussing at that particular moment. "People show a side of themselves you might not have otherwise found out if you were not asking about something they love," Nida Pafifer told me, and that stuck with me as well.

I had some years under my belt with journalism outside of the university, and I think though occasionally being assertive bordering on being aggressive to get information like Listley but being more subtle by asking questions when an interviewee's guard was down like Nida, I had learned a lot about what is called The Fifth Estate.

I thought it was time to have my own estate, the Fifth Estate, to supplement the powerful estates in Gillikin Country and even the entire Land of Oz itself. I would combine magic with my journalism skills (gleaned in the Out World) to have instant stories, presented news anchor style with commentary on the foibles of leaders and others sent all around Oz. There would be a scroll text beside the video image of my head. I would be a talking head and the "talking read" (pronounced like the color "red" in this case) – the "Andy Oz-zy" with more than 60 minutes of their time. Dare I say the "Walter Oz-con-contrite"? I could become a journalist like "Wood-words" (chronicles of a Tin Woodman as he helps bring down an evil ruler) and "Burn-stein" (burning happening and then water thrown on wicked witches comes to mind with the journalistic pun). Enough. Even I am almost sick of the puns. But an Out World-style hard-nosed journalist with the qualities of an avuncular news anchor seems needed in Oz.

My trusty Corgi staff could reproduce magical scenes of everything that occurred but with commentary and notes by me. Finally, not only the so-called progressive leadership of Oz would have access to the Magic Picture and the Book of Records, but Oz would have a virtual newspaper of record for the people and magic pictures which exposed the leaders' mistakes.

"Now what to do… these things must be handled delicately…Something with a poison pen in it… something with a bit of poison pen in it to be caustic towards those who need it… and to not put us to sleep… sleep… No longer at the news will we sleep," I said, making intentional jokes and parody lines out of the old Oz film before setting to work with the plans for all of what I described.

"First, a change of costume is in order," I said to myself.

I was wearing a long, gray robe, one of those "Gand-half-offs" basically. I never use a casted off staff, though. I have only ever used an inherited Cowardly Lion staff which was given back to my ancestor several years ago and my own Corgi staff after that. This staff is definitely "casted on".

Using my Corgi staff, I cast a spell, and the cute Corgi head at the top did what is called a derp expression, a Corgi smile with the tongue lolling out. Ziggy, who the staff head was modeled after, always did like it when I looked or acted slightly silly yet also in the mood for adventure and fun. He also did it when he rolled on his back for a belly rub.

With a flourish with Corgi cane or staff, I was back in my glittery green top-hat and suit from my last adventure. My gray locks had been to4uched up back with their rainbow colors, and my beard, which had grown as much or more than my long hair, now had rainbow streaks going all the way down it, covering the gray – a magical coloring technique Polychrome taught me. As my last adventure had ended, and I became an old man, I had just dyed the beard R.O.Y. G. B. I.V., but it grew out of those colors the past year. I had always kept my long locks rainbow-colored and had to change them toward the end of my last adventure as well because of becoming an old man because of a spell. The rainbow color had always kept well as a dye job until I became old. Polychrome's techniques really helped the facial hair and crown of hair retain their red, orange, yellow, green, blue, indigo, and violet hues. Polychrome allowed for my hair dying to be Less-Gandalfier Fruities (Garnier Fructis), more May-belle-lain (Maybelline), and more Rod-on Colormilk (Revlon). Maybe the Southern non-racist (but belle of the ball) wizard is born with it, maybe it's May-belle-lain.

The rainbow hues that once shocked now seem right at place in Oz.

I kept the dignity and wisdom of an aged face. I will leave the snake venom for face tightening for the truly vain. I wanted to be not only a news anchor for Oz who also did the field work for the reporting at the same time but more of a print news reporter who showed how he was proving broad statements with quotes and documents. Even in my small-town reporting back in North Carolina for a number of years, I always tried my best to do this.

Here, I wanted to become a different kind of anchor for a place that, though a fantasy world, a fairy's creation, could be an existential shipwreck – particularly when they forgot Lurline as the Creator and pretended they basically sprang up fully formed. I wanted to help be Oz's anchor in the storm and warn of approaching figurative mermaids who drown and do not help, harpies whose songs sound so gorgeous yet dash you on the rocks, and cyclops who stare at you with one seemingly wise eye but only want to eat you.

Chapter 2
"Eggs'es… EGGS'ES… PRECIOUS!"
The Kind Kalidah of Oz

I could finally disclose what the blue eggs were. The eggs were blue pter-Oz-dactyl eggs from the latest group of pter-Oz-dactyls. Pter-Oz-dactyls came from when pterodactyls flew into Oz when it was a barren area, and some were transformed into large blue birds with giant beaks and huge wing-spans, pter-Oz-dactyls, by Fairy Queen Lurline. Wherever they go, their songs sound like laughter, and they have been known as the blue pter-Oz-dactyls of happiness. In fact, they were said to make Munchkin Country an even more jovial country… if that's possible. It's all grrrrrrrravy, man.

I was hoping that if I brought the blue pter-Oz-dactyl of happiness eggs to the Phantfasms that they would hatch and make them happy and more willing to accept Kalidahs back into their fold… -Grrrrrrrr-andiose plans!

The Ork, who does have a name, but I will just refer to as Ork, grrrrr-ew impatient holding a large balloon basket, the original O.Z. Diggs' basket sans balloon, for the Scarecrow, the Tin Woodman, and me.

By the way, the Ork was not a bird yet had four legs like those of a stork and four wings shaped like upside-down bowls. The bowl-like wings, if you could call them that, were covered with tough skin instead of feathers. The Ork's head was shaped like an over-sized parrot's, and it had another bird-like feature – a plume of feathers on its head. What was really odd about the Ork was that it had a strange hodge-podge of skin, bones, and muscle composed into a propeller. This propeller was what the Ork is going to use to propel all of us in the basket. At that point, with finger-like claws on its front two legs, the Ork picked bugs out of the interwoven parts of the basket and flicked them away, occasionally munching on a few. Its back two legs were securely in the basket, and its posterior propeller protruded out the back of the woven means of conveyance. The basket had holes in the weave here and there. It was grrrrrrr-oovy! -Fig'rrr-atively and literally!

As it continued to flick some bugs away and eat others, the Ork said shrilly, "You really shouldn't put all your eggs in one basket."

I giggled despite myself and said, "Grrrrr…. But they aren't in one basket… they're in one Tin Woodman… with some of Scarecrow's straw to further protect them."

"Well, we Orks have never ruled over ptero-Oz-dactyls as we have other creatures in Orkland… I don't know if we can trust them when they hatch," the odd creature said, punctuating its sentence with a jab of its beak in the air.

Looking at the Ork, if it were not an Orkland resident, with its mix of cat-like claws and leathery bits and this and that, I would have sworn it was a Phanfasm, a mix of different critters as well.

I did not pursue my thoughts much further before Scarecrow said, "We can trust them. I have researched them, and they bring happiness wherever they go."

"And I have felt it in my heart that the beings in these eggs have much love," said the Tin Woodman, just pointing to and not rapping on his metal chest which carried delicate cargo.

The Ork fussed, "Well, the Tin Woodman will be riding in my basket, so that means he and the eggs will all be in one basket. You should never-"

I said, "We know… we know… put all of your eggs in one basket. Grrrrrr." Though some think kalidahs are dumb, we do not need this level of repetition.

The Scarecrow thought for a minute. The needles which had been placed in his head to make him sharp looked like they poked out more as he was in thought. His eyes, one more lopsided than the other, gave him more a jovial look as did his painted-on mouth. Grrrrr-inny fellow, he was.

"Nick (the name of the Tin Woodman), chop that big piece of blue birch bark off that big blue birch tree – just enough to make about the length of the basket," Scarecrow said.

Nick did as he was told – albeit a little more gingerly than usual because he was egg-specting.

The Scarecrow took the piece of long blue bark and shoved it right in the middle of the balloon basket.

The Ork asked, shrilly, "What good is that going to do?"

"I will show you," the Scarecrow said. He opened the Tin Woodman's chest and arranged his straw here and there, putting two of the eggs on one side of the inner part of his friend and two of the eggs on the other side.

The Tin Woodman said, "I think I know what he is going to ask me to do!" He tended to be able to predict some things the Scarecrow would do as they spent many years alongside each other as friends. He had grown wiser being around the Scarecrow just as the Scarecrow had learned to love others more platonically being around his friend. He told me all this. It grrrrrr-atified him.

The Tin Woodman straddled each side of the blue birch bark and whispered something to the Scarecrow.

The Scarecrow exclaimed to the Tin Woodman, "Exactly! I have made a virtual half basket and another half basket. It is never said that it's not good to put all of your eggs in two half-baskets! Because of how Nick Chopper, the Tin Woodman, is placed and the blue birch divider between his feet, one half of the eggs is in one half of the basket (albeit above it in one half of Nick), and the other half of the eggs is in the other half of it (albeit in Nick's other half)."

The eccentric Ork said, "Well, that's good enough for me… I can now agree to take all of you onward now that the eggs are virtually in different half baskets." He started spinning his propeller. Scarecrow was careful to load into the half of the basket farther away from the Ork so that his straw would not blow away.

He might even have blown away had he gotten too close to the propeller.

I loaded closer to the Ork. The Ork said, "I agreed to come help you because I know what it's like to be separated from one's people. You don't like eating Orks, do you?"

I shook my tiger-like head no and said, "Grrrrrr… No… I just eat meat from transplanted lunch-box fruit trees."

The Ork said, "Good…"

I whispered, "Grrrr… besides your meat is too tough." "What?" asked the Ork in a panic. "Nothing," I replied, and giggled / growled.

And with this, his propeller tail got buzzing so loudly that we could scarcely hear each other think.

The Tin Woodman latched on the front of the basket, still standing on either side of it with the blue birch bark below, beneath his metal legs.

The Scarecrow served as navigator, peering out the far-left side of the basket. He had already read a map and had it memorized.

I was coming along as an ambassador to the Phantfasms. –Grrrrreater than I was before.

Hopefully, our motley crew and their motley crew will grow to like each other.

Don't count your blue pter-Oz-dactyl eggs of happiness before they're hatched. Now the Ork has me saying old Oz sayings too! GRRRRRRRRR!

Chapter 3
Something About Frankenstein Can Really Bug One
H.M. Wogglebug, T.E.

That O.Z. Diggs the Seventh has been an ointment in my fly-like legs for quite some time! Why, I even heard that his son, Marteen, was only tutored in magic at home and does not have a college or university degree. Where are the verifiable credentials?

What kind of training is that? I had to have a way to get the news out about those two and their plans, but people will not always listen to an academic. My superior intellect is not always fathomable to them, so they do not always listen. Humans and non-insect creatures! BAH!

While on sabbatical from teaching, I have been working on something in my lab for quite some time – the perfect student. I do not mean teaching or tutoring a student to the point that he or she becomes near-perfect. In fact, I mean literally working on a student, a hybrid of several Oz-ian intelligent insects. I myself was a highly magnified insect with a magic lantern on a schoolhouse wall and overheard many lessons that way. Many aspects of a super-beetle are possessed by me. Even four of my arms with fancy gloves, and my two legs with fancy shoes show that. My trench-coat and three-piece suit do as well. I am dressed quite formally as a professor. Even my antennae are well-groomed. Unlike the non-academic Diggs VII and his lackluster mentee Marteen, I truly look the part.

My students have been given all their knowledge through pills, giving them more time for athletics. But these knowledge pills are on the primary academic subjects, and I have yearned for them to know more than that. I have wanted them to know about their holistic identities and how politics affects Oz and how they might change that. Also, deep down, I have longed for them to know that insects are superior to humans and that humans are superior to furry, feathery, and scaly animals. Arachnids are the lowest in the hierarchy, sworn enemies of insects and tricky beings – even trickier than me at times. I know it is going to take more than pills for that.

Well, I have taken that magic lantern which made me who I am today and have combined it with a magic telescope and other proprietary research devices paid for via university research. Using a dung-beetle, with its ability to spread dung, and a roach, with its ability to go in dark places and procure things, I have created the perfect propaganda pupil. I superimposed the images of the dung-beetle and roach with the magic lantern and combined and then enlarged them. I then had a hybrid bug that also had slightly magnified intelligence. Also, to make the creature trendy, I gave him a bug-bun with part of his antennae and some scruffy hairs on his ecto-skeleton. I also gave him a lot of cute qualities (the humans would say for an insect only, but his face resembles something I have studied in the Out World culture – the kawaii or cuteness factor in some characters).

Those who have only lived 100 years in Oz versus the hundreds or thousands many of us have or are sometimes called Oz-zennials. The Oz-zennials, such as my students, are in touch with all things vogue and trendy in Oz. It is those that people around Oz only tend to listen to anymore. They have found magic pods among the mushrooms in Oz and have used them to communicate with other Oz-zennials and do "podcasts". The younger and more attractive they are, the more influence they yield with their magic projected images. Sometimes, it is said they use the spores from the pods to wield influence, being podcast influencers. Old fogies like me are considered pase, though we teach the Oz-zennials themselves. We often do our best to teach them information that surpasses Ozian history and progresses them way beyond that. I wanted my creation to look like a typical popular Oz-zennial. Hence, the superficial aspects of the scruffy hairs on the head and the part bug-bun were added. He had to have cuteness to be an influencer as well. –A kawaii-chop… tee-hee… oh, bah, no one really appreciates my advanced academic puns the way they do that silly human wizard.

I made sure Ozian history was not as emphasized in my creation. I projected many LCD videos showing Oz to be a utopia and why we must not be warring people directly into the hybrid bug's brain. I also projected many Out World television news broadcasts, news narrative about oppressors and the oppressed and perceptions thereof, and Internet clickbait articles about politicians there into his mind as well. Some of these were materials I often used the past few years within my syllabi. My syllabi, the guides to taking the knowledge pills, are a virtual Lurline's book of life but not like Hers a`t all. My students know that to follow them through my courses is to prepare them intellectually and to make them devoid of harsh logic which they will not need in Oz. Converting them over into materials which could be beamed in-brain was quite the accomplishment! I patted myself on the back many times with many of my hands. Not since I invented information pills had I accomplished something so great!

And even greater was this creation before me of my own hands!

His brown eyes opened very wide. "He is now woke!" I yelled.

After doing this, I wrung four of my gloved hands together. It was all starting to come together.

"I-grrr, bring me the microscope and techno-combiner mechanism!" I yelled.

My hunchback assistant pill-bug, which some insects use as pets, was I-grrr. Some go as far as calling them pill-pugs (because they are cute) or rollie-faux-gies (because of how flexible they are like Corgis, how they roll on their backs, and are cute). But "I-grrr" likes to grrr sometimes like a dog and is a hunchback because I once tried to enlarge him and messed up his back. He became my assistant instead of my perfect student.

Anyway, I-grrrr, said, "Yes, master", and he put the telescope and combiner in his many legs, rolled up, and as a rather bumpy ball holding everything inside himself brought the equipment to me.

I set it up with the magic lantern.

"Now! Bring the extractor!"

I-grrr carefully carried something in all of his arms which looked like a giant syringe but with a fiber-optic sharp needle at the end.

He shook when he carried it because it made him very nervous (and rightfully so).

First, I shrunk the hybrid bug's heart very small with the microscope attached to the magic lantern with a special device. I wanted the hybrid bug to be almost heartless as a propaganda reporter but have just enough heart to fake being concerned. Then, I turned on an electronic component of the giant syringe. The fiber-optic needle glowed with a nether-worldly glow. It made a horrible hum like a dark chant. Then, a sort of blueish white version of the hybrid bug came out of him and was sucked into the syringe. And that blueish form stayed a kind of liquid there.

"I-grrrr, the Wobblebug University networked computer! Quickly!"

I-grrr brought it to me, and I, through fiber-optic cables placed directly on the hybrid bug's enlarged nervous system, which was now more like a mind, put electronic stimulation and loads of information directly in place of its soul. To give it a personality which would appeal to a younger demographic, though, I imbued it with young online video service celebrity commentators from the Out World. Yes, I have done lots of research on the Out World and have tried to emulate the progressive movements I have witnessed there.

The hybrid-bug twitched.

Who I will now start called H.B. said, "Hey, bru', where am I?! You are, like, really oppressive, and, like, I can tell like THE MAN that you have been trying to keep me down! I hate you, man!"

"He is dead! HE IS DEAD!" I yelled in my lab, and I-grrr and I laughed and lightning sparks sputtered from my many pieces of scientific equipment. I, of course, meant his soul is dead. He was very much alive in the clinical or scientific sense. Also, to use another of my scholarly puns, he is "a-WOKE-end." –Very woke!

Hybrid-bug's (H.B.'s) soul had been extracted, his heart shrunk, and his enlarged mind over-stuffed with visuals and information (but little to no history) and yet he lived to spread well-educated propaganda about Marteen and O.Z. Diggs VII throughout all of Oz! Yours truly, H.M. Wogglebug, T.E., now had his own perfectly made student, a student made in his own image, H.B.!

Chapter 4
That Which Resembles Flour Lands on Flowers
The Kind Kalidah of Oz

We were flying fine until the Ork, with our basket in tow, flew too low to the bluish-green Munchkin woods and to the Crooked, tall house of the Crooked Magician, Dr. Pipt -- blueish gray and only a little more colorful than the one Dorothy landed in Oz in but much taller. We ran into the roof which was somewhat flat but had corners. Hidden in one corner of the flattened roof's edges was a large container of Powder of Life. The lid loosened on it, and a soupcon on the powder blew out and landed on the flowerbed below the house. Grrrrrrr.

As the basket hit the roof, Scarecrow was jolted and hit along with it. He had been paying attention to Marg-rrrrrrrr-olotte, the Crooked Magician's wife, through the window putting together things for teatime. He noticed she was already drinking her tea but not doing what Dorothy had taught him, during a fake tea party, to do – lift a pinky in the air. He ges-g'rrrrred with his own stuffed pinky, accidentally doing a magic gesture around the Powder of Life which would soon scatter as he still held his pinky up in shock during the impending small crash. He said, "Woah" before the hit but, though not hurt as a non-meat-person, he still cut his word off when his straw-ey stomach was mashed, and said, "Woag" which sounded just like one of the activating words for Powder of Life.

The Ork had not been paying attention and, just before approaching the Crooked House, was also looking through a window at Margrrrrrr-ollotte, the Crooked Magician's wife, pouring tea and putting out delicious cakes and snacks. She learned about teatime from her visits to Wonderland years ago way over the Nomestic Ocean. The Ork loved to eat and yelled, "Tea" from his beak while not paying attention and that was when he too was cut off short by hitting the roof and ended with an "UGH"! He had even put one of his cat-like yet talon-like thumbs up in the air in a thumbs-up gesture when referring to the tea and snacks. We had not seen him at first. But he ended up sounding like he did the second Powder of Life activation word, "Tea-UGH", and body movement.

I had said, "Oh, poo," as in "Oh, crap," when I saw what was about to happen. I hit my stomach and said, "Ugh" as well, making the third magic activation word, "Peaugh." I also tripped, spun on one of my back paws in place, holding up both front paws up in the air with pads outstretched for balance. This was the final magic gesture with the final magic word. Grrrrrrrr!

Nick Chopper, the Tin Woodman, had not said a word because he was concentrating on being very still. The Tin Woodman was still trying to hold on to the basket, straddle the blue birch bark piece there, and remained a true steadfast tin soldier to protect those eggs in each half part of the basket.

Anyway, with the Powder of Life being sprinkled below and the words and actions for the spell being done, the flowerbed below us was probably brought to life. As we were somewhat crashed on the flat roof anyway, we knocked on a roof door, and the Crooked Magician who recognized Scarecrow, the Ork, and the Tin Woodman, invited us all down a crooked ladder for tea. The Crooked Magician could even recognize us through his very thick glasses as he extended his crooked back up just a little for a better view.

"Ya… ya… come on it," he said, "You are just in time for tea."

Only the Ork and I really needed it as the non-meat creatures had played tea party with Dorothy before but did not really eat or drink.

The Ork and I were munching on various sweet blueberry cakes and blue cucumber sandwiches and drinking tea from blue periwinkle porcelain cups when we started hearing the brought to life transplanted flowers from the open window. They had been transplanted from Wonderland by Marg-rrrrr-olotte, and the Powder of Life did its work on them. Unlike in a certain film's depiction, these Wonderland flowers made shrill noises. They made shrill, loud noises that made one cover one's ears. GRRRRRRRR!

As some animals such as rabbits get caught by predators, they make this noise (my father told me Kalidahs used to make other animals make that noise). But the flower noises sounded like animal screams mixed with the very few Munchkins who sang high-pitched and off-key (most were melodious) and Hammer-head shouts (think grunts and gr-r-r-r-rowls as speech)! Each time the flowers below opened and closed their petals, more horrible sounds ensued!

"Wonderland flowers!" yelled the Crooked Magician, "How I detest them!... The wife brought them back from Wonderland, but they were the non-speaking variety, ya? How were the flowers here brought to life, though?"

He peered at us. "You've been getting into my secret stash, haven't you?!" His eyes looked even more enraged in the magnification of his thick glasses.

We did not say anything.

Marg-r-r-r-rolotte said, adjusting her bun in her hair, "Now, you know how much I love Wonderland, husband. Why, that's why we have tea-time anyway." She turned to us and said, though a portly woman, that she loved to travel to other places and walk there, meeting and gr-r-r-r-reeting people. She defied the stereo-type of a large person.

"You know about my travels there and how I accepted some Wonderland visitors into this house years ago," she added.

The Crooked Magician grunted and whiny-grumbled the way only an old codger can: "How could I forget! I had to create a spell to write down her memoirs there... I grew to dislike the place immensely because I could not keep up with my other work and also record her adventures there."

The flowers still continued to make shrill, loud noises which could even be heard from the window which Dr. Pipt, the Crooked Magician, had now closed.

The Ork then made a foolish mistake. He said, "I guess we did knock some of the powder down below… and those noises and motions we made had to have coinciden—"

Scarecrow was trying to wave his arms trying to get the Ork to shut up, but it was too late.

The Crooked Magician flew into a rage and flung his limbs to and fro, "I knew you had stolen some of my powder. My precious powder! Now get out of here… you don't deserve our hospitality. Wife, bring me my garden shears!"

"Why, I will do no such thing," said Marg-r-r-r-r-rolotte, "They certainly can leave because we cannot have them stealing from us… sorry, boys… But, husband, there is no need for you to carry on so. And I am not cutting those flowers. They can be my little babies, and I will tend to them."

She gr-r-r-r-rabbed up a watering can from a closet, filled it in the sink with a hand-pump, and then walked to and proceeded to water the flowerbed. We could hear her sweet-talking the flowers as she watered them, and they finally stopped crying. Grrrrrrr.

Scarecrow explained, "We assure you knocking into the powder and using some of it was an accident-

"Sure, sure, ya" yelled Dr. Pipt, "Listen… I have grown to be a very old impatient man… I do not have time for these games! Now… go the way you came… out the roof! YA?!"

And we did. We loaded back into the basket as we had before, and the Ork took us further eastward. Wait? Is that the right direction? Grrrrr! Harumph!...

...   *To be continued in "O.Z. Diggs the Fifth Estate in Gillikin Country" in 2024!*

Not all of Ron's works are set in the magical land of Oz…

THE SHADE OF PAN OVER HALLOWEEN

Jumpy. Most jumpy was he. The twelve-year-old boy was fidgety in his Peter Pan attire on the bus, which would not have been unusual as we were on the way to an amusement park on a bus from a resort hotel for Halloween. But his Peter Pan attire was all in black, as if he were dressing as Peter Pan's Shadow. His cap almost looked like a mini-dorsal fin on a killer whale; it was so dark and the feather in it was more raven-esque than red. His tights made him appear to have ebony legs, and the rest of his attire made him look like a Shadow.

His eyes were hazel, but they did not have the sparkle of most hazel, and his hair was cottony and made him toe-headed but did not shine. Also, his hair always appeared to look wet, slicked down. It was not greasy. It was as if he had thrown on his costume right after exiting the resort pool. Though he sweated, he didn't even have a clean sweat smell, let alone a running boy stench. Boys and men usually have some kind of smell. Now, my smell is a strong deodorant and a kind of cinnamon-scented, bourbon-esque cologne scent. As a boy, I sometimes had what some perceived as a bad aroma. I try to remedy that as a man.

The scentless boy next played with a rubber knife as well as rubber chains. He even had one of those fake rubber earrings, so he looked more like a cross between Pan and one of the pirates. He sat right across from me on the other side of the resort hotel bus.

He looked at me and bent the rubber toy knife blade across one of his wrists. He was almost daring me to say something.

I said, slightly whispering, "You really should not do that. It's not nice to do that."

I looked around to see where the boy's parents were on the bus. They did not seem to be sitting by him. I turned to try to say something to them but could not find them. They did not speak up either.

"It's not real," he blurted, meaning that meant all the difference.

I replied, "When I was a boy, they always had these play knives that looked like they would disappear into somebody or make it look like they were stabbed. They stopped making those because kids were rigging them to stay put and hurt themselves and others."

"When I was a boy… when I was a boy," mocked the boy, seemingly dressed as Peter Pan's shadow, "Just how old are you, mister?"

I told him that I was fifty.

"Old… alone… done for," he replied.

"Well, not done for… I still like to come here… to this magic place… it takes me back to when I was younger… when things were simpler with my late father and—"

Young Peter Pan's shadow replied, tugging at the rubber chains, "Things were not simpler for me when I was younger. When I was close to the age I was now was when things started going wrong. By the way, they still use these sorts of rubber knives and the knives you are talking about in plays, sir." His hazel eyes stared out the window of the bus blankly.

I looked out one of the windows of the bus. The palm trees and the oak trees here in the theme parks in Florida looked eternally youthful, as if they were always in summer. Where we were going would have fall or autumn in stasis for all of us. Faux maple leaves of all earth-tones were there at the amusement park, which was decorated for Halloween, as were colorful fallen preserved leaves and pumpkins shipped in as well as faux pumpkins. Even the mums seemed fake at times. Mum's the word on that one! I still liked to fall in stasis, the still fall, of the amusement park. It meant things stayed the same. I did not feel like things were progressing in time, that I was becoming older and older.

"When I was young everything went right – especially here," I said, pushing up my glasses. "My late father worked all the time and was kind of mean to us, but when we came here, he was the kindest, gentlest soul you have ever met."

"Adults always say that," pouted Peter's Shadow. "They always say everything went right in their youth. It's because they don't remember so well. Not growing up could give them some perspective."

"You don't mean to say that you…" I shifted my girth in the seat incredulously. I was beginning to think that this boy was deluded into thinking he was Peter Pan or Peter Pan's Shadow. After all, he was just wearing a Halloween costume for his visit to the theme-park as hundreds or maybe even thousands were that night at this large facility.

He rolled his eyes. "No, I don't think I am Peter Pan. I am not Peter Pan." Then, he giggled shrilly a little. He said, "I am dressed as the shadow of Peter Pan for a reason."

"Early goth? A tween goth?" I joked.

"Ha-ha. No," he said like a nephew or niece does at an Uncle's bad jokes, and tugged on the rubber chains, continuing, "I played Peter Pan in a school production not far from here. There was a mermaid scene the director wanted to add in. I was to burst forth from a lagoon full of water through a trapdoor. Really, it was just a big water-tank decorated with fake plants."

I thought I was beginning to see why he appeared wet now. He had come straight from acting in that play. He had to have put on Peter Pan's shadow costume, though.

"Why is your costume all black, though? You weren't Peter Pan's shadow. You were the eternally youthful boy himself in the play. You should have been in green! Why did you change clothes?"

The boy just deadpanned, tugging at the plastic chains and seeming to change the subject, "I always liked Houdini. I always liked being a daredevil. Roller Coasters at this theme-park were always my favorite, that's why I am heading here tonight for the late-night Halloween event-"

"You mean rollercoasters always have been… always are your favorite," I corrected his grammar and pushed my glasses up.

"I need to ride the rollercoasters before going home," he said.

I replied, "Well, we all need to find thrills in our life. I am going to go on some thrill rides myself. Why, when I was in my teens and twenties, I would go on them at least 5 to 10 times apiece!"

"I just want to ride them all one more time before I have to go," the boy said. His face looked sadder than expected.

I sat up in my seat more, feeling more and more like a kid, talking about the rides, "I always wanted to ride the thrill rides one last time before we went home, too." I was thinking back to being a kid when I suppose I only thought things were easier. They definitely were not easier when Dad became aggressive at home, yet the amusement park was where we could always come together and be happy as a family. That was what I was trying to remember. Perhaps I clung to that idea too much.

As I was talking about liking thrill rides in the past and not referring to where we were going, I, too, was reprimanded for my grammar.

"You mean have always wanted. Do want to," corrected the boy this time, "You aren't dead, mister. You can live for now. You can be like a kid just as you are. Geez… you don't have to keep talking about the good old days." He continued, his voice getting a little shriller, "Sometimes, the good old days were not so good." He suddenly shoved the plastic chains closer to my face across the interior bus walkway with the slip-resisting grooves. He stared at me with those glassy hazel eyes that never sparkled. "They look like because they are plastic that they would be easy to pull apart or at least untangle, easier than metal chains, right?"

I nodded.

"That's why I picked them," the shadow of Pan said, "I picked them because I thought they would be easy. A regular Houdini prank."

I still was not following. He had just been in a "Peter Pan" play and had launched out of a mermaid lagoon thanks to a trapdoor close to the end of the play, had changed clothes, and came here. What did plastic chains have to do with it?

I thought about Houdini. Houdini often chained himself underwater, but why would this young actor have done that? Well, he did say he was a thrill-seeker, just the opposite of me.

We almost reached the theme park. The resort hotel bus was reaching a line of other hotel buses. I love the smell of diesel in the evening at the theme-park… It smells like victory!

"Don't live for then. Live for now," the shadow of Pan said as we were about to leave the bus. "Do it before it's too late!" His voice became shrill and cracked.

As we left the bus, I did not see him leaving with the crowd. I looked in the distance and saw the shadow of Pan seem to dissipate and fade into the darkness just on the other side of the fence of the coasters…

Thinking back to our bus journey, I suddenly realized that some time back the young actor playing Pan must have really died when he secretly tried to be Houdini during his mermaid lagoon scene, and truly became shadow…became spirit. And I knew that though the shadow of Pan could no longer live here that I must really, truly live for now…

THE GOOD SHEPHERD'S ASSISTANT:
A CHRISTMAS 2022 POEM

With my crook-less walking stick among the grassy fields,
I resemble a lowly shepherd during one Advent evening.

My Corgi, Ziggy, plays the carousel game, running around me,
leading me like an astray, black pea-coated sheep beneath the
black-lighted, blue-white shards of stars atop the black velvet sky.

Envision him as a Canaan Dog, leading me to the
bright, glassy star which seems part comet and part distant sun
yet with a descending downward tail.

My white-haloed fur-angel once nudged me away from sadness to
Yeshua,
But I had accepted the Great Counselor in the mountainous camp
wilderness
open wooden church at ten years old; sometimes all it takes for us
is a little nudge.

Now my Corgi, in my imagination, leads me as the lowly shepherd
to the Good Shepherd, a baby in a manger, whose hands gently
rub dog's fur
as a pure voice calls me back to simplicity and innocence.

And I know my fur-angel has always been… the Good Shepherd's
assistant.

THESE BOOTIES ARE MADE FOR TALKING

Anon Lilli Wooder had been working as a waitress at a Las Vegas diner for 30 years and had written many stories. She also had made many works of art but never exhibited the art nor submitted the stories. This was not for any reason of principle.

She really did want them to be seen eventually. Anon just thought they were much better than any other works out there. Anon hid her flashes of insight in her stories in mini-bushels of flash drives. Also, she threw clothing she had been working on into the closet or shoved fashion plates into drawers. She covered her small sculptures with bowls or threw sheets over her paintings when men came over to her studio apartment, which was always bathed in an icy blue neon light from just part of the many lights of the Vegas strip. And, from the Vegas strip, there had been many chiseled, lustful men in her apartment and bedroom up until about a decade ago.

About ten years ago, Anon, who had been a natural beauty before then, had finally started to get what some call a turkey neck and even figurative turkey wings on her arms. Her sandy blonde hair began to gray. Her crow's feet grew their own additional, compounded crow's feet like some sort of small hydras at the corners of her eyes. The type of superficial men she pursued stopped pursuing her. She was getting saggy but that boob job she saved up for years ago was still very perky; her breasts and her rail-thin, dry body were quite the contrast. Her well-draped, colorful, and stylish clothing could not hide the husk beneath. She was worn out in many ways.

Yet Anon took great pride in one thing. She could use her real name to remain Anon or Anonymous on various review and book sites online, showing what she felt was her writing prowess with reviews. She wrote a lengthy review about a culinary book she bought for the chef of the restaurant where she worked, though she knew nothing about cooking. "This book is bound to make you utter, 'Bon Appetit' in repeat," she wrote, among other trite phrases. The more mediocre works she gave lots of stars to and the products, art, or books she was jealous of, she tried to tear down and gave just one or two stars; "Just awful" or "Just terrible" would be one of her few remarks on those.

A few weeks ago, though, she had decided to expand on a succinct review of some black kitty fuzzy slippers she ordered from a homemade crafts place called Witchy Craft. She glared at the screen with the blue ice-balls that were her corneas. Her mouth wrinkled into a wicked smile at the damage she would be doing to the crafter.

"Two stars. I have been a waitress for thirty years, so I am always looking for something comfortable for my feet when I get home. And these are very comfortable and well put together. Though the black kitty fuzzy slippers are comfy, I cannot help but get grossed out by the kitties' mouths being around my ankles. Why didn't the crafter put the cat heads at the front? Also, isn't it a little too 'familiar' to have black cats be the signature craft of a place called Witchy Craft? How cliché can one get? The cats' eyes, though basically just like cat's eye marble buttons, appear to be a bit creepy. The cat slippers have an overabundance of whiskers around their round mouths which engulf your ankles. Their button noses are cute enough, but their scraggly felt ears make them look like they just got out of an alley fight. And the slippers are just so gross and ugly that I may just return them before the exchange time runs out," she typed. She submitted the review, and it was approved.

Two weeks later, the return time had almost run out, and after a big shift and a hot shower, Anon again slipped on a red silk robe with nothing underneath, and the black kitty slippers on her feet.

She saw the self-addressed black box which came with every Witchy Craft order on a pile of Lean Cuisine boxes she needed to throw away. On the Witchy Craft box read the white label in a font straight out of the Middle Ages, "If our dear ones are not completely satisfied, please return with our compliments."

Anon thought that was a nice touch.

As she moved to take one of the kitty slippers off her ankle and heel, it muttered, "Pleh! Pleh! I me-agree…meff disgusthin'"

"I agree, Hexth," said the other cat-themed slipper. It spoke with a huge, muffled lisp because of its mouth being filled by her other ankle and heel. Anon screamed and lifted her legs to take the slippers off.

She did not have to. The two black kitty slippers jutted themselves off her feet as she lifted her legs and were still sputtering.

One of the black kitten slippers said, "BLECH, POX! Some of the most disgusting feet I have ever been on. Meow-we both agree that having to have our mouths around her feet was a bad idea! We can agree with Miss Reviewer on that!"

"Oh, I agree, HEX! So dried up yet also so sweaty! ACH! ACH!" Pox acted like he was going to cough up a hairball.

Anon screamed some more.

Pox said, "Well, what did you expect with a place called Witchy Craft? And you really pissed off the boss. HISSSSSSS!"

Hex added, "But that's okay. If her dear ones are not completely satisfied, we can be returned. Meo-yoooo."

Anon stopped screaming. She could at least end this nightmare by putting the talking kitty slippers back in their box. She was one of the dear ones and needed to be completely satisfied and was not. Therefore, the black kitty slippers could be returned, she reasoned.

Anon said, using the same flattering voice she used to use for seduction, "Well…I-I…did say you were well put together…and I did say how comfortable you are…and those cute button noses."

She pointed to Hex's button nose, which he wrinkled at her.

Hex said, "Flattery would have gotten you everywhere with more of those magic stars, but you gave us two! HISSSSSSSSSS! You also said we had too many whiskers. And that our cat eyes creeped you out."

He stared up at her with yellow slanted eyes.

He used the sole portion of his slipper torso to jump up.

Hex rubbed his faux fur and whiskers against her calf beneath her blood-red robe.

He muttered, "Do our over-plentiful whiskers tickle too much? P-r-r-r-r-r-r."

Anon giggled despite herself. She was being put at ease by the two, for want of a better term, characters.

As Anon was giggling, Pox said, staring from her other side with twin yellow eyes, eyes which glowed like some otherworldly suns, "You mentioned our scraggly ears as well. HISSSSSSS! Do you realize why we have such scraggly felt ears?"

Anon shook her head no.

"We've been returned before," he said.

Anon started getting indignant then, "I knew it! I knew there was something rough about those ears!"

Truth be told the cat slippers had been in a fight like alley cats before but not with each other. Someone had tried to fight them off.

Hex had returned to the ground from tickling Anon, "Calm down meow…speaking of ears…you have lovely ones."

Anon pulled her nearly silvery long hair behind them. "Well, thank you," she said, "I used to get compliments on them among other things." Her ears were quite petite and well-shaped, and the rest of her body was, too. However, she had just had too many debauched liquor-filled nights, and the mileage was starting to show.

Pox said, "Yes…meow-I would say your ears look scrumptious."

Anon laughed. She said, "Well, many men have nibbled on them."

"I think we would like to nibble on them, too," said Hex.

Pox said, "Hisssss-ome like to leave the ears for last. We like to do them first. We like you to hear the initial crunching and munching as best you can."

"What do you mean?!" Anon asked, starting to panic.

Hex kicked a sheet down as if he had a magic foot within his mouth, a solid form within his slippery body.

Anon had painted an oil of a former lover and made him out to be a true Adonis. The painting was finally revealed.

"Too bad you hid this beauty from the world… and only shared ugliness," Hex said. "A pox on you."

Pox leapt up, with needle sharp teeth, dangled by Anon's earlobe as he chewed. She screamed, but all the younger ladies and fellows in her building were out on dates or were out on the town – things she had done in overabundance years ago.

"A curse on you, too," said Pox between chews, "You are to be hexed."

Hex leapt up at the other ear and started to chew as well.

Streams of red flowed from where Anon's ears had been and looked like vermillion streams around the well-formed marble rock of her head.

The monstrous slippers chewed downward until they arrived at her plastic breasts. "Blech!" one of them said. The other said, "We'll leave those alone!"

At this point, Anon passed out…

Two days later, the owner of Witchy Craft gave the Federal United Parcel Service four stars for shipping back a pair of black cat slippers and a couple of breast implants.

The raven-haired witch, as gorgeous as Anon had been years ago but kept youthful through dark magic, thought she might be able to make the well-used breast implants into a neck pillow for a male reviewer who complained about everything and suffocate him with them. She giggled with delight.

She said, petting her black cat slippers, "Just as I always say in my disclaimer, if my dear ones are not completely satisfied, they can be returned with our compliments. Isn't that right, dear ones? My lovelies! Thank you! Thank you! Thank you, my dears!"

Hex and Pox purred in her arms. They had not been completely satisfied with the Anon merchandise as parts of it were fake – especially the attitude. They were happy to be returned and to be dissatisfied with the dissatisfied once more. Maybe one day they would get a fully tasty meal or leave a fully formed person alone that shone with too much light. For now, they could not wait to devour another human book, a very real one, and hoped to remain hungry for more.

XCALIBUR AND THE KNOWLEDRAGON

Xcalibur, who did not even know that his namesake was a truncated version of the legendary sword of King Arthur, was, nevertheless, an extreme smart aleck in his 8th grade English class.

His bespectacled and shabby-chic-attired teacher, Mr. Terbax, attempted to go through a Greek myth lesson on Prometheus bringing down the flame on a torch from Mount Olympus, the teacher running the gamut from acting out parts, drawing illustrations, showing a digital film on the myth itself, and, of course, reading the myth aloud. Xcalibur offered cross-curricular tangents.

Xcalibur, a curly-haired youth, asked, without raising his hand and giving that feigned nascent look which betrayed his intent to get the class off subject, "Wouldn't the torch have become galvanized and perhaps have cracked because of the trip from the very cold top of Mount Olympus to the very warm beaches of Greece below?"

Xcalibur had learned this fact in science class. Mr. Terbax wasn't the type of teacher who tried to thwart such teachable moments that crossed the curriculum. However, every time Mr. Terbax introduced a new topic, Xcalibur purposefully brought extraneous science facts into the conversation. At times, Mr. Terbax felt like saying, "Dammit, Xcalibur, I'm an English teacher, not a scientist."

Mr. Terbax gripped his podium a little tighter. He unfurled his shaggy black eyebrows, took a deep breath and smiled. He said, "That's a good question, Xcalibur. But you've got to remember the genre of this tale. It's a Greek myth. It takes liberties with natural events. In fact, what is one of the traits of a myth, class?"

Approximately 10 droned, "It contains elements of the supernatural."

"Good," said Mr. Terbax, adjusting his corduroy suit coat. He wore it to appear tweedy and even authorial. One of his good lady friends said that, given his paunchy-ness, he was "Corduroy Bear" whenever he wore it.

"This is stupid, Mrs. Terbax," said Xcalibur and shifted his slightly portly frame in his desk.

Mr. Terbax said, "If you would like, you can always submit a bonus paper critiquing the Greek myth and stating why it is stupid. And you are lucky that I don't report you to the office for disrespect for that last comment." The teacher had not ignored what Xcalibur intended as a gender insult.

Xcalibur looked at Mr. Terbax with buck-brown eyes, shining with loathing, "Maybe I will. -May be the only way I can get a good grade in here since you don't teach us anything."

Mr. Terbax, against his better judgment, said, "What do you call the various steps that we've just gone through? The mini lecture. The dramatization. The digital film with questions that I composed."

Xcalibur said, "Yea, but we've got to provide all of the answers."

Mr. Terbax said, "You learn better that way. Besides, I always let you know if you're off course."

"You're the one that's off course," said Excalibur (at this point, other eighth graders were giggling, taking on a pack mentality)

Finally, Mr. Terbax stated the eight wisest words any parent or teacher can utter to a young adolescent, "I am not going to argue with you."

This shut up Xcalibur and ended his little argumentative game. Had Mr. Terbax continued, Xcalibur was planning to mention his Nationally Board-certified teacher mother and how much she knew. Xcalibur often resorted to this to condescend to the teacher, who was relatively new in comparison to other teachers at the middle school. He couldn't wait for the school year to be over, which was soon. This Summer, his wealthy grandfather, who he also discussed ad nauseum, was taking the family to Greece. Perhaps there, he would run into a great scientist, a post-cedent of Aristotle or Archimedes. Xcalibur hoped to show off all he truly knew and none of this English garbage, this unrealistic myth that didn't have anything to do with his life. The Prometheus myth had nothing to do with him…

Prometheus had much to do with mankind, its wisest moments, and its foibles. Little do most people know that when he carried his flame of knowledge from the gods to the mortals that some of the flame leapt from its torch and landed in the sands of a Grecian beach. From this sand, a gnarled yet translucent being was formed. Given that it was made of glass, the limbs of the beast were elongated and curvy as were its three necks. Its wings were antique bottle green, light green and size of a demonic cherub. The way the glass dripped downward gave the glass dragon slightly goofy tongues that lolled out of its three mouths. Yet these goofy glass tongues could aim fire and were to give the dragon a benign appearance for his trickery. Knowleddragon was his name, and he took great pride in his knowledge of everything of all time. He was ecstatic over the fact that he could grant six wishes, two for each head. Knowledragon knew that he was given this gift because he was forged of the flame of knowledge itself, knowledge creating all possibilities for fabricated creation. Pure creation came from creativity and spoken word. Fabricated creation came from accrued knowledge.

Knowledragon had naught left to accrue. His one pleasure in life was giving unsuspecting souls wishes and seeing how foolishly they squandered them. Knowledragon often twitched his long, bumpy tail in thought on the beach. But that Summer day that Xcalibur approached during his Greek vacation, Knowledragon kept his tail very still.

A scientist was on the beach, one with a long white beard and scraggly patches of hair with a bald spot. Liver spots that looked more like burn marks donned the spot. He wore Bermuda shorts with black socks and sandals, the trademark of the elderly geek on the beach. His eyes were strangely dark in the pale gaunt face around them, like pieces of onyx shoved into stretched Sculpy clay.

The scientist used a laser device to take measurements of a gigantic marvel of a sandcastle of all things. The precision amused Xcalibur, but he could see from all of the instrumentation that here was the scientist that he was looking for. Xcalibur had walked many miles down the beach, ignoring the warnings of his grandfather and parents. He did not realize he had undertaken an epic journey over the sands. He opened his mouth in wonder at the colossal sand walls.

"Did you make this, sir?" he asked as he approached.

"Yes, I have made the perfect sandcastle," said the scientist, "I have taken into account the force of gravity and various other factors. I have created the most perfect, strong structure you can create out of sand. I spent a month of my sabbatical drawing out the architectural plans, architectural plans coupled with physics equations!"

The elderly scientist shoved plans into Xcalibur's hands. Here were facts. Here was something he could do something with. Planning and building were real, not that garbage his English teacher taught him. Here was measurement, precision, something tangible.

The elderly scientist pointed to the three turret towers of sand as they swayed only slightly in the forceful wind of the Greek isle.

"I have reinforced those towers so that they will stand up to the winds, so that they will stand the test of time."

Xcalibur wondered what the man's castle of sand was built upon.

The gigantic sandcastle had bigger dimensions than many boulders and was as tall as some of the craggy cliffs behind them. The cliffs were a pure white, a pure white that Xcalibur remembered from a Greek restaurant that his grandfather took him to. Zorba's had sculpted clouds and depictions of the Greek gods. He often liked trying new dishes there, testing them. Xcalibur did enjoy trying new things, and this was wonderful. However, his looking down his nose at those who had not experienced what he had was not.

Xcalibur said, "Oh, I've built many sandcastles on trips to Edisto Beach with my grandfather. I even saw some really huge ones one time during a trip to Miami. I don't think I've ever seen one this big, though."

The scientist looked very tired when he spoke again. He winced a little. His dark eyes were closed under purplish lids. He had a baggage compartment under his eyes, not just bags. He said hoarsely, "You will see bigger soon. I plan on building a palace of sand on the sandy cliffs there. I shall live there forever, away from everybody, thinking my great thoughts."

Xcalibur asked, "Why wouldn't you want to share those thoughts with everybody?"

"Not everybody can think the thoughts that I do. I have theories that would explode your neurons, son."

Xcalibur had a moment where he was slightly remorseful for being condescending to people, for being such a smart aleck. Yet this didn't last too long when he thought of the greatness of the scientist and the wonders that he had and would achieve.

He was about to say something to this effect when he noticed that the scientist was dragging all his equipment, drawings, and charts to the cliff top. The scientist rudely walked off without saying goodbye, mumbling to himself about his plans.

"Sir?!," asked Xcalibur, "Can you teach me about constructing houses of sand?"

The scientist ignored him. On the horizon, because of the brightness of the sun, he dissipated. Xcalibur convinced himself that the elderly scientist dissipated in his eyes because of the bright sun. Still, he didn't hear the mumbling of the scientist after he disappeared over the horizon. Xcalibur said to himself, "It's the waves. Yes, the waves. I cannot hear him because of the waves crashing against the shore."

"SH-O-O-O-RE!" yelled a voice suddenly.

It was more of a roar but through a mouth used to hissing replies.

Xcalibur convinced himself that it was an echo from the cliff walls or the castle walls. He examined the castle walls further. He ran a hand along them.

A green, clear talon-ed hand shot out and grabbed his.

Xcalibur screamed.

The three turret towers of sand of the castle fell and the three glass heads of the dragon shot out of them. The castle of sand was quickly vanquished. The glass dragon had been beneath it the entire time. The glass dragon shook the remaining sandcastle off of his back like a gigantic dog.

Xcalibur screamed some more, "You're impossible!"

"You're thinking of the demon Imp Possible. No, my name is Knowledragon," said the clear green head far left.

"What happened to the scientist? Did you eat him?"

"No, blech," said Knowledragon's middle head, "I do not eat humans. I only consume knowledge, and I am well satiated. He probably disappeared off somewhere."

Xcalibur laughed nervously and tried to relax. He said, "So you're a friendly dragon then."

"I am not friendly at best, but I am the best kind of friend," said the third head, "I shall give you anything you want."

"Anything?!" asked Xcalibur.

"Yes, I can give you s-s-six wishes, two for each head instead of the usual three. I was made from Prometheus' flame. Fabricated creation is my s-s-s-s-pecialty," said all three heads in a hissing fashion. Their elongated necks gave them a serpentine look.

Xcalibur said, "I don't believe in Prometheus, and I don't believe in wishes. I only believe what I can see. I like facts."

Knowledragon said, "You will soon see with your eyes what your head cannot believe. I do not need your belief. You need not believe in anything. I only need your desire to know more."

"Kewl," said Xcalibur, "Well, I guess what I want more than anything else is to know more than anybody else in the world."

Knowledgragon's heads jutted out towards Xcalibur. He could smell his smoky, glassy breath.

"There is a certain protocol here. You do know what the word protocol is, don't you?"

Xcalibur nodded, lying. He hadn't been paying attention in English when they went over this vocabulary word.

"You must actually state the wish as a wish. Haven't you read a lot of wishing tales? In my mind, I have everything from Arabian nights to Grimms, etc., etc.," said Knowledragon.

"Okay… okay… I'll wish like I'm in a little kid's story or something. I wish that I had more knowledge than anybody else in the world."

"Taken for granted," said Knowledragon. He directed this toward Xcalibur in more ways than one.

Xcalibur found himself with a doomsday device of his own invention in a secret underground bunker. He was a military scientific genius, and gaunt looking grey aliens with onyx eyes were attacking and destroying the Earth. Xcalibur pushed the button on the doomsday device. It was to destroy the entire Earth along with the aliens. He rushed to escape with an elite group of scientists and thinkers to another planet. But he had not thought to fuel the escape pod. His mind had been on too many higher thoughts. "No-o-o-o-o-!" he screamed. "I wish that I don't know anything."

"Taken for granted," he heard echo in the bunker.

Suddenly, Xcalibur found himself in a hospital bed, a complete vegetable, being kept alive by machines. However, wishes would come from the heart. He felt in the core of his being that he wanted nothing more than to be back on the Greek beach with the glass wish dragon.

And he was there.

"You tricked me!" screamed Xcalibur, "That isn't fair."

Knowledragon's three heads chuckled a gurgly, glassy chuckle, "You tricked yourself. When you only **think** you know everything, that isn't hard to do!"

"Oh, really," said Xcalibur. He looked at the glass dragon. He thought back to what he had said in English class when he was trying to get everybody off subject. He thought of how the torch of Prometheus could have been galvanized and possibly shattered.

He stared at the clear, soulless eyes of the dragon with his buck-brown eyes, and stated, "I wish for you to go from very hot to very cold."

"Taken for granted," said the dragon.

Suddenly, the sun became excruciating. Xcalibur's skin, being a little fair, began to burn. He had a horrible red sunburn. Still, he didn't ask for the wish to go away.

Then, it became very cold. Xcalibur began to shiver. He watched in anticipation, hoping that Knowledragon would shatter.

When it started snowing on the beach and Xcalibur feared catching pneumonia and getting frostbite, he said, "I wish it to be normal temperature again."

"Taken for granted," said the dragon.

Knowledragon's three heads lolled in laughter sunlight, causing green designs to project on Xcalibur and the sand. He roared and hissed a laugh.

"You tried to destroy me with science!" he roared, "I am science! I am all knowledge! I am not only glass! I am supernatural, of Prometheus' flame itself! You will never destroy me!"

Xcalibur thought and thought. He wondered about what Knowledragon was truly made of and believed him. He believed in something extraordinary, something he could not fully see with his eyes, something supernatural. He believed that the glass dragon before him was made of pure thought. Perhaps it was time to send him something impure. He said finally, "I wish Knowledragon was ignorant!"

"No-o-o-o!" screamed Knowledragon.

Knowledragon could not bear being ignorant. The flame of knowledge left him. He went through a reversal of the glass-making process. His molecules shifted around and around until he converted into sand. Then, he was part of the beach itself.

Before he died, his head a specter of sand, a sandy jaw lifting, Knowledragon said, "You have one more wish."

Xcalibur thought of the scientist on the cliff, the one building the giant sandcastle. He thought about how he wanted his secrets, how he wanted all this knowledge. He wasn't quite Excalibur, a grand sword that could fight all, but he thought he was.

"I wish to know more than Knowledragon did before he was made to be ignorant," said Xcalibur. And then he screamed as he felt a gigantic burning. An all-encompassing burning. He became Prometheus' flame itself. Then, he plummeted into the sands on the beach. Painfully, one limb extended outward, a green translucent serpent limb. He sprouted one serpent head.

Xcalibur was then known as Faustuserpent. The glass wishing Faustuserpent formerly known as Xcalibur made his home on the beach. And, until the end of time, he was always available to argue with teachers and students, grant them dooming wishes, and prove them wrong, believing in nothing but himself and his own knowledge.

VON MAL TO GOOD

Jose von Malidiomus grew up in a second generation away from two immigrants, and people in his Southern U.S. city took to shortening his last name to von Mal. Though the von Mals' had idioms of their own in their own two respective countries, Germany and Spain, Jose and his five sisters and one older brother, made up their own new idioms in their parents' pet shop – particularly Jose.

In the pet shop, for example, Jose would say that he and his sisters were fighting like cats and guinea pigs. They sold kittens in the pet store, but Jose spent more time with the guinea pigs. He made little costumes for them and showed them how to escape from the kittens should they get out of their cages. In fact, Jose had developed a little network of tunnels for them. If a kitten got away from any of his siblings and him, the inevitable hissing and chasing would ensue. Thanks to Jose's tunnels and training, the little felines never caught one. Still, the guinea pigs would chirp loudly at the kittens, and the ferocious mini tigers would hiss. Hence, Jose started using fighting like cats and guinea pigs as an idiom.

Jose and the others' parents' pet shop was named Sumo Idi Lam Exotic Pets. People thought it had an Asian sound to it which was intended by the clever marketer Hamish, and it was decorated with silks, Chinese screens, and Asian prints with bamboo frames. But, really, part of the name of the shop was Malidiomus spelled backwards and split up. Except for the five-year-old girl, Julieta, all the children worked in the shop informally after school. Jose's sister, who was just a few years younger than him, Dreisel, and his older sisters, Bina, Faitel, and Martina, as well as his older brother, Anshel, all worked there.

Jose von Mal's German Ashkenazi father, Hamish, and his Spanish mother, Maria, had Sumo Idi Lam Exotic Pets on Broad St. in Augusta, Georgia since the fifties. Hamish had escaped the Nazis in the forties and met Maria in New York City, but she grew up in a farming family in Spain which mostly sold flowers. And Maria longed to get away from the large city.

Therefore, she searched for a place that would have a lot. She saw, in her research at the New York Public Library, that Augusta, Georgia was called the Garden City (it does have small gardens and greenspaces / parks in places). But she also saw lots of photographs in the newspaper of Augusta National and its many red and pink azaleas. As a little girl, reading Oz books translated into Spanish, she had also always longed to go live in the mostly red foliage and floral covered Quadling Country in Oz and be a princess alongside Glinda, who ruled that sub-country of Oz. Having been on a farm, she also liked animals but longed for the comfort of the city.

Having had to flee Germany through all sorts of European backwaters and growing up in a city, Hamish did not want to move to a rural area of Georgia. Maria soon convinced Hamish to take all their savings, give up their New York City apartment, get a larger apartment down South, and start the pet shop in the small city of Augusta, Georgia with its green spaces. It seemed like a good compromise.

As per Hamish's and Maria's next to oldest boy Jose, a delicate looking child with long curly black hair, dressing up the guinea pigs, the matriarch of the Spanish side of his family, the abuela, did not like this. The abuela had to stay with them in her old age, and she used to corner him in the apartment when others were not looking and listening and call him a mariposa. He did not know Spanish as well as his mother and looked it up. He saw that it meant butterfly, and he thought butterflies were beautiful – particularly the Monarch butterflies that flew to the flowers in the box on their apartment windowsill (Maria did not get all the flowers she wanted in the Garden City because she was in a part of downtown that had few of them).

As Maria thought of the public gardens they would travel to in Augusta, she often wondered if they should have opened a flower shop. But she went with Hamish's idea and made the best of it with him.

Jose asked his Mama after Abuela's confrontation, "Que es mariposa?"

He told her his abuela called him that.

His mother flew into a rage and ran to fuss at her mother. Spanish words Jose had never even heard from his mother were uttered. Then, there was some crying in the other room. Finally, silence.

After a while she came back to explain to Jose that it meant "boys who were a little different."

Hamish, who was in the main room of the apartment and knew a good bit of Spanish from Maria, said in his style of English -- English with a Yiddish syntax at times, "Oye…what is it that a boy makes clothes? Plenty of Jewish people made clothes back in New York City. What do we care if for guinea pigs? He practices. It is fine."

The thing was that Jose eventually found out that mariposa meant gay, but he did not really feel attracted to guys in the modern sense. He just wanted to be close friends with them the way he was with girls as well.

But the von Mals still allowed the abuela to corner Jose when others were not looking, and she would hurl little insults at him. They never gave her an ultimatum about it.

One day, when others were busy in the shop, Jose was asked to look after his abuela in the apartment. She had been so hateful to him for so many years and she was lying so still in her bed that he felt like rejoicing. He did not even see her chest rising up and down, but he dared not test her breath. Instead, he screamed, "My grandmother is dead! My grandmother is dead!"

She opened one eye and in her gruff voice said, "Jose, tu abuela no es muerta!"

She did die a couple of years after that, though, and she was one of the few people in life that Jose said "Good riddance" to.

Next, another false idiom or a sort of malapropism idiom that Jose used was that is raining snakes and fish. They had an incident one time in the shop where his clumsy brother Ansel, who was on a ladder cleaning above Jose, knocked and partially spilled an aquarium with fish and a terrarium with some snakes down on

Jose's head while he was cleaning below. Snakes and fish rained down on Jose in the spilled, tepid water from the fish tank. Jose had to quickly gather the reptiles and underwater denizens and put them back in their respective habitats. Jose then mopped up the water quickly and loathed having to smell fishy the rest of the day.

"Mashugana", he yelled to his brother Ansel, which was a word their father used when either did something dumb. His brother, who had already descended the ladder and was not bothering to help Jose but laughed at him, became enraged at what Jose called him. Ansel punched him so hard on the shoulder that it left a bruise. The older boy was a tall, muscular dirty blonde fellow who contrasted Jose's skinny arms and short height. Jose did not tell his mother but hoped one day he could leave this bad family. They were not all bad. But there were enough bad examples that he just wanted to get away.

Yet another malapropism idiom Jose used was "minding your Cs and Ms". Usually, that was "Ps and Qs" and used to refer to pints and quarts but meant as an idiom to mind your manners. Whenever customers were around and his brothers and sisters were rowdy, he would say, "Mind your Cs and Ms" to them. This delighted the customers and some even made a little fun of the usage, thinking it came from their ethnic diversity and lack of understanding of idioms. But it was not that at all. Yes, being second generation, they did not grasp as many idioms as their peers because their parents did not, but they were learning them more than their parents did. They just found it fun to make up their own. So, it was not all bad in the Mal family.

By the way, minding your Cs and Ms meant minding your crickets and mice. The van Mals had two hole-filled drawers with them in the shop close to the separated iguanas and the boa constrictor respectively. Those terrariums looked like a military section with all the greens, browns, and light browns appearing through the translucent covers of the reptile habitats. The chirping of the crickets was constant and a bit annoying. Jose did not mind feeding the crickets to the iguanas, but it was not because of the noise. It was because they were insects and did not seem truly alive but more robotic. But Jose loathed feeding the mice to the boa constrictor. The mice seemed communicative when they squeaked and nuzzled Jose as he always took great care of them. The crickets just lunged for orange slices when he threw them in. The mice gently took food pellets from his hand. Jose had probably just trained them well.

When he had to clean out the acidic and fecal smelling mouse drawer, he would allow the mice to play. Sometimes he would have a little guinea pig ranch set up with a mini-fenced area and would clean out the guinea pig cages first, putting in fresh cedar shavings. (His abuela's old closet at her old place when she moved to the U.S., after his mother did, had smelled like cedar and moth balls and was put in at great expense. His abuela was a dancer well into her sixties and had to protect the many dresses she wore. Having been a dancer, she deemed herself some authority on which male dancers were masculine and which were more effeminate. She had some old-fashioned ideas of the harmful variety. Just because a male dancer was a bit effeminate did not mean he was gay; just because a man danced professionally did not mean he was gay, either. Jose's abuela could accept that the more masculine-acting dancers were straight as she had some of them as her lovers. But if any of them had any effeminate behavior whatsoever, acted in any fashion outside of machismo, she passed instant judgment. Jose's actions as a little fashion designer for his guinea pigs incurred her wrath for this reason.)

After Jose put fresh cedar shavings in the guinea pig cages, he would let the mice play in the guinea pig tubes and area while he cleaned out the mouse drawer. Finally, he would switch them back again, and the mice, to him, seemed almost grateful, nuzzling him again as he returned them to the drawer. This happened quite a few times each week, and Jose bonded with all of them.

Next, Jose did not mind feeding the crickets to the iguanas because he felt like they did not feel pain like the mice did when the boa constrictor got them. Though his father often ended up being argumentative and angry with him, calling him names at times, Jose remembered taking the crickets and putting hooks into them with Papa at the Savannah River, where they would catch fish and where Jose would always remember that muddy smell. Papa had a way of inserting the small hooks just below the exoskeleton of the cricket but not piercing the flesh inside. He taught this to his youngest boy many years ago. With this method, the crickets could jerk around in the water and attract more fish. Jose's papa, Hamish, taught him to pull up the cricket every few minutes so that it would not drown. His father, even in the city where he came from in Germany, would fish in the river there. They shared this as a bonding experience, and kind words were given there to him as they were to his brother. Hamish always complimented his daughters which was the way of his culture. But Hamish could be an obstinate, harsh man to all his family members. Jose would soon find out.

When Jose came up with a plan to no longer feed the mice to the boa constrictor and shared it with his father, he was called a bad boy, the worst boy ever. His father told him he was behaving like a "soft goyim" and that Jews are made of stronger stuff than that.

Jose was also called this because, in the pet shop, he led a protest, with his brothers and sisters, that once they sold the boa constrictor that they never get another one and sell the leftover mice as pets and not as food. The soft boy stood in front of a hand-embroidered silk work from China of some butterflies near some flowers with some Chinese characters in a vertical line to the right. The butterflies behind him were many colors and created the illusion of the boy looking like he had parts of a colorful coat at his sides. The piece had a red background and was framed in black bamboo. Red passion met black bars on each side. Jose just stared at his father after he made the demands of the protest.

From the corner of the front room of the shop, leaning against the corner with her cane, Jose's abuela whispered, looking at him in front of the butterflies in the silk work, "Mariposa." Despite her great age, Abuela still had soft brown skin and was fit but had an almost permanent scowl on her face – particularly at

Jose – and this aged her. Her beetle-brow descended into a capital V darker than an accidentally doubly printed or bold letter. The tendons in her neck looked like baby snakes stretched out in the sun above her high-collared floral dress. Abuela kept her frown. "Mariposa," she whispered again.

Maria, who was with the family, shot her mother a look but the rest ignored her. There were proverbial bigger Savannah River or Rhine River fish to bake. (The von Mals preferred it baked, and they did love to change those idioms!)

"What a son I have!" Jose's father said, and not in good way when Jose explained that his brothers and sisters would contact the Department of Labor and turn the von Mals in for child labor, that only rural people could have children work for businesses. He said that technically no child should work in a business and especially not in a city.

"Worked I did from when I was a kleyntshiger until now…and…you…you all come to me with this rubbish!" Hamish yelled. He took his yarmulke off as if to throw it at the boy and then thought the better of it, returning it to his head. He then tried to calm down, stroking his long, white beard.

Jose said, holding one of the white lab mice and petting it as he talked to his father, his brothers and sisters folding their arms in solidarity behind him, "Papa, we know where you get the mice, and we will tell on you about that as well."

The mice were leftover mice from medication experiments from a local medical facility. Hamish and his Spanish wife had both agreed to purchase the mice at a much lower rate than they could get from a distributor. This was not a case of a Jewish man being stereotypically cheap or thrifty, if you will, and Spanish people were not always known for being cheap either. The multi-ethnic couple had made this bad decision together as husband and wife. They knew that by feeding the boa constrictor the tainted mice for the past months that the boa constrictor would not have long to live.

Jose said softly, "I am going to take care of the mice until they pass away. If you sell one, you are going to tell people they are rescued medical mice and that they may not live long—"

Jose stroked the mouse like a Bond villain, or the Godfather stroked a cat. But he was not intending to look the part of the villain.

"And one more thing, Papa—"

"What? What a *schlemiel* of a father I am to have such a son as this!"

He pulled at his beard until nearly pulling hairs out of it.

Maria had been standing by Papa for some time quietly. Maria looked on at her children with pride. She had taught them to stand up for what was right and felt convicted. She told her husband this, too. He had just lost his way a little.

She looked at the children who said they were "like elevators": all up and down. The common Southern U.S. idiom was to say if you had kids one after another that they were like steps. But some of hers had enough age between them that they were all up and down. There had been a year or two when business was bad that Hamish was so stressed out that they did not make love. This was hardly the norm for them both, though.

As a Catholic, she did not convert to Judaism but did allow her children to attend Temple as well as Mass (they could never be truly Jewish in the traditional sense as Hamish married a non-Jew). Maria strongly opposed birth control in any form. And she was well acquainted with Hamish's kosher, cut German sausage. So, she ended up with quite the brood. And they were, as Maria said, "like elevators."

When they were all in the shop or when she was out with her children on errands, she was distinctly called Maria "von Mal" with her many dirty blonde- and black-haired children of all up and down heights looking like the von Trapp children in "The Sound of Music" movie. However, she never dressed the children in curtains, but they could often be seen in smocks they wore over their clothes in the pet-shop. Anyway, being a fan of musicals herself, she thought in this case it might be, "How do you solve a problem like Jose?", not "Maria".

Meanwhile, Jose continued, the mouse squeaking contentedly in his hand, "You will sell the boa constrictor at a deep discount and let them know it may not live long."

"A child telling a parent what to do! Spare the rod, spoil the child… I should—" Hamish grabbed his walking stick from behind the counter.

"Parents, provoke not your children to anger," Jose replied, "The sins of the fathers…"

Hamish muttered something about that mashugana priest of his mother's teaching them the scriptures. At least the rabbi had them learning Hebrew and the Torah.

Hamish did listen, though, and put the walking stick down, threw up his hands, and said, "Do what you want… never could I imagine when I escaped the Nazis that I would have such children at this!"

Some of the others said, "What we are doing is not bad, Papa", and "We are only trying to do the right thing." Some of the girls approached him and grabbed his hands.

Maria said, "I follow you as my husband, but we must both recognize when we've done wrong. There is a saying in the Catholic Bible… and a child shall lead them—"

"The Catholic Bible… bah… I agreed to having them raised in both faiths, but I did not know you were going to bring yours up so often… Hear about it every day, I do!"

Maria said, hugging him, "How about from the Torah then…from Proverbs? 'My child, hold on to your wisdom and insight. Never let them get away from you. They will provide you with life, a pleasant and happy life.' You have wise children."

Hamish softened with this and relented.

Anshel nearly dropped the mouse drawer he was holding as Jose held that one mouse. The others had their mouths open. They had seldom if ever seen their father give in to anyone or anything.

"Oye, vey," Anshel said as the holey mouse drawer nearly hit the wooden floor of the shop.

"I have a schlimazel!" Anshel half-joked about his clumsy son.

Jose then joked, in a quasi-falsetto in a cheer as his voice was still high at the time, grabbing one his sister's arms, *"Schlemiel! Schlimazel! And then there's Faitel!"*

Faitel, his next to oldest sister who liked such fun and games, did a little skipping walk with him.

Hamish said, "Oye, vey," but he laughed a rolling, bass laugh at his children's antics.

The boa constrictor was eventually sold, the snake had left its terrarium garden, Abuela eventually died, and Jose was able to tend to sickly white mice, only selling them to those who he knew were the most caring with rodents.

Scott Blanke

Scott Brian Blanke is a retired Mayo Clinic surgeon whose interest in the continuing saga of The Wizard of Oz began as a child and now, as an adult, he reads the stories to his children and now grandchildren. His personal collection of Oz titles numbers in the hundreds and he is a member of several Wizard of Oz clubs.

His novel, 'Oscar Diggs, The Wizard of Oz' was published in December by Black rose Writing. It is available on Amazon.

Scott lives in La Crosse, Wisconsin with his author wife. He has three grown children and trips to visit them make up a large part of his life, though that may be just an excuse to try out new restaurants and wines. When not writing, Scott enjoys gardening, specializing in exotic garlic, and amateur photography, particularly taking photos of his grandchildren.

THE OZ ALMOST COVEN

"Double, double, toil and trouble," chanted Mombi, The Evil Witch of the North. She bent so far over and stared into the boiling cauldron's putrid contents. She inhaled. "It needs mortal's blood and more swamp water."

"Eye of newt, and toe of frog," screeched Bastinda, The Wicked Witch of the West. She stalked around the pot. "Death to these pesky locals." Bastinda went over to a young girl, crying in a small cage. "Damn, it needs more blood. We might need to use yours after all deary."

The girl looked up with bloodshot eyes. Her dress was filthy and torn. "Leave me alone, I want my mommy."

"Wool of bat, and tongue of dog," shrieked Gingema, The Wicked Witch of the East. "Adder's fork, and blind-worm's sting. Um...?" She paused and looked up at the ceiling, taking in the cobwebs and dust. Gingema lowered her gaze and traced the blood oozing down the pine walls. The witch scratched her greasy head and three cockroaches jumped off her hair and scurried away. "Oh, yes. Lizard's leg, and owlet's wing."

Together, the three witches howled the next line. "For a charm of powerful trouble, like a hell-broth boil and bubble." They lifted their hands to the roof. "Now, fire burn and cauldron bubble. Cool it with a baboon's blood." They silenced themselves and held hands around the cauldron. The released cockroaches stopped mid-stride and the pot's contents ceased to bubble. They screamed in unison. "Then the charm is firm and good!"

Gingema scuttled over to a wall and ran a finger down its splattered, clotted blood. She held the digit up, turned it from left to right, then licked her finger. "Do you think?" She turned back to her fellow witches. "We can use the blood from the family whose hovel this is. Or must it be from an ape?"

Mombi shook her head, then spit her response. "There isn't enough blood to our cauldron from those three puny bodies, though it was gratifying to see them die in terror and pain. I will save the girl for further torture or use her to stir if Pippt has to be killed. Also, the spell is quite specific." She held a large butcher's knife at arm's length, its edges razor sharp and bloody. She grinned, her eyes shiny with delight. "I loved slitting the parents throats." Mombi put the blade down and lifted her wand. "Why waste magic when you can be hands on?"

The young girl screamed. "Who are you people? What did you do to my parents and brother? Please let me go, I did nothing to you!" The girl wiggled against multiple rope bindings and pounded on the cage bars. "Please, what are you going to do with me?"

Bastinda walked to the corner, where a thin man, bent and crooked, huddled. "You, stand up," she ordered. She grasped his arm, dragged him to the cauldron and forced him onto a tall, wobbly stool.

"Please, release me," begged the crooked man. The man's joints creaked even after he sat on the stool.

"Shut up," yelled Bastinda. She waved her wand and a moment later a large stirring paddle secured itself to his leg and an equally sized spoon did the same to his arm.

"Stir and keep stirring until we tell you to stop." Mombi put her face to his as she spoke. He turned away from the stench of her breath.

Gingema sidled up to him and whispered in his ear. "Now, Pipt, unless you want to end up like our friends here?" She pointed to the murdered family on the floor. "Or should I prove how serious we are? We can demonstrate on little Amanda's throat." Gingema made a slashing motion across her neck with a long-pointed fingernail. "You shouldn't even stop stirring long enough to scratch your pathetic crotch."

He whimpered. "Please release me and let me return to my wife, back in Oz."

She moved to his other side. "Stirring is all you are good for. You are an incompetent magician." She pinched his earlobe between her long black, broken, nails. "All we found in your house was a small pinch of your Powder of Life. That's not even enough to bring a patchwork girl to life."

Mombi pointed her wand at him. "So trapped you are here. We need someone to do our bidding… and stirring."

Gingema stoked Pipt's bald head. "If you're a good boy, we won't harm your fat little wife, back in Oz."

He jerked to look at her, his eyes wide and he sniveled as his mouth opened and closed.

Bastinda's voice rose above the noise. "When this magic potion is done, we three will dominate here with evil power." She thought, *Pipt and his wife will then die, as will thousands here, before we are done.*

Gingema lifted a wand and pointed it at the crooked man. "Quiet Pipt. If you don't want to end up like this dead family, shut up and keep stirring. It's too bad we had to come here and then found out our wands and brooms were so limited in power. Yes." Gingema hissed. "Our Flying Monkeys have your wife. So, you will sit here and stir all day until I say you're done." She threw out her arms and her head back and let go a shrieking cackle that caused the blood on the walls to turn black. She pointed at the cauldron. "So just STIR!"

Dr. Pipt shuddered. When the clamor around him settled, he asked in a hoarse whisper, "You promise to release my wife?" He grumbled and continued to mix.

Mombi stared at Pipt with an impish smile on her face and crossed her fingers behind her back. She widened the smile, revealing blackened teeth and gums and missing spaces. Her putrid breath rivaled the potion's horrible aroma. "Of course, we will, Pipt my boy. You know you can trust us!"

Bastinda cackled and bent over a crystal ball placed in a tall metal stand. She motioned to her compatriots, and they angled their bodies around the ball so that only they could see its contents. When she waved her wand, an image materialized inside the orb. Margolotte, Pipt's wife, was inside the castle, chained hand and foot to a castle wall. Three winged monkeys impaled hot pokers into her belly and a fourth slowly bit off one finger after another from her hands. The crystal ball emitted no sound, but her screams were evident. "Yes, Pipt, it looks like she's doing fine."

He sputtered. "Dear witches, you are power, and I am just a minor wizard. Please do not harm Margolotte." With his crooked free hand, he easily massaged the small of his back. "With all this stirring, my back is killing me." Pipt whined. "When are you going to get the rest of the ingredients? When can I just stop and just go home to Oz?"

Mombi shrieked. "Stir, Pipt, or suffer the consequences."

Dr. Pipt said. "Ladies I am. Besides, I'm doing all the damned work." He vigorously stirred the cauldron with the one paddle tied to his crooked leg and pointed the huge spoon at the witches." You can sing about the ingredients, but what you require are in short supply. Where can you acquire 'eye of newt' in the middle of a New England winter?"

The door of the hovel crashed open at this moment and snow interspersed with sleet blew in. The flames of the cauldron danced sideways in the gusts of frigid air and almost went out. Pipt shivered but Mombi waved her wand and the flames roared upwards again.

"It's all your fault Mombi," said Bastinda. She walked over and slammed shut the door. Bastinda turned and went to the cauldron and took a deep breath of the fumes. Then she stuck a finger into the bubbling liquid and licked her digit. "The aroma is coming along famously, the odor of wet cat. She sighed. "But it definitely lacks a kick. We could have easily gotten all the ingredients in Oz, especially with the help of the Flying Monkeys. But no, Mombi is bored and wants to travel far from Oz." The witch pretended to dance around, like the cauldron flames, her tattered dress billowing about her spindly legs. "I'm Mombi, I'm bored, let's go somewhere different. Let's go to America!"

"I thought it would be an interesting idea," said Mombi. "I've never been here before. How was I supposed to know our powers would be severely diminished and we would have to brew a restorative potion before we could have any fun?" She also sniffed the cauldron's aroma and frowned. "It is much too weak. There's been evil witches out here for centuries. I wonder how they do things?"

The evil Witch of the East looked around the cottage. "I thought the flying monkeys would have brought the next ingredient already. It should be coming here any second."

"How were you able to get the magic flying monkeys to agree to come to America?" asked Mombi. "I thought their powers weren't strong enough to work in the outside world. You never see flying monkeys; only squirrels in this neck of the woods."

Gingema pointed to her bare feet. She wore black smelly socks with huge holes in them but was missing her silver slippers. One big toe, with a twisted sharp toenail poked through the largest hole. "I lent them my slippers to send our package back to us. The monkeys are going to harvest the item in Oz, put it in the slippers and then tap three times. It should be here soon."

Bastinda looked into the cauldron. "What is it, what is it? What ingredient are we getting?"

"You'll see soon enough." The evil Witch of the East wiggled her big toe. A visible miasma of odor rose from it.

A pair of giant frog legs wearing ornate yellow knickers, suddenly, materialized next to the witch. On the feet were bloody yellow and red striped stockings, encased in unusually shaped silver slippers. The legs ended at bloody stumps. They were still twitching.

Dr. Pipt stared at the only remaining part of the Frogman of OZ, slid off his stool, and fainted dead away. Amanda screamed and screamed.

The evil Witch of the East pulled the legs from out of the silver slippers. The shoes were wide and almost flat. As soon as the witch removed the bloody extremities from the shoes, they began to transform. First, they narrowed, then shortened and finally developed a small platform to the heel. She kissed the footwear and slipped them back on.

The witch walked over to the wooden kitchen table and picked up a rusty cleaver. She hacked off one big toe from the bloody leg, peeled off the sock, remaining on the digit stump and threw the toe into the cauldron. "Oh dear. It appears that the Frogman of Oz has croaked."

Mombi walked over and slapped the little girl. "Quiet you, or I'll use your legs next." She then walked over to Pipt and kicked till he awoke. The crooked magician groggily shuffled over to the stool and sat down again.

Dr. Pipt began stirring with his crooked leg but used the huge spoon to point it at the three witches. "So now you have two ingredients. Gingema got the toe of frog and Mombi ripped a poor poodle's tongue out of its mouth yesterday. Now where and how do you get all the rest of the items? How can I ever leave, you three keep forgetting the exact spell and what is needed. I want to go home."

Bastinda raised her wand. "Quiet Pipt, or I'll turn you into a mouse. My wand at least has that much power."

Gingema raised her wand also. "Sisters, I do have an idea. Separately, our wands are impotent 'til the potion is brewed. But together we do have some power. Think how mighty we would be if we could summon a true coven."

Mombi raised her wand. "But we are only three. Pipt doesn't count at all. We need a full thirteen for a coven to raise full power." She wrinkled her forehead. "I wonder if the wife here had any witchy powers?" Mombi shook her head. "No, she would have protected her two children better, before we done them in."

"The closer to that magic number, the better," said Bastinda. "We could certainly start with our three sister witches from Macbeth. They should be able to remember the exact spell and ingredients. They said it enough times during that dumb play. We could also get their head witch, Hecate."

"I vote no," said Mombi. "That woman was too bossy. But we should also try to summon Morgan le Fey, Circe, and Baba Yaga." She began to wave her wand and chant.

Bastinda looked confused. She waved her wand around aimlessly. "I'm certainly familiar with Morgan le fey and Circe, but who in the world is Baba Yaga?"

At the same time, Gingema winced and turned pale. "Mombi, Mombi, Mombi, not the best of ideas. We need all of them, but even I am afraid of Baba Yaga. She is the most evil creature there is."

Bastinda turned to her. She asked, "But who is she?"

"A witch found in old central Europe. She started eating children before the witch from Hansel and Gretel. Some say she is immortal, and her spit can transform people into living furniture." Gingema shivered, "I don't want to be a living nightstand."

Bastinda looked serious. "We need all the help we can get. So, Hecate is in also. Great idea on summoning Circe. She can definitely help us obtain the rest of the animal items. I think we have to recruit the mighty Baba Yaga, despite the danger."

Gingema nodded. "Pipt, stop your stirring, get over here, and draw a pentagram on the floor."

Dr. Pipt stopped stirring, straightened up as much as he could, and shuffled over to the table. He pushed aside onions, garlic, turnips, meat cleavers, huge butcher knives and a sharp ice pick. The magician found a short piece of black chalk. He went to the center of the room and quickly drew a pentagram on the floor. Then he carefully inscribed a large circle around the star. "One of my better figures." Pipt lifted his head and furrowed his brow at the witches. "Now what?"

Mombi, Gingema, and Bastinda took their wands and stood carefully outside the drawn circle. They formed a perfect equilateral triangle. All began to chant and waved their wands in a counterclockwise direction. As their words became more frenzied, their circles moved faster and faster.

First to materialize in the pentagram were the three Weird sisters from Macbeth. One witch held a large spoon and was attempting to stir even while they manifested inside the star. The three sisters all blinked rapidly and looked around in bewilderment.

Next substantiated was a stately beautiful woman with streaked brown hair. She was in the process of petting an African lion, who was purring loudly. "I am the great Circe. How dare you summon me?" The two attempted to leave the pentagram but were repelled. The three witches outside the circle, changed their chant, reversed the direction of the wand circles, and the lion vanished.

"Goodbye cat," Mombi cackled. She continued the chant and waved her wand counterclockwise again.

Next came a squint-eyed, bent over crone. She held a large tree branch as a staff. The woman put her hand out and an electric charge pushed it back. The witch glared, "I be Baba Yaga, pay the price of your insolence." She turned towards the Weird sisters and spat on one of them. The sister nearest transformed, screaming, into a large, overstuffed chair. The crone cackled and sat down. "That's better, more comfortable. When you let me out, I might turn this woman back. If not, I have plenty more spit for all of you."

Two bloodshot human eyes, on the top of the chair, blinked and then glanced frantically around the pentagram. A large mouth opened widely and screamed, "Oh the pain, the pain. Help me sisters!"

The two remaining Weird sisters backed as far away from Baba Yaga as the pentagram allowed.

Mombi, Gingema, and Bastinda all took several steps back from the pentagram. They trembled as they stared at the witch sitting in the living chair but began to wave their wands again.

Almost immediately another woman with vivid red hair materialized. Her body rotated in the pentagram slowly. But a distinct, separate face was able to glare at Mombi and the two Wicked Witches, all at the same time.

"Ack!" Gingema screamed. "She gots three faces, on one head!" Her mouth fell open, and drool dribbled out. The witch stopped waving her wand and her hand fell to her side.

Next to the woman with red hair, was a pack of pitch-black dogs. They all growled and barked excitedly. The woman looked disdainfully at the pentagram and raised a regal staff. "It is rather crowded in this pitiful star." She waved the staff, the top burst into flame and the woman and dogs easily stepped out of the pentagram. "Now who summons Hecate, the Queen of the witches?"

The beautiful woman with streaked brown hair, raised a wand and waved it. She also stepped past the pentagram's lines. "Where did my pet go? My subjects need me so." Circe turned towards Pipt and waved her wand. He immediately became a crooked pig. "Bah, pitiful, but I need creatures to worship me at all times." She then turned toward the little girl. Amanda screamed, crouched down in the cage, and hid behind her arms. Circe murmured, "So loud, I'll make you an appropriate animal." She waved her wand.

Amanda changed into a Howler monkey. She screeched, slid through her ropes, squeezed through the bars of the cage, and tore around the room. The monkey climbed into the rafters of the hovel and began to throw feces at the witches. The witches ignored her.

Pipt ran around in circles and squealed. Finally, he came over to Circe's feet, bowed, and looked up at her with a worshiping look on his face.

The two Weird Sisters beat at the invisible barrier inside the pentagram and kept getting thrown back. They next waved their wands and chanted futilely. The chair continued to scream.

Baba Yaga just sat and stared.

Hecate faced Mombi, the two wicked witches, and Circe, she asked. "Really ladies, I thought I taught you better." Hecate waved her staff again and all the lines of the pentagram and circle vanished.

"Oh no," cried Mombi. "We didn't summon Morgan le Fey."

Circe nonchalantly waved her hand. "Why have you summoned me and these other vile creatures?"

Baba Yaga just sat and stared. "I could have eaten that child. What a waste."

The remaining two sister witches bolted out of the center of the room and ran up to Hecate. They all prostrated themselves at her feet. One exclaimed, "Thank you, oh great one!"

One of Hecate's faces turned as red as her hair as she glared at the three Oz witches. "How dare you drag me to this dreadful place against my will! Why shouldn't I destroy you as you stand?"

Circe pushed pig Pipt to the side with her foot. "This ugly three-faced one speaks the truth. Why shouldn't I destroy you all and return to my island?"

Baba Yaga just sat and stared.

"Sisters," cried Mombi. "Hear me out. We are from the land of Oz, just visiting this place. Our powers are unsurpassed in Oz, but here, we have found them wanting. We are here for just a short visit and then we will be out of your lives. We are attempting to duplicate one of your most powerful spells." Mombi pointed to the bubbling cauldron. "But are having trouble obtaining some of the components."

Three wads of spit cascaded to the floor. Hecate's other two faces turned red. "Bah, I repeat. Why should I help instead of destroying you?"

Mombi held up both her hands, palms outward. "Strictly for the idea of pure evil, sister. We will enslave these mortals." She turned towards Baba Yaga. "Plenty of fat children for you to eat." Now she faced Circe. "Lots of stupid men for you to transform into animals to worship you." Finally, she faced Hecate. "When was the last time you and your coven did anything against these puny mortals? When was the last time you were truly wicked? "

Hecate's faces turned back to a more normal color. "I'm listening. This idea does intrigue me." She waved her wand and eight wooden chairs, and one padded throne appeared. The queen witch waved the wand again and Pipt turned back into a man.

Baba Yaga slowly stood up. "I will assist. I was bored back in Hungary." She waved her tree staff and the Weird sister chair turned back into a woman, screaming all the time. "I already had a chair, but I'll accept this one." The old witch haltingly trudged over to the throne and sat down. She looked over at the girl, bound in the cage. "Is that a snack for later?"

Hecate muttered. "That was my seat." She waved her wand over one of the wooden chairs and an even larger, more padded throne appeared. Two out of three of Hecate's faces merged into just one stunning countenance. "I could tell some of you were uncomfortable with my appearance." She lowered herself into the throne, regally with her back straight, as if she were sitting only on a cloud. "What do you require from my royal presence?"

Mombi recited, "Um, we have toe of frog and tongue of dog. I also got a lot of green swamp water for the boiling liquid. But we still need a newt eyeball, a lizard's leg, and um…. I don't remember the rest?"

"Mombi you're hopeless," said Gingema. "We still need fur of a bat."

"Wool of bat," sang the Weird sisters. "Not fur."

"Picky, picky, picky," said Gingema. "What's the difference?"

One Weird sister scratched her head. "I have no idea, but I know my chant. I said it enough times for Will."

"What is an adder's fork and a blind-worm's sting?" asked Bastinda. "And where can we get baboon's blood in the middle of winter in America?"

"That's why I recruited you ladies for help," said Mombi. "The Weird sisters will be quality assurance experts and will continue to stir." She turned to Hecate, bent over, and whispered. "Pipt is a typical male, worthless." The witch straightened up. "Circe is an animal expert. If anyone can get wool of bat and baboon's blood, it's her."

"And my role?" said Hecate.

Mombi chortled. "The rest of the ingredients are reptilian. As a witch, you are known to be extremely cold- blo…."

Hecate's three faces appeared again and turned very red. "If you value your existence, don't finish that statement."

"Mombi turned pale. "No, no, no. I just meant you are the ultimate in evil. So very respected, so knowledgeable." She took a step back and hid behind Bastinda. "So very cold-blooded and evil."

Hecate's three faces merged back into one. It then turned back to a tannish color. "I will accept that statement and let you live. But I still have one problem. I have no idea what a blind-worms sting is or where one finds that creature."

Circe said. "It is a very poisonous snake with very small eyes. I don't know if they really exist?" She turned to the three sisters. "Do you?"

The middle sister shrugged her shoulders. "Not really. I think the author just couldn't think of anything to rhyme."

Baba Yaga pounded her staff on the floor three times. "What dost you require of mine self? These arduous chores sound tiresome."

Gingema bowed to her. "You evil one will be our security specialist. We only have a limited time before the moon is full and if any mortals attempt to enter our abode, we will need you to fend them off."

"As for the rest of the tasks, I have an idea," said Mombi. "Weird sisters, keep stirring. Circe, take my broom and find baboon's blood. You can find it in Africa. On your way back, pick up an owl's wing and shave a bat." She bowed to Hecate, then did a terrible curtsy. "Queen Hecate, you procure the eye of newt and the adder's fork. Take Gingema's broom and have Bastinda with you."

"What of the blind-worm sting?" said Hecate.

Mombi smiled. "I will take care of that with Dr. Pipt's help."

The witches opened the door and snow billowed in. Circe, Hecate, and Bastinda mounted their brooms and took off.

Through the open door, two children carrying a pail and milking stool could be seen. Baba Yaga rose up from her chair and screeched, "Dinner!" She waved her staff and the two-lock stepped into the hovel. The pail dropped and fresh milk spilled out onto the dirt floor. The door slammed shut. High pitched screams began.

Seven hours later the witches returned.

All the ingredients were placed in the cauldron. The weird sisters stirred vigorously, and the liquid boiled. Foul smelling bubbles popped. The three sisters chortled, chanted, but continued to cast frightened glances at Baba Yaga.

Baba Yaga sat in Hecate's chair and picked her teeth with a small finger bone. A pile of mangled clothes was at her feet. Hecate's black dogs lay beneath her, chewing on leg bones.

On the kitchen table was a rolled clay snake. It had small eyes, and brightly painted stripes. A thin, serpentine tongue protruded from its inert mouth.

Hecate looked at the snake. "Nice clay work Mombi, but of what use is it to the spell? The chant calls for a live reptile."

"Watch," said Mombi. "Dr. Pipt, it is your turn."

The crooked Magician took a crooked arm and reached into an inside coat pocket. He removed a small vial and uncorked it. The man motioned to Mombi to be ready and then poured a pinch of the Powder of Life from the vial on the clay snake.

Mombi immediately grabbed the reptile just at the back of its head as it came to life. The snake bared its fangs, venom dripping off them. Mombi threw the serpent into the pot.

"The potion should be ready soon," said Mombi. "And then our evil witch's powers will be at their ultimate apex!"

Hecate stood up and faced the door. The black dogs stopped chewing and began to yap. The witch cried, "I hear hammering, and yelling outside. We are found out!"

The front door smashed open. Standing just outside the door frame were dozens of men holding pitchforks and torches. The two men in front lugged a tree trunk, using it as a battering ram. Everyone was garbed in dull black or gray, wearing baggy pants with large shiny buckles and loose-fitting jackets. The leader pulled off his flat-topped hat and waved it in front of him. "Witches, you face the wrath of God. We will test your virtue and Godliness by a Witch's Trial. Those who fail will be burned at the stake."

Hecate stood up from her throne. "Begone, foolish mortals. We laugh at these trials." Her face metamorphosed into three faces again, each one turning red.

The leader lifted a bible. "Parishioners, we don't even have to do the Witch's Mark test on this one. Behold, she obviously has the sign of a witch. And that thing…" he pointed at the crooked magician, "is a warlock. Burn them."

The crowd pushed forward with pitchforks ready. A dozen men were blasted back by Hecate's staff, but these were replaced by a dozen more.

Baba Yaga spit on the lead man with the two men holding the battering ram. While screaming, they metamorphosed into a twin bed. "Bah," she swished her tongue back and forth in her ancient mouth. "I now be out of spit." She sucked on the finger bone. "Nothing!" Baba Yaga waved her tree staff. "Back to my home." She vanished.

Hecate waved her staff and blew apart five more men. She shook her three faces. "Foolish mortals, you would have been perfect slaves. We flee. Come sisters, let us leave." The Weird Sisters, the pack of black dogs, and Hecate disappeared.

The leader shouted. "Let us capture these other witches. Their leader is gone. And the three brewing in the cauldron were obviously making witch cakes or such." He pointed at Pipt. "We still have the warlock."

Circe preened in front of the Puritans. Although their eyes bulged out at her beauty, they still advanced on her with their pitchforks. "I should just turn you all into the pigs for the way that you are acting. But I think I'll just flee." She waved her wand and vanished.

One of the men screamed and dropped to his knees. "Pastor Elijah, such evil is afoot. What do we do with these last three evil doers?"

The man pointed at the Oz witches. "They will be destroyed by God's holy fire. But as pious men, we still have to offer them a Witch's Trial to prove if they are innocent. Evil woman, do you wish to undergo the 'Prayer Test'?"

Mombi said, "No problem. Here I have never trespassed or transgressed… yet."

The Pastor said. "The Incantation Test?"

Gingema said. "That might be a problem, I never can remember all those words."

Pastor Elijah indicated that the three be bound. "Therefore, we must do the Dunking Stool test. It will sort out the righteous!"

"Water!" The three Witches screeched. "Never!"

Mombi raised her wand and waved it. A pitchfork flew from the hand of one of the men in front, reversed and pierced the abdomen of the leader. The fork moved by itself, first side to side, then in a rotational motion. She waved her wand again and the fork tore out through the man's back.

The pastor screamed and attempted to hold in his intestines as they slithered to the floor, from his gaping wound. "Dear God, I am done in!" His black pointy boots became soaked with blood and feces from his ruptured entrails.

Other Puritans advanced on the three witches.

The witches danced gleefully, then stopped. "No, we must flee." They grabbed their broom sticks, waved their wands, and vanished.

A disembodied arm reached back and grabbed Pipt by the shoulder. He disappeared also.

The caged girl in the corner cried out. "Pastor Elijah, Deacon James, free me. Please!"

Deacon James smiled wickedly at the caged girl. "Here at least is a witch, we can burn. Take her men!"

With his dying breath, Pastor Elijah cried. "We must be ever vigilant against these transgressors. These evil ones must have been just the beginning. We will continue to search out others and kill them. Let it never be said that we will allow any evil to brew in Salem, Massachusetts."

Jerry Bridges

Jerry Bridges is the author of "'INTO THE LAIR", a sci-fi fantasy epic novel that was a decade in the writing and is the first book in the "Taming the Chaos" series. His novel is available on the YBR Publishing website store.

Jerry is a proud graduate of LSU School of Horticulture and has been a practicing horticulturist for most of forty years. He began his practice in Baton Rouge, but when that city experienced 48 percent unemployment, he moved back to his ancestral home of Columbia, SC. After many years there, he followed work to Beaufort, SC.

An avid gamer, his writing is based around the magic system found in one of his favorite Role-Playing Games. Jerry reads constantly, accompanied by his dog beside him and his cat on his lap. He is a proud husband to Vickie for 37 years and father of four incredible children. A committed Christian, he is an active member of his church choir.

STRAWBERRY MYLANTA

I believe that every husband should be supportive of their wife. So, when my wife, Vickie, was in her third month of pregnancy with our fourth boy and she came out at 10 PM complaining of an upset stomach, I was up in a heartbeat getting her some Mylanta. When she complained about the taste, I said, "Well, think of something whose taste you like better, like… oh… chocolate or strawberries."

She said, "OK."

I repeated, "So which would you like better, chocolate or strawberry?"

I was shocked when she said, "Strawberry." I don't think I had ever heard her prefer ANYTHING to chocolate. When I heard that little something in her voice, that's when the horns began growing on my forehead, supporting my halo.

"Ok, I'm going to paint you a word-picture and I want you to really, really picture it. Ok?"

Her "Ok" was so filled to the brim with trust that my barbed tail just naturally joined my horns in supporting my halo.

"Ok, now imagine bright, red, fresh-picked strawberries diced and freshly melted in sugar, like you put on short cakes."

"Hmm, hmm."

"Can you just taste how good and sweet they are?"

"Oh, yes."

"Now picture a second taste coming in to blend with sweet, melted strawberries just waiting on a spoon right at the edge of your mouth."

Her eyes closed and her head moved forward to the imaginary spoon.

"Are you ready?"

"Um, hmmm."

"Ok, then picture this… strawberries and… Mylanta!"

And she KICKED me!

She went to bed in a huff and woke up an hour later. She had had a dream of strawberry Mylanta. She kicked me again.

When I suggested going to the store to see if they carried strawberry Mylanta, she kicked me again. It's a good thing for me that she can't kick very hard.

That was a Saturday night, so the next workday, I came home with cherry Mylanta, apologizing because they didn't make it in strawberry flavor. Guess what, for some reason she kicked me again. When I checked for it a month later because I needed Mylanta, I discovered she had thrown it away. I wonder why…

So, you see guys, with a little imagination, you can help your wife with her physical needs and with helping her to dream and even aiding her in getting her unfocused aggression out.

SWORD PLAY

(This short story takes place after the "Taming the Chaos"
series)

Drip, drip, drip—the sound of the water deep within a cave was interrupted by the distinct sound of a hammer striking a chisel. The light of three torches set in a circle around a small pool disappeared in the immensity of the cave. Several partially dismembered old skeletons were visible within the light, as if a battle had been fought here long ago.

Centered within the torches and embedded at least two feet into the cavern's stone floor, a magnificent sword still stood five feet high. Inset in its pommel was a huge diamond; a green falcon was embedded along the Ricasso of the transparent blade. The chiseler, a man of proportions to fit the huge sword, was kneeling inside the light as well, was working his way deeper into the rock encasing the sword. The unusual blade had been a gift from a Wee Folksmith for services rendered. More than the old man's size and girth paired the two, the beaded green falcons decorating his tabard also matched.

Wiping his forehead, hammer in hand, Duncan said, "I have you now! Once more and you're free!"

A pulse began in the pommel and shot through the blade and fifteen feet of stone disintegrated, leaving a circular hole just wide enough for the two-foot-wide quillons to fit as the sword plummeted out of his desperate lunge.

Laying aside the chisel and hammer, the hero paced until his anger abated. Calmed, he knelt and pulled a neatly folded rope and hook out of his pack. Hour after hour after tedious hour, he tried to hook the sword like a fisherman going after a particularly canny fish, but to no avail. The sword kept dodging his hook.

Exasperated, he shouted to the sword, "Quit moving, Glennfallis!" Drawing a deep breath, he said, "Yes, I *know* if I hadn't sunk you in the stone ten years ago, you wouldn't be mad at me now!" He paused as if in conversation with someone, but no one was present but the sword. He continued, "But you killed my grandson. So yes, I stabbed you into the stone and swore never to use you again."

"How did that make you *feel*?" the sword asked.

"How should I know? You're a sword! A bloody, stinking sword! Quit moving and let me catch you! I need you!

"For what?"

"To kill enemies! Stupid talking sword," he grumbled as he continued to work his rope and hook.

"I have you now," he shouted as he rapidly pulled the rope up. As the blade reached the edge of the hole the diamond flashed blue and the sword flew to the cave roof ten feet over the hole, hovering there. It was a dancing sword, after all.

Duncan had been an athlete and warrior his entire life. No longer a young man, he could still make that jump, but just as his hand was about to close on the pommel, the sword spun around and spanked him! He fell with a crash.

Worse, as he regained his feet, the sword was now completely invisible. The Wee Folksmith was talented and had poured all his abilities into the forging of this blade for his favorite Hero. After surveying the entire cave and walking in complete silence as only a true hunter could do, he finally gave up and crawled around searching the cave on his hands and knees. +The much-humbled warrior mumbled, "At least no one is here to see my shame." He heard footsteps from the cave entrance…

"Duncan! Honey! You've been up here for three days! Haven't you gotten Glennfallis free yet?"

Duncan whimpered and collapsed.

Rana, his tiny wife, hurried to him.

"Honey! Are you hurt?"

"No," he answered, a low moan escaping his throat. He whined, "He's hiding from me. I finally got him out an hour or two ago and he spanked me. Me! His master! Now he's invisible and he's hiding from me."

"Sounds to me like he's mad at being stuck in the stone for so many years without even a visit," Rana said.

"He's a sword! A bloody, stinking…"

"Shush now," she spoke gently, like she would to one of their many grandchildren. "You know he hears everything you say. Did you tell him *why* you needed him?"

"No." Duncan snapped.

"Did you mention the new enemies from the south who attack us with our own dead, making our brave lads run in terror?"

"No," he said more quietly and slowly, almost a mumble.

"Did you mention how your brother Sean told you how you were the last of the Great Heroes still alive?"

"No." His lips moved almost soundlessly.

"Honey, don't you think you should?"

She lifted his chin to gaze into his tear-streaked eyes and kissed his forehead.

Gathering himself to his full nearly seven-foot height, he cleared his throat, "Glennfallis, you heard why I need you. Come to my hand," he said holding his hand out.

Nothing happened.

"I said I needed you. Come here!"

Again, nothing happened.

He called over and over, ignoring Rana's hissed advice to apologize.

Duncan just kept going on about how it was a "bloody, stinking sword", that it had killed Camlain and deserved to be stuck in the stone.

Finally, Rana stepped in front of Duncan and held up her hand. She said, "This is about your guilt over Camlain's death! You couldn't help it! He ignored your orders and stepped in front of you while invisible. You never saw him till he was dead!"

In battle, Duncan had never left a foe standing. As Rana's words sank in, his features fell and he collapsed to his knees, the damning word, "Kinslayer" escaping his lips. His own conscience proved a master of him again, leaving him heaving gut-wrenching sobs.

Tears ran down Rana's cheek as she continued. "Honey, I don't blame you for that. Nobody does. Exiling yourself as "kinslayer" has only hurt you. Everyone was so happy when you returned last week."

When he couldn't stop sobbing and listening to her, she shook him. When that didn't work, she shouted, "Duncan, listen to me!" When that didn't work, she slapped him.

He was such a powerful, hardened warrior that he never noticed her blows until she closed her fist and repeatedly punched him as hard as she could until he caught her hand. He had stopped bawling and with a move almost too fast to follow, caught her hand in an immovable grip. He looked up at her and released her.

She took his cheeks in her hands, gazed into his eyes, and said, "Duncan, honey, listen to me. You aren't responsible. You were never guilty. The only thing you did wrong was let a headstrong boy use your ring of invisibility. Honey, darling, I give you permission to forgive yourself. Give yourself permission to forgive yourself. Camlain is dead and you have punished yourself for too long. You have punished *me* for too long."

His tortured look became confused as he sniffed and held her hands gently between his. "I punished *you*?"

She hesitated before answering. "You, dear, dear fool. Where have my hugs been for the last ten years? Where has my joy at seeing you play with our grandchildren been? Yes, you've punished me. For too long."

"I'm… sorry. I never thought about it like that."

He took her tear-streaked face into his own massive paws. "Rana… I'm so sorry. You're right. I was wrong. Can you ever forgive me?"

She wrapped her arms around him as they cried together. After a while, he stood and said, "Glennfallis, I was wrong about you, as well. I'm sorry for blaming you for all those wasted years."

Glennfallis appeared instantly in his hand and jerked him toward the cave's mouth. Regaining his balance, he resisted being dragged for long enough for Rana to lug his pack to him.

Pecking his cheek, she said, "Go! Save our people again."

Jennifer Burns

Jennifer Burns is a writer, artist, poet and varied creative type. She enjoys writing poetry, prose, short stories, and scripts. Often her poetry comes to her in the form of lyrics or song and is influenced by personal life events. In her spare time, she enjoys what she calls "creature making", which is sculpting strange monsters and cryptids then hand painting them. A full moon will almost never cease to hypnotize her and create a frenzy of lit candles and moon bathing. She has a deep love for oddities, horror, gothic decor, October, and vintage toys. Jenn is inspired by the beauty found in scars and the ability to rise above while expressing the pain.

$5 DAD

He had an excuse for everything.
The late birthday, the nonexistent birthday card, the non-existing parent,
He had an excuse for everything.
"I had to go, had to leave state to get away from your mother,
If I had seen with another man, I'd have gone to jail."
"The alcohol made me call you a little bitch on the phone when you were 13."
It's that whole Cats In the Cradle with a gender swap.
He had an excuse for everything.
He needed validation for marrying a stripper.
She couldn't have been older than 18 when he met her if you do his math.
Transforming from an abuser to the abused
Maintaining that while still abusing.
It's ok if you admit to your sins.
You can keep committing them and wear them like badges.
If you own it, it redeems it.
It's like a coupon for being an asshole.
If you say you're doing better, trying harder,
That's the proof, right? Saying it?
He has an excuse for everything.
He contorted and bent into the shape that was the thing he hid best:
Fault.
I contorted, bent backwards and faced blame in any direction,
Until I was gripped with two firm calloused hands that turned to me to face facts.
It wasn't anyone's fault that he wasn't there.
It wasn't anyone's circumstance or fear or obligation that devoured the drive.
It wasn't money, it wasn't love, it wasn't alcohol or strip clubs.
It was *choice.*
The voice came rushing from behind in an echo,

Teaching the lesson well.
"If you remove the obstacle and the behavior continues,
You must accept that the obstacle was never really there."
I took a deep breath to accept the Oracle's words,
"He made that choice, he continues to, and that will never
change. It's just the way it is, it's not ok."
"I know" was my reply.
Yet I had never considered this before.
Feeling guilty for blaming the dead,
But it all lifted in that moment, brushed away leaving a kink in
my neck.
A spasm in the lower back accompanied by a strange calm;
It's just his fault.
But it's also mine for accepting it.
I had an excuse for everything.

WAR CRY FIRE

Something came over me.
It tried to smother me.
But like the Phoenix I rise—
I won't let the atmosphere cover me.

Crude, an awakening.
Moments painstakingly.
I want to walk but I run.
Evacuation—a panic spree.

Salt of the devil,
Wrath of a million,
Dirt of a scholar,
Mouths of civilians.

Bread breaking something,
Mass making mum-things,
Keep your jaw closed,
Don't say a word or I'll cut strings.

This is the enemy.
Doubt-guilt-fear-pain.
This the child,
Walking in circles—going insane.

How dare you butcher me?
Make it your bragging right.
13 years old—
But it was all just another night?

How dare you color me?
Paint me the shame you bleed?
I see it now—
I find the weak spot and tear away.

Suffocation is not the choice I will make.
Lying to take- is not the claim I will stake.
You smile so wide in your scrapbook display.
But you know the truth, you know you can't run away.

Tried to demolish me,
Tasted the salt of me,
I see your words,
I heard your curse how it bothered me.

Beat on the battle drum,
Unsheathe the beast in me,
I tame it now,
So, I control what consumes of me.

This is my battle cry!
My silent surgery.
This my plate, it's full—
Serving the best of me.

Jack Gannon

While Jack usually writes with co-author Cyndi Williams-Barnier, receiving 5-star awards for three of their joint novels, and one 5-star award for his solo Christmas book, "I Walked In Santa's Boots", which was the book that launched YBR Publishing. They have four other books together, and after a few planning sessions he is at work on the next two in their "Task Force" series.

Jack's career was in print media, starting as a carrier for The Beaufort Gazette before a summer job as an intern reporter. He later returned to the Gazette as the mailroom supervisor, working his way up in the Circulation Department to Circulation System Manager for both the Gazette and The Island Packet. After 23 years in management, Jack entered retirement.

From 1993 to 2016, Jack also appeared as Santa Claus for Beaufort, SC, and the surrounding areas of upper Beaufort County. Although he retired from the couple dozen-plus major events he anchored in Beaufort County every year as St. Nick, he continued to appear at a couple smaller events in neighboring Jasper County for children's events as well as Toys For Tots. Jack was given a Toys For Tots pin from attending US Marines for his years helping to gather toys for needy children. His "Santa's Boots" book showcases his over two decades of major event appearances. He finally hung up his Red Coat after 30 years.

His and Cyndi's books are available at the YBR Publishing website store.

ANCIENT FOOTSTEPS

A stream of light crept through the darkness and the half-opened bedroom door. The position of the dim hallway lamp gave the illusion of shadows that were thin and ridiculously elongated. Layton Burroughs was dead asleep, until he heard the low creak of the bedroom door swinging completely open. Startled at first, he turned his head slightly on the pillow, blinking hard, trying to focus on the silhouette tiptoeing in. He listened as the sound of tiny footsteps approached the bed. Layton quietly sat up, grinned, and waited. In the near darkness he was barely aware of the human object hurtling itself at him before the impact forced him backwards onto the bed, knocking the breath out of him.

"Daddy, Daddy, today's the day!" six-year-old John squealed. Layton's wife moaned and rolled over following the forceful intrusion into her world of slumber.

Layton smiled and wrapped his arms around his son, forcing himself to suck air back into his chest at the same time. His words came out raspy at first. "Yep, John, today's the day; your first trip to the museum!" Layton effortlessly lifted the small boy upwards in the darkness, holding him in the air while the pajama-clad boy giggled.

"First, though, there's some breakfast to be had." He sat up and set his son feet first on the floor. Feeling extra groggy, Layton shook his head to clear the fog.

Hopping from side to side, John pleaded, "But, Daddy, I don't wanna miss anything!"

Layton looked at the digital clock on the nightstand. "John—it's only four a.m.! No wonder I'm so tired," Layton groaned. He smiled at his son and rubbed the boy's hair. "I think we have more than enough time for our breakfast, showers and then get dressed."

The retired pilot kissed his wife goodbye, gathered his son in one arm, and threw a picnic lunch bag over the opposite shoulder. Traffic was light for a Saturday, but Layton still preferred to take the city shuttle, just down the block at the corner kiosk station.

John was fascinated with ancient archaeology, even though the subject had barely been touched on in school, especially for children of his young age. His interest had grown from his father's expansive library collection of old textbooks and electronic publications. It was his father's favorite subject as well.

One series of articles attracted John more than all the others: writings that highlighted historic human footprints preserved in ancient lava-ash or mud. He would sit on the floor in his father's den for hours, trying to read and comprehend the periodicals. Once he even pulled off his shoes, placing his tiny feet atop scores of pictures of Homo erectus and Homo heidelbergensis footprints found in Italy and Kenya long before he was born, trying to compare the differences.

John's mother walked in one time, snickering at John with his pants legs hiked up. He was staring down at his feet. "John, what in the world are you doing?" When no response came, she leaned against the wall and crossed her arms. "What would you like for your birthday, John? It's coming up soon."

That statement got his attention. "To see the old footprints, in the stones! Can we go there Mommy, and see them?"

"I'll tell Daddy what you want and let him make the arrangements; how 'bout that?" John screeched with excitement, hopping and jumping through the room, occasionally stopping to give his mother a hug around the waist.

The trip to the museum was relaxed, aside from John eagerly looking out the windows of both sides of the shuttle bus as it gently navigated the city streets. At one point, John looked up at his father and hissed an impatient whisper, "Daddy, there's too many stops, too many people, can't we just go and get there now?"

After what seemed to be forever to the small boy, the shuttle arrived at the museum entrance. The vehicle came to a stop, and temporarily made a humming sound as it lowered itself closer to the ground, allowing the passengers to disembark safely. John was so excited to get started that Layton literally had to hold John in his seat until it was their turn.

John jumped out of the shuttle, not bothering to use the steps. Layton steadied himself trying to hold on to John, who bounced up and down like an astronaut on the moon.

The child stared up, wide-eyed and open-mouthed, at the grand entrance, with its sculptures of scientific discoveries and inventions, and likenesses of the people who made them. Beyond the museum entrance, John could barely make out the special dome-shaped structures where the exhibits were located, the ones he longed to see. Just inside the entrance promenade, there were miniature models of ground transportation vehicles from ancient Rome to modern day. Suspended overhead were models of flying vehicles: hot air balloons, supersonic aircraft, early earth-orbiting capsules and satellites, Apollo missions, the International Space Station, and space shuttles. The display was vast and multi-cornered, and John felt overwhelmed by the enormity of it all. It did not matter, though, because he knew he was about to enter the depths of the museum and be engulfed by all the exciting knowledge within. Every other word out of John's mouth was "wow". Layton chuckled at how mesmerized John had suddenly become.

Layton paid their admission, and then pointed at the floor plan on the wall display. "Where do you want to start, son? Any location you want." He was not surprised at John's answer.

The map displayed color-coded rooms, based on the time-periods of the various exhibits. John immediately pointed to sections A11, A12, and A14 through A17, all colored gray on the map. The most direct route would require them to pass through early transportation and modern civilization. John looked up at his dad. "Can I meet you there?" he asked innocently.

Layton wrinkled his forehead and smiled down at his son. "I don't think so, little man. It's ok, kiddo. C'mon up and save your walking energy for your favorite area." He lifted John to his shoulders and headed for the gray sections.

As they approached section A11, John pivoted forward in excitement and nearly jumped off his father's shoulders. Layton wobbled, and then lowered his son to the floor. John grabbed his father's hands and squealed, "We're here, Daddy! We're here!" Little John dragged his father forward as hard as his tiny arms could pull. Other museum guests smiled and nodded politely, most privately enjoying the enthusiasm of a youngster who willingly entered the sanctuary outside of the school's virtual educational tour.

Exhibit A11 was a series of glass-walled cylindrical hallways with all exhibits viewable up close, even underfoot, but preserved in a special vacuum where there would be no chance of accidental damage or deterioration of the exhibit. The hallways hung from intricate rigging overhead, simulating a floating environment above the exhibit. The policy and design allowed visitors to view the various artifacts as discovered many years before when the city was growing and looking for new areas to develop.

The hallways made it look as though guests were spacewalking over the exhibit. Even the walkways were transparent. At various points magnifying lenses in the walls allowed closer examination of artifacts. From the exhibit entrance, the first two intersecting walkways ran east to west, and the main walkway continued north, made a semicircular curve to the west, and joined up with the western ends of both the east-west hallways. However, John wanted to see the first east-west intersection the most. After John was told about his museum trip for his birthday, he had obsessively studied the museum floor plans online from home and knew exactly how the "A" exhibits were laid out to the minutest detail. Using his dad's virtual 3-D holographic computer, John would sit on the floor and finger through screen after screen, zooming in to study everything.

Three feet into the right hallway, John came to an abrupt stop. He stood, mesmerized, mouth open wide. There was a protection rail to keep guests from touching the glass walls, so the exhibit view could remain as clear as possible. John looked down through the reinforced Plexiglas walkway and peered at the line of footprints. The impressions ran under the walkway off into the distance.

"Wow! Daddy, see that? This is so cool!" John plopped himself down on the walkway and took off his shoes comparing his feet to the preserved tracks beyond the glass wall. His little eyebrows wrinkled, and he looked up at his father. "They don't look like mine, Daddy," he said, confused.

Squatting down next to his son, he said, "John, those were left by ancient man. See, the sign says, 'Studies show that these are the earliest tracks known to exist here.'" Pointing with his finger, he guided John's eyes east and west. "And these tracks go on for about fifty meters. The next walkway has tracks that go for about seventy meters, and then back the way we came. There's more over there at the hall curve. There're tracks that lead to artifacts."

"I know, I read about them! Let's go see!" John shouted. He got up and started to run but Layton gently grabbed his son by the arm. "Forgetting something, kiddo?" He pointed at the discarded footwear. "Oh," said John with a crooked smile, and sat down to put his shoes and socks back on.

At the far western end of the hallway, the glass wall allowed the father and son to view a huge archaeological display. "That looks a little like Granny's fancy table!" John said, pointing outward.

Layton smiled. "Well, your Granny has a lot of people to feed when we all visit." He looked at the exhibit with a bit of seriousness. "Hum, yep, it actually does look like Granny's table now that you say that."

John giggled.

"What's that way over there, Daddy? Why is there a cloth on the ground? It doesn't belong there."

Layton looked beyond the table-like structure and peered at a white cloth laid out in a triangular-shape on the ground of the exhibit. "Could be something new they're adding and not yet ready to show?" he wondered in reply. He looked at the exhibit sign. "Actually, it's supposed to be there, it says that it originally stood---"

"Are those shoes?" John interrupted while he jumped up and down excitedly. He pointed at objects lying on the display floor.

"Sure look like shoes," Layton agreed as he squinted. They were a couple mostly buried items which resembled large old-fashioned boots. "Certainly nothing like what we wear today." He pointed at his own footwear, smooth, seamless, and much more comfortable looking than the ancient ones on display. He thought of all the various ancient footwear he had seen in museums, and how uncomfortable they all looked. "How anyone could ever walk in something like those beats me. But that was early man, I guess. You think those look hard on the feet; I remember seeing some ancient Egyptian footwear in the Smithsonian. Now those looked hard on the toes!"

There were many other larger artifacts on display, most covered by loose dust and dirt. Using the circular magnifying lenses, they could focus on many of the unusual, shaped bulges just below the dirt's surface. By city law, the signs clarified, scientists could not touch any of the artifacts, which included digging them out of the ground, because of the fragile nature of the site. Therefore, the museum signs clarified that the objects' uses were guesses and deductions based on aboveground scans. Also, according to the signs, scientists concluded there was probably some sort of central force, like an explosion in the long past, which scattered them across an area up to fifty to sixty feet across. There was an apparent hand-held tool lying in the dirt in the distance, mostly dust-covered on one end, shaped like a modern drinking cup with a strange handle.

There was another series of circular magnifying lenses in the glass wall to allow closer view of the greatest concentration of footprints, and John went from one to the next to take in the entire site. "Daddy!" he called. "Come look! There musta been a lot of 'em here! Maybe it was their home! Look at all the footprints!" John's voice squeaked with excitement.

Layton joined his son at the magnifying lenses and looked through one at the adult level. He was impressed with the sheer number of preserved footprints. Even to his untrained eye, it looked like a gathering place for many individuals, he agreed. However, so many were disturbed long ago, probably from the theorized disturbance. They were mere outlines in the dirt, smoothed over. He looked through one lens toward the "table" and could see no footprints anywhere near it.

Layton and John continued their trek through the elevated walkway above the preserved site. John pointed at another line of footprints that led to an obvious cylindrical object with a pole that pointed to the sky, with a line of flat frames on either side. Layton was impressed with early man's ability to create tools and early inventions. He wished he knew what their purposes were, to help his son learn. On the other hand, he was thankful that they had left it all behind for his generation to view in the present time.

They got to the end of the walkway that returned to the main museum hallway and the early transportation exhibit. He looked down at John and saw his son was already slowing down. He had used up all his youthful energy in A11. "Worn out, kiddo?" Layton asked.

"A little, I guess," John confessed.

Layton led his son to the nearest dining court and retrieved their lunches from his shoulder pack. After their peanut butter and preserves sandwiches were eaten, Layton asked, "Where would you like to go next?"

"Can we go to A12?" John asked back.

Layton looked around for an information board, finding one over the entrance to the adjoining exhibit for Local Fashions

Through the Ages. "Sorry, kiddo, we just missed the tram for A12. We can come back another time though."

"That'd be great!" said John, smiling wide with peanut butter and red fruit preserves in his teeth and on his cheeks.

Layton gave John a napkin to wipe his face. "Tell you what, there're a few closer exhibits we can do today, and get home in time for your mommy's most excellent slow-cook roast."

"Yay!" John said excitedly.

Four hours later, as Layton and John were walking through the modern medical equipment exhibit, an announcement came over the speaker system, "The museum is now closing. Thank you for visiting us today. We hope you enjoyed your adventures and look forward to welcoming you back again soon. Please proceed to the exit."

Layton and John left the museum, hand-in-hand, and went to the transportation kiosk to wait for a shuttle to take them home. "So," said Layton, "how'd you enjoy the museum?"

"I loved it!" John's face beamed with joy, but his dad saw how tired his eyes looked. Layton knew that John would sleep on the shuttle. "But there's one more thing I'd like to see one day."

"What's that?" Layton asked.

John pointed a tiny finger up into the starry sky beyond the protective atmospheric dome. "There."

Layton looked up into the sky at the distant Earth. He then pointed back at the museum and the workers putting up a new sign. "I'll do even better. See that sign? Next year is the thousandth anniversary of the Apollo 11 landing you just saw, and there's going to be new interactive exhibits so you can pretend to be part of the launch and flight and landing… more than just looking at the first footprints and ancient tools and the landing site here." He leaned closer to his son. "And I've been asked to 'un-retire' for a few months to do one of the special Moon-Earth daily shuttle flights for next year's special events, and I got permission for you to fly with me any time you want! So, you ready to visit your great-great-grandpa's home next time, on the Earth?"

John shrieked in delight and jumped up into his father's arms, hugging him as tightly as he could. The shuttle arrived, and they stepped into the transport for the trip home to their apartment in Tranquility Sea City… on the Moon…

THE SQUAD

Jack's father had been a medic on the front lines of the Korean War, and he heard so many stories of his duties under fire, and that gave Jack an idea for a very different war story...

Lieutenant Grant brushed aside the tall green forest stalks, leading his four soldiers through the growth in search of their quarry. The recent rain had turned all the dirt on their path to mud but were dedicated soldiers and wouldn't let wet ground slow them down.

The five soldiers reached a clearing, a small area, no foliage in roughly a twenty-pace circle. The ground was solid rock, with spattering mud about halfway into the area. The five made their way to the hard surface in the center where the mud had not reached. In his proper English accent he ordered, "We'll make camp here, men. Antson, Bryant, Assante, make a perimeter search. We don't want any of those Red bastards catching us unawares when we're this close to our goal."

"Yes, sir," the three non-coms answered, and they departed to make a sweeping search of the foliage surrounding the clearing.

Grant eased himself down to a squat on the stone and stretched out his legs.

His First Sergeant, Hildebrandt, stood before him. In his best Queen's speech, he inquired, "Sir, how far until we reach the target?"

Grant looked up into the blue sky over the clearing, the sun directly overhead. "If the reconnaissance information is correct, we should make it before sundown."

"Permission, Lieutenant?" Hildebrandt extended a hand toward the rock next to his sergeant.

Grant turned his head away from the sun to his subordinate. He nodded, and Hildebrandt sat down beside his commanding officer. "I'm getting tired, first," said Grant. "Don't tell the men, but I feel this is going to be my last mission."

Hildebrandt turned to stare at Grant—and wiped his arm across his forehead, leaving a smear of mud across his dark face. Shaking his head, he replied, "I can't accept that, sir. We've been through so many campaigns, all those engagements, the victories." Hildebrandt picked up a small branch, fiddling with it nervously. "Do you remember the last battle in The War? We were outnumbered, sir. Casualties on both sides, but we still won! You led the charge that day 'For the Queen and the country!' No soldier has ever rallied like that in all my days!"

"Days," Grant sighed. "I feel it in my joints, Sergeant. This ol' body wants to push on, but just doesn't have much juice left in it." He stretched his arms and legs out full, hearing the cracks of his joints.

Even the sergeant heard them. "Ouch," said the sergeant in a whisper. "That echoed off the overgrowth here."

Grant rested his hands on his legs. "We'll see this mission through. We've been lucky so far not to have run into any of those Redskees. Bad enough we have to fight them, but it'd be nice if they'd scream their death knells in our language. It's hell trying to understand what they say as we impale them in combat."

Hildebrandt chuckled. "You could be down to just one arm on the ground, and you'd still kill them all."

This time Grant laughed. "Oh, indeed, I've heard the 'Legend of Grant and The Hill'. Let's just say that the entire company exaggerated beyond reason."

"So, you're saying that you didn't kill that whole Red squad single-handed?"

Grant sat back comfortably. "OK, so yes, there's truth in that. We were on surveillance when we were surrounded by a platoon of Redskees. My troops were cut down where they stood, practically cut in half by those butchers." He reached down to his legs and brushed away mud that had dried from the sunlight. His legs felt lighter. "So, there I was, trapped against a stone cliff, the hill going down on all the other sides, but those bastards had me surrounded. There was no way out."

"Let me finish it for you, sir! As it goes, you drew your blade and with a war cry leapt into the Redskees, slicing away until you were the only one standing, surrounded by their rotting corpses until long after the sun set!"

Grant groaned. "Is that how it goes now? Please!"

"Well, sir, it is inspiring! Made for a great recruitment story."

"But that's not what happened."

Hildebrandt looked Grant in the eyes. "Okay, sir, tell me. I promise not to tell another soldier." A stern look from Grant made him amend, "Or anyone else."

Satisfied, Grant said, "The truth is that I did end up standing amongst all their bodies, just as the search team found me. But what really happened is this: I was facing that horde of murderers when out of nowhere there came flooding rain, and a mudslide poured over the stone cliff and washed those Redskees away. For a time, it looked to me like I was inside an air bubble surrounded by flowing mud! Barely a drop landed on me, while it washed away all the Redskees. I was just fortunate to be in the right spot at the right time."

Hildebrandt couldn't help but laugh out loud. "That's the most preposterous thing I've ever heard! OK, I understand. You're just a humble lieutenant who doesn't want all the attention. If you wanna say it was a sudden mudslide, that's ok with me, sir!"

Corporal Bryant abruptly broke through the overgrowth, stifling the conversation. "Sir! I found it!"

Grant got to his feet. The secret whistle was tweeted to bring the other corporals back from their sweep. When all five soldiers were gathered back together Grant said, "Lead on, Bryant."

"Yes, sir!" said the young smooth-faced corporal.

It wasn't long before Bryant led the squad to another clearing. They found themselves at the forest's edge, and they could see that the clearing stretched on past the horizon. Before them was a huge structure, smooth and arced at the base but pot marked beginning just one story high. "Look at that damage," said

Grant as he pointed up. "That's typical Redskee attack marks. Look sharp, they could be anywhere around us."

Hildebrandt pointed up to the right corner. "There, sir. A sentry!"

Grant looked up where the sergeant pointed. "It is indeed a sentry. I don't like this," said Grant. "There's never just one. Eyes sharp, men." With a subtle nod, Grant led his men forward.

He didn't like leading his squad across open ground. There was nowhere to fall back or regroup, or even use as a base camp. The only choice was to keep going.

When they were within paces of the nearest overhanging edge, they saw movement of several sentries that had been hiding above. Grant and his men went into assault mode, not giving any time to wait for the Reds to attack. The Reds charged without a sound, their squad of six only one soldier more in count. The largest one made straight for Grant. It was a typical military move, attack and kill the commander and the troops would lose their fight and be easily killed. But Grant was a seasoned warrior, and he wouldn't give up.

The engagement was short but furious. The Red soldiers were determined, but they didn't have the experience Grant and his soldiers had. In short order only two remained standing: Hildebrandt and Bryant.

Surrounded by the carnage of the gruesome battle, the sergeant leaned down, cradling Grant's head in his arms. Grant gasped, "So... how... you gonna... end the Legend?"

Hildebrandt said, "That you single-handedly killed the final Redskee patrol as you led your men to the goal. Two of your men met their deaths at the hands of the bastard Redskees, but you avenged their deaths before succumbing to your own wounds."

"That's very... noble... almost... god-like. I think... I think... I... prefer... a mudslide." Grant's eyes closed and gasped his final breath.

"What do we do now, sir?" Bryant asked.

Hildebrandt looked at Bryant as though the corporal was a moron. "We complete the mission, corporal, what else?" He set

Grant's body on the ground. "Gather what we can from up there. We take evidence back to the captain. Let's start going up."

They began to climb the large structure just as it began to shake...

...when the little girl picked up her sandwich from its paper plate on the driveway, she screamed when she saw the two black ants climbing onto the sandwich. She quickly dropped her sandwich back onto the plate, grabbed the plate by the opposite side and tossed the plate and sandwich in the trash can...

ODE TO BIRDBATH

Jack started 2011 very ill and was confined to his home for a couple weeks. It didn't help that ABC's "Extreme Makeover-Home Edition" was doing a rebuild on the street behind his house, and for over a week his sleep was always interrupted with all the spotlights for the workers and television crews that lit up his back yard all night and glowed into his bedroom window. The Nyquil barely helped as they worked around the clock. The only company he had during the day while he was sick and his wife at work was his dog and cat inside the house...and the regular visitors outside the back door...

Dear basin disc of concrete
I note your start-of-day plight
That dryness which really doesn't bother you
But I notice at dawn's first light.

I start my morning fix of caffeine
Before giving you your first day's filling
I must be quick before they all wake
And signal to the rest with their "water's-ready" calling.

'Tis my daily duty, ah 'tis quite true
Which I must do calmly and go slow, not dash
Those waiting for me to go must not be scared
So they can come drink and splash.

From the window I often check
The continuing lowering level
Due to the constant splish-splashing
Of many a dozen feathered devil.

Like my cat and dog I have been well trained;
They are smart, these little finches and jays
For when their water level gets too low
They up and fly away

So that I may come back out
And scare not so much as one
That I may refill that stone bath
And they return for more wet fun.

One large blue jay
Half a dozen of finch
When I watch them from inside
I move not even an inch

For my movement's sound
Would warn and give them fright
And send them to instinct
Of winged flight.

This goes on all day long
Watch, watch, and then refill
And watch as they all return
To splash and drink their fill.

Then the day does end
And the last has flown away
I give silent nod of thanks
To the guardian of my guests each day.

Though my day is mostly alone
As cat and dog sleep on and on
I know I'm never lonely
At the arrival of each new dawn.

Again, I'll do my duty and when they return
There can never be anything wrong.
I am comforted by the flutter and splash
Of that wonderful birdbath song.

Frank W. Howard, Jr.

Frank was born in Montgomery, Alabama. At 18 years old, he enlisted in the US Navy where he served as a hospital corpsman and recruiter for a total of 12 years.

In 1980 he met and married Mona Lanier. They have 3 sons and 4 grandchildren. They have been married over 42 years.

Frank has worked in several trades. He enjoys church, song leading and guitar. He currently resides in Guyton, Ga.

Mona and he are moving back to Beaufort, SC soon to retire.

THE DEAD DON'T MOVE, BUT I DO

When I was a young fella, I got a crazy notion that I may want to go into the funeral business. I should've known that was a bad idea since I slept with a Snoopy light in my room 'til I was 30.

I was living in South Carolina and thought I would moonlight at a local funeral home in addition to my day job. The next day I stopped at a local funeral home to speak with the owner.

I entered the room and talked to the owner, Mister Brooks. He was sitting behind a large desk in a dimly lit office. He was a tall thin man dressed in a black suit, pale with a high-pitched voice. I wondered if he was the owner or one of the residents! He invited me to come back that evening and he would show me the ropes.

At sundown I returned, and he showed me the facility. Around 8:30 p.m. he received a call that an elderly lady had died, and her body was at a morgue 30 miles away.

The night was warm, and the moon shone through the ghostly oaks full of hanging Spanish Moss. At the hospital, we entered, stretcher in tow, and walked to the morgue. We pulled out the drawer containing the deceased lady, moved her body to the stretcher, covered it with a sheet and fancy carpeted blanket, and headed for the hearse.

He opened the hearse's rear door to put the collapsible stretcher and lady inside. He told me, "Frank, lock the stretcher to the side." I later learned why this is very important.

We were traveling along when suddenly a raccoon ran out in front of us, so I hit the brakes hard! At this instance the stretcher violently shook, and the lady's body flew forward and her arm flopped over the seat between us!

Instantly I opened the door and took off away from the hearse when Mister Brooks yelled, "Frank! You can't run out on a body transport!" Mister Brooks was wrong. I don't know how he managed but one thing is certain: I got back to town before he did!

James W. Krych

James Walter (J.W.) Krych had his first novel, *From Neptune to Earth*, published as a collaborative work between him and David Cuciz, a member of the Swiss Army at the time. *The Flight to Oz Book I: Arrival* was his first-ever Science Fiction/Fantasy story based on the characters and world of L. Frank Baum's *Wizard of Oz* series. *The Flight to Oz Book II: Anusha of Oz* is a direct sequel to *Book I* and includes a new Original Character with Asperger's Syndrome. *This Point in Time* is the first book based on his *Flight to Oz* universe and deals with the Holocaust and forgiveness. *Book III Odyssey in Oz* continues the series and is split into three acts with Act 1 titled "1530." Act 2 is titled "The Enchantress."

Starting in 1988, James served in the US Military, retiring as a CW2 in 2011. As a Warrant Officer, he was first assigned to the Joint Force Headquarters in Columbus, Ohio, preparing for natural and/or man-made disasters. After relocating to South Carolina, he became a member of the 218th MEB and finished his last two years of service on active-duty orders as the Brigade S-6 IT Signal Warrant Officer for the CCMRF, the CBRNE (Chemical, Biological, Radiological, Nuclear and Explosives) Consequence Management Response Force, Mission, where circumstances would have had to be terribly bad in order to be called up. He and his wife, Lori, and their two special-

needs boys live in the Charleston, SC, area. He can be reached at the following on Deviant Art and Facebook:
https://www.deviantart.com/centurion030
https://www.facebook.com/TheFlightToOz

THE FLIGHT TO OZ

The Vultarian and Dawn flew over the city next to the hills and towards the Capital. As was before, the vines were everywhere and everywhere that the vines had touched, death and dust had resulted. Upon reaching the ruins of the statue that overlooked the location, both were amazed at what they saw, and, quickly, they ascended high enough to get an overall look. A vast collection of large, greenish vase-like pods was laid out with inhuman precision.

Descending once again, they commenced the mighty chore of counting. Up they went until the last pod was counted, and it numbered 300. Then they traversed across, and this took some time until the two had enumerated the answer and, for both, it was the same: 6000.

"More than enough," she stated in Enochian, and the vile bird grunted its approval. They could see that each pod was equally distant from the other. Each pod had vines running from it, and those were all intertwined. Every pod seemed to exhale and inhale at the same time. Indeed, every pod was identical to its neighbor and so on for all to see.

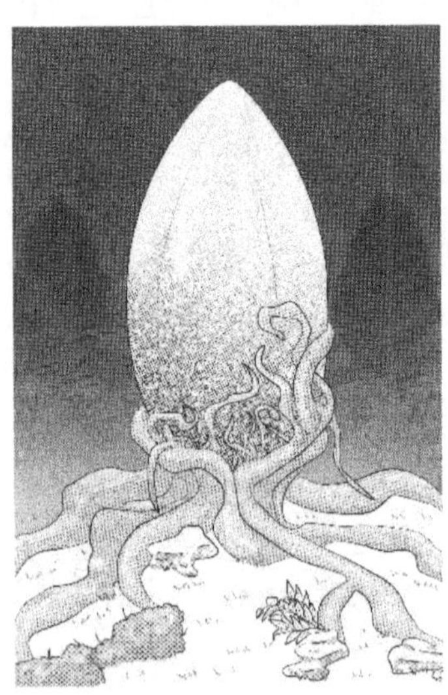

She directed the evil bird to hover around one. Cautiously, she touched the surface, and it felt leathery. Whatever was growing inside the pod couldn't be seen clearly nor could either the bird or she tell just how thick the walls of the pod were.

Rising once more, they observed the incredible mind-numbing sameness of inhaling and exhaling at the same time. All pods acted in an indistinguishable way for no other series of motions…until something caught their eyes and they hurried towards the disturbance.

The trip took several minutes…

"This must be the center," she remarked, and the Vultarian looked back and nodded with its beak.

"Look, the vines have crumbled into dust," the bird noticed and commented in its evil tongue.

"Yes, now we can land," the girl ordered and pointed just where with her hand.

Height-wise, the pod was as tall as the Vultarian, which was nearly ten feet, and it expanded outward and inward. The exhales and inhales became more intense as the top seemed to inflate out like a balloon. A doll laying right next to the pod captured their eyes and ripped clothing could also be seen.

"Must have been a girl," both said in response.

Rip! They looked up just in time to see something tear through the pod like it was tissue paper and its revealed leathery walls. *Swoosh!* A river of dark green gel poured out onto the dusty ground and quickly congealed. *Thump!* One leg of sorts stepped out onto the ground. *Thump and thump!* Finally, they beheld the end product.

It stood and looked at them. Both had been told what a Mandorian female should look like, and this thing in front of them was certainly not that; at least, not anymore. The outward appearance now matched what its heart was. What would have been a cute tail had been mutated and corrupted into a third leg. The feet were clawed and consisted of just three pointed toes. The monster's skin was tight and had a jaundiced tinge to it. What had once been smooth had been turned rough and tough.

Looking up, the girl and bird further observed the abomination. It had three arms and the third waved every so often. Worse yet, the third arm wrapped around from the back and was longer than the other two, much like a tentacle. Where the forearm and hand should have been, a club of bone was in its place. They could see that the bone was jagged and had been honed to an edge like a knife, and they grinned with malicious glee; it was this "arm knife" that had so easily cut through the pod's strong walls.

The creature's face held a perpetual scowl. The eyes were soulless with a piercing hate. What had been feminine and soft was long gone. The head was bald and its once cute cat ears had been replaced with holes and lumps of tissue. Finally, the chest was rugged like body armor and displayed three letters that had been grown into the skin. They were initials.

The transformation had forever marked and branded the creature, the SIM, Sirenae Iustinianae Milites or Sirena Justinia's Warrior.

The creature picked up the doll with its two normal arms and used its bony fingers to construct a crude necklace from the pieces of ripped clothing and put the necklace around its horrible neck. It threw the doll to the ground and crushed it with one of its mutated legs and tore across its cute feminine face with the bony-built-in knife of its third arm, the fluff from inside the mutilated doll scattering to and fro. It finally released a loud shriek and howl and spoke to the two in a harsh, smoky voice, "Suut suvres mus ogE!"

Dawn and the bird nodded in approval as they instinctively understood the reversed Latin. Together, the three howled loudly as, all around them, the remaining pods began the same birth dance – all one million, seven hundred and ninety-nine thousand, nine hundred and ninety-nine of them.

> *"So much grace, femininity and beauty lost.*
> *So many ruined lives."*
> – Mallory Millet

THE GARDENER

In a most unusual location, located in one of the most inhospitable regions known to mankind, a little plot of the Garden of Eden had been recreated. In the very middle of the garden were three pairs of date palms, Abraham/Sarah, Isaac/Rebecca, and Jacob/Rachel—descendants of the Judean Date Palm named Methuselah.

Stationed underground, based at Tsiolkovsky Crater on the far side of the moon, it was rectangular in shape with a domed ceiling. Off to the side were three compartments – rooms – which housed the "real" business for which the garden had been designed; two were for vertical gardening and the last was for aquaculture. The vertical gardening compartments each housed several panels on which plants were grown and LED and fiber-optic lights provided the needed illumination. Finally, the aquaculture compartment contained a large tank which held duckweed and tilapia, a kosher fish.

Overlooking its little ponds here and there, the grapevines, cherry shrubs, and dwarf trees – of which cherry and plum were included –and several electric grills and a faux stone fire pit, was the dome ceiling with a too-good-to-be-true feature: a high-definition display made up of rollable LED screens. With a suspended sun-globe and using soothing fiber-optic provided light, the ceiling could provide breathtaking night and day views of anywhere in Israel. These would also be previously recorded or streamed from several locations in Israel itself.

Though not technically kept as a secret, knowledge of its existence was limited to the various crews that had manned the station and to the friendly space-faring nations that had been given an opportunity to visit – especially after a long voyage. And delightful shock at what the Israelis had accomplished was always expressed.

This should not have come as a surprise, for the Jews of Israel had made the deserts bloom back on earth and what is the moon but an airless desert?

However, there were a few more steps that had to be taken before this patch of lunar soil was turned into a small piece of Eden.

Initially, it *was* a well-kept secret. When the Israeli Space Agency (ISA) had announced its intentions to build a radio observatory base and locate it at Tsiolkovsky Crater; they had given the international scientific community no less than four artists' conceptions of Base Esther. However, once construction had begun in the late summer of 2030, the actual base, for security's sake, was nothing like it had been portrayed. In fact, the garden's plans were never mentioned.

It was only after all other construction had been completed that work on the garden commenced in earnest. First, an extremely large inflatable structure was placed at the exact location where the garden would eventually stand. Then automated construction diggers were run around the clock to excavate the site. The excess lunar regolith, the layer of deposits on the surface, and the underlying material were then added to the berms around the landing pads one kilometer away.

Once the target depth had been achieved, construction crews excavated a tunnel to the base and installed a multi-stage airlock. This prevented lunar dust from contaminating the air, for lunar dust was quite abrasive and a hazard to the lungs and eyes. They next dug out where the three extra compartments would be located. Finally, the crew lowered the inflatable structure. The Chief Civil Engineer of the project, Yonatin Rawsonson, conducted load and soil bearing tests to calculate the footers needed to handle the weight of the structure. With the footers in place, it was time for the next step: strengthening the structure.

Wire mesh was first planted throughout the interior. Next, ribs manufactured from lunar titanium were connected and then anchored to the footers. Finally, the inside was filled with a type of lunar concrete, using lunar dust, water from lunar ice, a powdered resin, and synthetic fibers. Once all of that had been hardened and cured, the roof was backfilled with lunar soil and made flush to the surface, a depth of about five meters. This would protect the garden from radiation and micrometeorites.

Work then commenced on readying the three compartments. This included installing the water lines, electrical, fiber optic cables, and ventilation. As vertical gardening and aquaculture began, the most important step in creating the garden was implemented: preparing the lunar soil.

By itself, lunar soil cannot be used to grow crops because the needed nutrients are locked up in tough minerals. However, in an experiment conducted by NASA, it was found that the addition of cyanobacteria – originally found in hot springs in Yellowstone National Park – along with water, air, and light produced acids that broke down the tough minerals.

Section by section, the lunar soil was dug up and placed into tanks where the cyanobacteria worked its magic. Thus, when each batch was deemed ready for the next step, the now-processed soil was placed into another tank where a source of nitrogen was added – which was readily available from the base and construction crews.

As the soil for the garden was prepared, the interior of the structure was sprayed with a specially designed type of water-proof insulation that would hide the wire mesh. At the same time, the three pairs of Judean Date Palms were transferred over from Base Netanyahu in pots – already two years old by that time. Finally, the rollable displays were attached to the ceiling and turned on to provide both daytime and nighttime scenes. The crews installed the sun-globe and numerous speakers for future ambiance.

For the time being, the displays projected only an empty field, for which the speakers were but silent witnesses. Had one only viewed the soil, they could have imagined it was from Israel or even from Kansas! However, it was entirely on the moon and ready for planting.

The plants wouldn't be safe for consumption by the base personnel—not yet. The reason for this was quite simple: lunar soil contained an abundance of heavy metals.

In large concentrations, this could be quite dangerous to humans. Common heavy metals included barium, arsenic, chromium, cadmium, mercury, lead, silver, and selenium. The trick then would be to remove these hazardous materials before anyone tried to eat any of the plants grown here.

Fortunately, there was a low-tech solution readily available to solve the problem. The answer was to use something called phyto-remediation. Certain plants had the ability to concentrate heavy metals and literally do the dirty work of cleaning the soil.

For the first year, the phyto-remediation processes relied on Indian Mustard Greens and after seven weeks they would be harvested and placed into air-tight containers. The soil would be plowed, and another crop begun. In total, seven crops were produced, placed into containers, and then sent to a smelter.

Finally, the on-site botanists utilized a plant known to be a hyperaccumulator to slurp up everything else that could have been left behind. That plant was the *Salix Viminalis*, otherwise known as the osier willow or the basket willow. The soil was temporarily made wetter than normal for the willows as they grew and performed their phyto-remediation. After a year of growth and extensive testing for heavy metals, the willows too were harvested, removed, and sent to the smelter.

At long last, the garden was ready, and the three pairs of Judean Date Palms were the first transplanted, followed by grapevines, shrubs, dwarf trees, and many others. Then, all that was needed was time as everything grew and matured at different intervals.

As the seasons went by each year, the transition would bring a different crew to maintain the garden. Over time, the need for a support staff diminished with each crew iteration until only one chief botanist—listed on the crew roster as "The Gardener"—was permanently assigned.

Chatulah

It was late afternoon of the 23rd of Sh'vat, 5805, which in the Gregorian Calendar meant February 10th, 2045. The garden was still, the ambiance turned off for the day. The overhead displays presented an incredibly breathtaking view across the Sea of Galilee, towards the skyline of Tiberius, from the cliffs of the Southern Golan Heights.

There was only one person in the entire garden at the time: a woman in a light blue jumpsuit wearing tennis shoes, zipping around using a push-reel mower. The mower was an ideal tool for garden upkeep; it was pollution free, didn't need electricity, the clippings provided a free source of fertilizer for the remaining grass, and as a bonus it offered a great cardio workout. It was also nearly silent, only the *snip-snip-snip* of the blades indicating the machine was working.

After a few more minutes, she finished mowing with a customary hard sprint. Then, after returning the mower to a storage shed and having a pleasant cool-down, she began her weightlifting at the resistance training station, which also had a nearby treadmill for normal cardiovascular exercise. Everyone at the base had to conduct two hours of daily exercise: one for the heart and one for the muscles. It was a major way to stay healthy while residing in the reduced gravity of the moon.

She commenced her lifting regime with gusto. She was a thin woman, but by no means frail; she had an athletic build due to exercise and great genes which included a Romani great-grandmother. Her eyes and hair were brown with her coiffure long and wavy. Her nickname was Chatulah, Hebrew for a female cat, though truth be told, the Hebrew for date palms better attested to her real name.

She was the oldest of five children, the tiebreaker when it came to boys and girls, and her 45th birthday was only three weeks away. In all her family, she was the favorite of her great-grandmother because she had hung onto every word of the heroic stories of fighting in the Palmach during the Israeli War of Independence. With tears, she had quietly hearkened to her great-grandmother's recollections of traveling through Europe after she had been liberated from Auschwitz.

Chatulah was also the only relative that ever believed the fantastic tale of how her great-grandmother's people came to wander through the countries of Southern Europe.

Shortly after high school, Chatulah joined the Caracal Battalion of the Israel Defense Forces to honor her great-grandmother's memory. She continued to do so after the mandatory 26 months of service, as a reservist, finally becoming an officer after attending Bahad 1 at Camp Laskow.

She had come from a family of farmers, so it was only natural that she would earn a bachelor's and master's Degree of Science in Agriculture from Hebrew University – concluding with a PhD. Outside of Reserve Duty, she would divide her time at her family's farm and any one of several kibbutzim—communal settlements—her favorites being Kfar Masaryk and Kibbutz Sasa.

She hadn't been the first of her family to go into space. That honor went to one of her brothers. Once she had listened to his own experiences in orbit and on the moon, she felt wanderlust to explore. Fortunately, Base Netanyahu and its lunar agricultural center needed experienced botanists and after training with the ISA, she was part of the crew there, gaining vital hands-on experience that in time would enable her to volunteer for duty at Base Esther.

Buzz! The alarm announced that her hour of weight training was over. Smiling at the feeling of having had a great workout, she stretched. Then, grabbing her towel and a cold grapefruit-flavored sparkling water, she ran towards a three-meter-tall platform that oversaw the entire garden. With a powerful jump, Chatulah took advantage of the 1/6th gravity and leaped up to the top with a single bound and landed deftly on her feet.

Sipping her water, she was reflective as she looked out over the entire garden. She sighed and smiled, for not only had the garden been fruitful, but it had multiplied its bounty much more than normal. This was a problem. Normally she'd only need herself to handle each harvest, but not this time. Everything would be ripening close to Purim and her birthday, and with the yearly station audits, no help could be spared.

Still, she blessed the harvest as it was a daily routine she'd had ever since she was a little girl working on her family's farm. *"Baruch atah Adonai Eloheinu Melech ha-olam borei pri ha-etz."* (*Blessed art Thou, Lord our God, King of the universe who creates the fruit of the tree.*)

Chatulah lifted her head and with a heavy heart, prayed for help. *"Elohim sheli ha pa bemitzi chazra."* (*This time, Lord my God, this time I truly need help.*)

A few more gulps of water and she was done. She jumped off the platform and landed on a patch of soft grass. Satisfied with everything in the garden, Chatulah headed towards the main compartments of Base Esther, bunny-hopping all the way.

Passing through the multi-stage airlock, she made a quick detour to her stateroom, which was about five meters away. Grabbing her evening clothes, toilet kit, and a pair of sandals, she continued to bunny-hop to the female washroom module. Once there with the door shut behind her, the dirty clothes were thrown into a container, and she placed her clothes and kit on a nearby bench.

The module held four showers, three vacuum toilets with privacy stalls, three sinks with a large mirror, and a large hot water on-demand system. The male washroom module was identical and even though lunar ice was readily available, conservation was king to the efficiency of the base.

She swiped her ID badge as she stood up to a shower head. The system used her credentials from its database and prepared the temperature to her liking. Then she received a rinse that lasted 30 seconds. Quickly using her body wash, Chatulah pushed a little green button and 45 seconds of water rinsed everything down. The dirty water was already being sucked into the water recycling system.

Back in her stateroom, she rested on her part of the bunk bed. Normally, there would be another person sharing her quarters, but there currently wasn't a need. It was a rather spartan affair; other than a couple of desks that also had drawers for storing clothes, there was a small water closet with sink and several rods that held fresh jumpsuits. Of course, there was a base intercom with video, connections for her tablet or workstation, and a smart screen that was an alarm clock and played music or movies.

She prayed again, asking for help before she read her Tanakh (The Jewish Bible). It was a habit that her grandmother and mother had installed within her. Yawning, Chatulah set the book aside after only a few passages, prepared her blankets, and then walked up to retrieve a picture she hid behind one of her and her great-grandmother taken a year before she had passed.

The stories flowed through her heart as if she was still there at her great-grandmother's hospice bed. With all the craftiness of cats, she was told, they had to be while traveling after liberation. It was her great-grandmother who had bestowed on her the nickname Chatulah, and she gladly accepted it. Even after liberation, it wasn't safe, so her great-grandparents fled south until they were met by the miracle of miracles—The Jewish Brigade Group in Tarvisio, Italy.

It was in Tarvisio that they were taught how to fight with the weapons the Jewish Warriors possessed. Then they were transported south and loaded onto ships to be smuggled into what would soon be the restored state of Israel. Together, with her Jewish husband and many other brave souls, they fought for Israel's freedom.

Chatulah remembered her great-grandmother's plea to her as she unfolded the picture: the yellowish paper that revealed the One. Drawn when her great-grandmother was only eight years old, the very one that had sent her people from a magical land to the countries of Southern Europe. Her fingers grazed the figure, traced the long hair, the circlet, and finally stopped at the twin poppies the young girl wore. Chatulah sighed deeply but was determined. Somehow, someway, she would indeed carry out great-grandmother's wish.

"Chatulah, zichri zot ve-tinkemi et nikmati im ei paam ya'aleh be-yadech. Hayiti ha-yachid mimishpachti she-sarad et machanot ha-hashmadah. Hayinu tish'a bnei mishpachah k'she-yaradnu mi-kronot ha-bakar ha-amusim. Simnu li lifnot yamina, ve-ha-sh'ar hunchu lalechet smola la-miklachot.... At ha-yechida she-ma'amina li! Nikmi et nikmateinu!"

(Chatulah, remember this and avenge me if you ever can. I was the only one of my family who survived the death camps. There were nine of us when we came out of those packed cattle cars. I was directed to go to the right, the rest were told to go left to the showers... You are the only one who believes me. Avenge us!)

"The gypsies she banished from Oz altogether, sending them by her magic to wander through the countries of Southern Europe."

~Ojo in Oz by Ruth Plumly Thompson, 1933

JC Sulzenko

This Canadian poet's work has won awards and appeared in anthologies and journals in print and online, either under her own name or her pseudonym, A. Garnett Weiss.

In 2022, her work featured in releases from Public Poetry (Houston), Hidden Brooks Press, Poetry Superhighway, and at the Puppets Up! International Festival in Almonte, Ontario.

In July 2021, Aeolus House released *Bricolage, A Gathering of Centos*, a finalist for the 2022 Fred Kerner Award from the Canadian Authors Association.

Point Petre Publishing issued her debut collection, *South Shore Suite…POEMS* in 2017.

JC has written books for children and families and a play about dementia. She co-authored two poetry chapbooks with Carol A. Stephen, *Slant of Light* and *Breathing Mutable Air*. In the US, Silver Birch Press and *The Light Ekphrastic* carry her poems.

She has offered workshops through the Ottawa International Writers Festival, the Ottawa Public Library, and many school boards and Alzheimer societies, among others. She selected for the online journal *Bywords and* founded and curated Poetry Quarter in the *Glebe Report*. She serves on the Executive Committee of The Ontario Poetry Society.

MENS REA

Whodunnit? A perp? A stooge? A snitch?
Take your pick. Choose 'em all!

What'd they do?
Fraud. A word clipped short like a buzz cut.
You think you'll see it coming. But smooth as silk,
soft as velvet, *presto,* you're the rube, the dupe,
the fall guy. They have your money, you don't.
Larceny. A fine, rich word, whereas "theft" sounds
flat as a white bed sheet. Results the same:
They take what's yours.
Vandalism. You see graffiti, hear glass smashing.
You feel the invasion, contamination at the heart
of where you live.
Violent harm. Assaults, the colour of rage, inflicted
by hands or weapons, scar victims who happen
upon a wrong place at a ripe time.

Why? Out of greed or need. Or in retaliation.
And, sometimes, just because they can.

[*Mens Rea* refers to criminal intent. The literal translation from
Latin is "guilty mind."
https://www.law.cornell.edu/wex/mens_rea]

SOUTHERN TRIPTYCH

I

"Get on or off at the Dot stop."
Free bus routes frame historic squares, pass
steeples, fine houses in this southern-belle city.

Genteel facades belie the elegance of the past.
Brass plaques illuminate truths about what

made those fortunes, that way of life thrive.
Stone cellars where slaves lived
become museums, reveal to every tourist

what happened behind ochre walls of lime,
oyster shell, water and sand.

I step onto the bus on Liberty Street,
move to the back, choose to sit
where people of colour were forced to ride

behind anyone with light skin
not that long ago—the animus still fresh.

In front of me a Gullah man takes a seat.
I am the invisible one now. Between us, two
pale mothers with three children in tow gossip

as though the kids—their giggles, high-voice
excitement in taking the bus—weren't there.

We circle a park with picnickers, an alabaster
fountain, busy tennis courts, dogs off-leash.
Two hammocks swing low under Spanish Moss.

The small boy nearest me babbles about what he sees
until his mother hands him a smartphone and silence.

II

Along the river, souvenir stands, fudge stalls, popcorn
vendors wait for day trippers on trolley tours through
the old town for a few hours. No time to look beyond

the magnolias, the manicured gardens, the mansions
to where people sleep in front of shuttered stores.

Above the river, boutiques and restaurants
nestled in history stare at visitors across
wrought-iron walkways above cobblestones.

A hot-pink balloon floats "Valentine Love" next door
to an antique shop going-out-of-business.

The dealers, partners in life and work, offer wares
at half price, bemoan their landlord's choice: fancy
flats over treasures they've collected for decades.

Beyond window shelves laden with tiered, glass plates,
the progress of a huge container ship heralds the future.

III

I glimpse a fawn, greyhound-sized,
on the verge of the parkway

into an enclave open only to holders
of a yoke-yellow pass.
Except for the fawn.

Caught in the headlight's glare,
it stands as though sculpted to beautify

private properties and patches of ultra-green
golf courses, hemmed by canals and lagoons,

their dung-brown water host to diving ducks,
Anhingas, stark-white herons, and alligators
that discreet wooden signs announce.

I hear the sea rouse to high tide.
Where is the moon? Where is the doe?

LONG AFTER DOROTHY

That she had so much to do with my early life is no surprise.
Best friend in preschool years, we played house, hopscotch and dress-up,
rode in backseats to the country, shared fries and hotdogs to the last bite.

We were nine or ten when she started taking hours to pick out
what to wear. Every night, she washed her hair, slept in hard
plastic rollers while I left my curls uncombed.

> I stand near Impatiens in a shaded summer garden,
> wait for eleven blue candles on my cake.
>
> Every year the same white sponge with orange zest
> and icing that screams purple.
>
> Dorothy slips in, slender in a cotton shirtwaist with red
> cherry print. She perches on a wooden deck chair, undusted,
>
> speaks with an accent like our new neighbour from England.
> Her hands, nails polished pink, rest in her lap.
>
> I look at my wrinkled knee socks, my scuffed scandals
> and my rumpled skirt…

Until my father's funeral, hadn't seen her for decades.
She'd kept fashion-model thin—Her sling-backs,
navy trench coat, high cheekbones, all in vogue.

She spoke of bearing her son at twenty-two, her first divorce
at twenty-five, her work in travel and escapades abroad.
She smoked. Smoked a lot.

Then she told me I was beautiful still—
now *that* was a surprise
She left me messages after the service I never answered,

thinking there was nothing there. No friendship glue.
Now she's dead at fifty-five. Again to my surprise,
I miss the yellow brick road of our childhood.

John T. Wayne

John T. Wayne, the American Civil War and Historical Western author, is the grandson of legendary actor John Wayne ("The Duke"). Growing up attending schools all over the state of Missouri, John learned the true history of the US Civil War. John is a chip off the old block, believing in God, individual responsibility, and the idea of a free America (following in true Ronald Reagan fashion, "A True American").

John began writing his stories in 1985 while attending the University of Oregon. He left Oregon after daughter Kimberly passed and returned home to Missouri. After 30 years of marriage together with Donna, there are incredible stories of traveling together to share.

These days, John is on the road a lot with speaking engagements and book signings. Traveling about 50,000 miles a year and attending between 50 to 75 western festivals and book signings every year.

John has written and published seven western novels telling the story of "The Gaslight Boys": *"Ol Slantface"*, *"Blood Once Spilled"*, *"Captain Grimes"*, *"Peace In The Valley"*, *"Catfish John"*, *"Showdown At Scatter Creek"*, and *"The Treasure Del Diablo"*.

John has signed on with YBR Publishing for his autobiography "An American Heritage" planned for fall 2023, plus a new western series to follow.

BLOODY BILL QUANTRELL

I was told once that Bill Quantrell wasn't bloody, that it was Bill Anderson who was the real Bloody Bill. I answered by saying, quote: "Anyone who can put on his resume the burning of Lawrence, Kansas and orphaning 248 children in one day is bloody in my book." But why, why was the man so vicious? I found some of the answers in old southern folklore which I believe explains the man's character.

Chapter 1

A cold miserable rain-soaked night beset the Quantrell brothers as they began their crossing of the Kansas plains headed for Colorado. At a small creek several miles from the town of Lawrence they held up on a low ridge and made camp. Huddling beneath their wagon next to a woefully insufficient fire the two men did their best to keep warm. As the rain continued to fall a sound in the distance warned of oncoming riders, a lot of riders; an army troop would have been riding in a column, so the two brothers guessed this to be no army troop. As numerous horse-mounted men began to circle their wagon, the brothers arose from the warm confines of their blankets to greet their unexpected guests.

Thirty-four men were riding home from a night of vigilante justice across the border in Missouri, a night which had gone terribly wrong for the bedraggled bunch of Kansas Red Legs. Two bodies lay draped over no-longer-needed saddles tied like unwanted baggage, making their ranks thirty-two. The troop of Red Legs, unfit Kansas Representatives they were, paused before returning home to Lawrence. Several of the others carried evidence of wounds they would have to nurse for some time before they would ever again be self-sufficient or thought of as complete men. The party presented the picture of a disheveled lot of rabble as they rode up to the fire of the unsuspecting brothers. On this night the vigilantes were by no means finished.

"Howdy, we've some coffee on to boil, but not near enough for this many men," Charles William Quantrell offered, trying to break the ice which hung rigid upon the wet, but open, prairie. Except for the steady fall of rain upon everything in sight, no other sound was heard for a good long minute. The men just sat on their horses and stared at the two brothers before them.

"Where are you two from?"

"Ohio, headed for California," Bill said.

"Did you come through Missouri?"

"Everybody comes through Missouri, you know that."

"You are trespassing."

"Trespassing? We're just passing through on open range."

"You just left Kansas City heading west. That makes you a no-good four-flushing Missourian in my book. I think I'll just shoot you now." The man speaking wore a badge visible by the gleam of the firelight coming from under the wagon. Marshal Dixon of Lawrence Kansas was a hard bred lawman, a man who didn't take kindly to strangers, and he looked upon the brothers with disdain.

"We have mighty little we could afford to share. We have a long journey ahead of us and we need most of what we have."

Marshal Dixon drew his pistol and leveled it at the stranger. "Not any more you don't."

The pistol spat fire, then several other men opened up from all around the camp, drilling the two brothers full of holes front, back, and side, until there was no mistaking their demise.

"Round up their animals, hitch up the wagon and let's get home," Dixon ordered.

"What about the bodies," one of the men asked.

"Let the buzzards have them. We're too far from town to be noticed and any evidence we might leave behind will be wiped out by this rain."

While the men followed his instructions, Marshal Dixon noticed that the brothers had fallen on a good blanket pitched fairly beneath the wagon. Stepping down from his mount, he dragged William Quantrell off his dead brother's body, then removed their boots. Had he left the blanket the brothers would have been run over by two thousand pounds of wagon, yet providence had chosen to laugh in the face of certainty on such a miserable rain-soaked night. When Marshal Dixon pulled the two brothers out from under the wagon wheels which would have crushed them beyond human endurance, he unknowingly spared the life of one of them, the schoolteacher known as Charles William Quantrell.

For the next twenty-four hours Charles William Quantrell lay unconscious, motionless, more dead than alive. Then as he awakened shivering in the cold the following evening, he vowed to hunt down every man who had been involved in the killing of his brother. Of course, he had to live, but that was a small order now. He was still breathing, and he was awake.

As the day waned buzzards began to circle and soon were trying to pluck what they could from the dead man. Bill swung at them with a stick, but the pain was unbearable. Ultimately, he had to let them do their deed. He passed out again and was awakened by the vultures that were now picking at him. If he didn't do something to scare the scavengers off, they would eventually eat him alive.

Bill hated the fact he could do nothing for his brother, but he was struggling to keep the birds at bay. His ankles were raw from being pecked at by the hungry beasts. The vulgar fowl continued to pick and peck at him with beaks meant for tearing and ripping flesh from dead animals. It was working well on a live one. Each time one of them struck home Bill yelled in pain and cursed at the God who would allow such a thing to happen. It might not be a good thing to curse God, but for the moment it helped him live through the ordeal.

The now mad schoolteacher had no idea how he was going to accomplish his revenge as he had concentrated on none of his assailants faces except for the man who wore the badge, knew none of them by name, and could not identify any of them save for the red band tied around the left leg of each rider. For the next three days the elder Quantrell struggled to live, lost more blood and defended his brother's body from the gathering onslaught of buzzards.

Buzzards! So, they did have a use after all.

Early on the fourth morning the Buzzards flew up, startled at something or someone. Had it not been for the circling buzzards the old Indian known as Buck, who was looking for his lost dog, would have never found Bloody Bill lying on the open range guarding his brother's corpse. Horror struck, and the old warrior bundled up the one man who still lived and packed him back to his small single room cabin over the nearby ridge. There he began the treatment necessary to bring Bloody Bill Quantrell back from the brink of death. A slow yet methodical recovery began on that day, and the Indian never complained of having to share what little provisions he had, he only hunted more meat and worked twice as hard so the wounded man would sufficiently recover.

Slowly the two men became friends, for the Indian was a good teacher and Bill had a purpose. It didn't take long for the man to master the art of seizing an enemy by hand-to-hand combat with a knife, move silently upon any terrain, or the art of war and strategy itself.

The old warrior was no fool, for he understood the reason why Bill wanted to master the art of killing. Although never spoken between them, the old Indian was not uninformed as he had seen revenge capture man's heart before. Revenge was the lowest form of human behavior on planet earth or in the heart of men. Entire peoples had succumbed to the evils of revenge. This he had learned from an old Witch Doctor many years before. Having seen the carnage and how the two bodies were left for dead, the old Indian had no desire to speak of the evil behind revenge and was sympathetic to the cause for which he knew the man to be engaged. So, he taught, he imparted his knowledge to the white man for he knew also that his days were numbered.

As he was an old chief, his tribe had deserted him, not wanting to follow a coward who would no longer fight the white man; but he was no coward. In this they did error, yet only in death did his tribe understand. The old chief had known that to fight with unmatched weapons would bring death for all his people. The young men did fight and proved him. His tribe had followed the younger stronger leaders, but not the wisest. All were dead now, all but he himself, and soon he too would die. For this reason, he passed on his knowledge of battle, his skill in hand-to-hand combat, and taught the young white warrior his ways in battle, for through him the old ways might live on. If he did nothing to pass on his knowledge the warrior's way for his people would die upon his death.

Thus, it was Charles William Quantrell would become the most feared of men. No one could match his skill with a weapon or in planning a raid. None could speak against his ways for they were far superior to anything the men who followed him had ever known. Indeed, had the incident with his brother taken place a few years before the Civil War, it was quite possible General Grant would have met his match in Quantrell. However, as the war had only just begun and revenge Quantrell's only modus apparent, fate never allowed the two commanders to meet on the field of battle.

During his recovery the student known as Bill was able to get the old warrior to ask about the Red Legs and found them to be residence of Lawrence, Kansas; not only did the old Indian find them but he was able to get the names of all thirty-two men who were involved in the killing out on the plains that fateful night several months before. The men were braggarts; all Buck had to do was listen in the white man's tongue. By August of 1861 Quantrell was ready to exact his revenge. He said his goodbye to Buck, the old Indian warrior who had taught him so well, and Bill walked all the way to Lawrence Kansas where he spotted the first of his prey. There he goaded the man into a fair fight. The fight which ensued was the kind from which legends are made.

Quantrell had an idea in mind, while not completely formulated, the idea was there basking in revenge mode in the deep recesses of his mind. As he walked up the main street of Lawrence, Kansas armed with nothing but his pride, he spotted his first victim entering the Pottawatomie saloon. The man was in his mid-twenties, armed with a colt .44 while having a long knife tucked into his right boot, the red band around his upper right leg signified to Bill Quantrell the youngster was a target, guilty for the raid which had taken the life of his brother.

Bill had nothing with which to fight but his bare hands, yet onlookers would swear he had extracted the man's knife from his boot and then fed it back to him before the Red Leg knew what was happening. Not satisfied to leave the man bleeding to death in the middle of the street he picked the man up by the hair and removed his scalp then slit his throat Indian style while he still breathed. Leaning over the still twitching dead man he stripped him of his gun belt. Then with his hands full of the dead man's hair, guns, and knife he looked into the eyes of a terror-stricken crowd.

"Which outfit belongs to him?" Bill asked, pointing to the dead man.

"He's got him a saddle and horse down to Emporia Stable," one of the onlookers said.

"How do I know which one belonged to him?"

"I'll show you," the man stuttered, swallowing hard.

The crowd stood stunned as the two men made their way up the street to Emporia Stable. None among them had seen the likes with which Bill had dispatched such a well-armed adversary, and to have done so with no weapons of his own! Even Marshal Dixon was in shock for he had seen the beginning of it. He had seen the man enter town on foot, had seen him call the Red Leg out and had seen the initial challenge from the unarmed man. He had thought what kind of fool is this man to call out such a well-armed adversary and challenge him to fight? He had not intervened only because he could not believe such a situation would transpire into what he had witnessed with his very own eyes.

Originally Dixon had thought someone was playing a lark, and he being the Sheriff was the beneficiary, or so he thought. Now he stood with the rest of the townspeople looking upon a dead body in the middle of the street, and suddenly Marshall Trinity Dixon felt the cold fickle hand of the grim reaper. With sobering clarity everything came back to him. The face of the stranger was that of the man from whom he had pulled the blanket out from under months ago on their spoiled night raid. As Marshal Dixon stared into the face of death, he felt himself becoming very ill. He was uncharacteristically silent in the moments after the fight. As the two figures entered the stable up the street, Marshal Dixon turned and ran for his office, leaving the crowd wondering what had gotten into him. The Marshal was convinced the Grim Reaper was coming for him in the person of Bill Quantrell, though he did not yet know the man's name.

Had Dixon been wearing his red bandanna he quite possibly might have been the first target of Bill but being the town marshal, he felt it inappropriate to wear the Red Leg Colors along with his badge. One thing had absolutely nothing to do with the other.

As Dixon stumbled into his office he ran over to his desk, grabbed his Red Leg moniker and stuffed the red bandanna into his desk drawer. Sweat began to run down his cheeks as he wondered how it was possible the man had survived. "He couldn't have, he simply couldn't have," Dixon mumbled to himself, knowing full well what had just happened.

Marmaduke Mabry stepped into the doorway behind the marshal and stopped in his tracks, unable to fathom what he was witnessing. He had never in all his years known Marshal Dixon to cower from anything or anyone, but his actions following the slaying of young Willoughby indicated something else altogether. He stood in silence as he watched the marshal sweat.

Slowly Dixon lifted his head to see the silhouette standing in the doorway. He stood stark still once he had his eyes focused upon the man. The light outside was bright, leaving only the black outline of a silhouette standing in the doorway. A shiver slashed down his spine, the spasm causing him to palm his six-shooter and fire repeatedly into the target which had manifested itself in the doorway of his office.

"Don't shoot, Dix," the man said as the marshal palmed his weapon, but it was too late. Three bullets leaped from the gun barrel faster than Marshal Dixon could recognize the voice in the doorway. Dixon had mistaken his friend for the cold-blooded killer he had just witnessed down the street. Unfortunately for his friend Marmaduke Mabry his frame was built much the same as Bill Quantrell's. Mabry hit the boardwalk outside Dixon's office door, a dead man.

At first Dixon could not believe his mistake, he had shot a good friend and neighbor. He ran to the doorway to confirm his suspicion, but he knew even before he looked. Marmaduke Mabry was dead, and he had pulled the trigger. He was washed up. No town would keep a lawman who shot and killed the good honest citizens of the town. This he had now done. To make matters worse, Mabry was one of his casual friends.

Marshal Dixon stood overlooking the body of his friend as town folk began to gather around. He was holding his pistol in his right hand as the crowd moved in. The silence was almost deafening. The shooting had been a mistake; surely the town would see how such a thing had happened and forgive him.

Horse hooves sounded from down the street and Marshal Dixon looked in the direction of what he heard. There, fifty yards away and coming was the man he'd thought to be killing. His name was still unknown, but soon Bill Quantrell would introduce himself to the citizens of Lawrence, Kansas and they would forever remember his name. Slowly the man on Willoughby's horse ambled down the street heading straight for the Grizzly scene playing out at the office of the town marshal. Dixon watched as the killer paused long enough to spit some chewing tobacco onto Willoughby's body, which still lay in the middle of the street, and then watched in horror as the man slowly walked the horse behind the crowd gathering before him, staring at the Marshal. "Killing your own men, are you?"

Turning his head back to the front, William Quantrell nudged his new horse and rode by the carnage he had helped create. Dixon wondered for a moment about putting a bullet in the man's back before he could get out of range, but the crowd which now gathered had grown and there were too many witnesses. They were going to have enough trouble believing he had mistakenly shot Mabry, but if he shot Willoughby's killer in the back now, he was unquestionably a marked killer. He would be hunted, tried, and hung. If he stood and faced his mistake, he at least had a fighting chance. Dixon holstered his pistol and knelt at his friend's side.

"My eyes weren't adjusted to the darker confines of my office yet. I thought Mabry was the man who killed Willoughby," the Marshal explained to the horrified crowd.

"You killed him," someone said.

"It was an accident," Dixon defended.

The horrible silence was broken by the man on the horse who had just scalped Brock in the street. He began to whistle an old-time tune as Brock's horse carried him by, a tune meant especially for the marshal. Everyone stared at the man riding away wondering just what he meant, everyone but the sheriff. He understood the man with utter clarity and from the back the fellow looked just like the grim reaper!

Chapter 2

Bill Quantrell was reveling in the fact Marshal Dixon had helped him eliminate an enemy today. A broad smile crossed the lips of the man known as Quantrell while he cleared the meadow only a short distance from town. Reaching into his pocket he removed his list and crossed off two names. "Willoughby and Mabry," he said as he crossed the two names out. "Thirty to go," he added.

Willoughby had apparently been a well to do young man. Bill had taken five hundred dollars off the young man's body and saw it. The money had been tucked into the open chamber of his rifle. Bill had pocketed the money and saddled the man's horse without any onlookers. The man who led him to the stable, having departed immediately, could not have known the young butcher was carrying so much cash.

An hour later Quantrell rode into the yard of his faithful Indian teacher and friend. He put his new horse into the nearest stall in the barn and fed him some oats. Then unsaddling the mount, he picked up a handful of hay and began to rub the animal down. The horse was a beautiful sorrel and for the rest of his days Bloody Bill Quantrell never rode another.

THE LIQUID FOREST

Chapter 1

There was nothing I could do but stop and continue sucking for air. My lungs felt as though they would rip from my chest at any moment. My body folded, forced to surrender, my legs hurt beyond comprehension. No longer able to move my limbs with normal coordination, they crumpled into a grotesque position beneath me and sent a sharp pain from my right foot all the way up my right side into my back. A spasm wrenched my entire body around, tossing me face down into the black water swamp at my feet. Immediately I flipped upright in the murky liquid and rose from the depths to gasp for more precious air. I had to stay upright on my feet for the water was too deep to lie down in or rest on my knees. I needed rest yet I was afraid because time was not on my side. My dress had been fairly shredded by the invisible jagged edges hidden in the swamp and I knew too little of swamp life to do me any good. No matter what direction I looked, all I could see was a natural prison, impenetrable by mere mortals.

My only desire was to lie down and rest under a big Cypress tree somewhere and sleep, but there was no land in sight, no hammock or rise, just water and trees as far as a man could see, yet I was no man, I was a ten-year-old girl running for my life! If the gator's got me so much the better, for I had a sneaking suspicion my destruction would be less painful than the nightmare which lay in wait for me back there in the swamp.

Unable to stop and rest for the fear of being caught, I struggled to move forward. I forced myself to spin around to get my feet under me, then began to stagger desperately through the swamp which seemed the end of my world. Ominous trees stood straight and upright reaching toward the heavens emerging from the blackened water like towering giants, although at times I came across one which was down laid over by age or a storm or some other cause of nature; those were lined with turtles and gators which dove into the water the moment they spotted me. I could not rest on a log, not without offering myself up as gator bait.

Mother and Father had left behind no wisdom for me when they died, no guidebook, not a thing I could use to survive the Okefenokee Swamp, yet in my heart I knew what my life had become was not anything they intended. Neither of them could have envisioned the direction my life had taken after their death just a few short days ago. People just didn't think about such things, only now I had to because my very life depended on my ability to escape and hide.

I had to literally out-think the sick and evil man who was after me. How does a ten-year-old girl do such a thing? He had twisted and tried to shape things in my head which were lies from the beginning. Did I ignore all he said, all he had done, or did I try to separate truth from lies and use what I could for survival? How could I even identify the truth, and how could I spot the lies? How could a girl of ten figure out such mixed-up stories and survive? If grown people could get themselves killed such as what had happened to my parents, what chance did I have? The very same man who had killed them was now on my trail or soon would be, yet he had for all intents and purposes been my mentor these last few days.

He tried to teach me what he wanted me to know and how he wanted me to view things, yet now he'd failed, and his failure would illuminate itself. For that reason, I must be disposed of. From the moment I put enough facts together to identify him as the man who killed my parents, my fate was sealed.

It was when I'd found the graves, all seven of them! They were well off from the cabin I suppose so no one would find them, but I did. A ten-year-old child can get bored. Lester had gone to town and left me alone for the day. He instructed me to stay in or near the cabin because of the wild animals and snakes which lived in the swamp. He didn't want any of them to get me, he said. It seemed okay for him to do whatever he had a mind to do with me, but for some reason I felt I was in less danger from wild animals than him, so I ventured out early this morning.

When I found the graves, at first, I couldn't believe it. I just stood and stared down at them. Oh, by the way, my name is Elizabeth Ledbetter, but Lester had been calling me Sally Ann since the moment he brought me home. I never understood his reason for this. Then when he got me to his cabin out in the swamp, he began to treat me just like I was his wife. It didn't take long for me to understand why he was calling me Sally, but I still did not grasp the real reason behind such a name. The moment I looked down upon those seven graves, all of them marked with the name of Sally Ann, I knew Elizabeth Ledbetter was never going to leave this swamp alive unless I ran for my life at that very moment.

I had no idea what child molestation was. He made me wear a dress and all, but I thought, at first, he was just playing some sort of silly game with me, a game of house; now I knew his evil desire was no game.

As the full weight of what those graves meant settled upon my shoulders I began to panic. Elizabeth Ledbetter was next if she didn't cooperate, yet I could not. There had been seven children before me, seven girls and they were all six feet under! Were they all young girls like me? There was little time to look for answers, weapons, change clothes or anything else. If I planned to live, I had to get out right then. I could not endure another day of his hands all over me.

At first, I returned to the cabin to look for anything which might help me make my escape, yet there was nothing. Anything I might have used was in the boat with Lester. The dogs had been fed, so I turned them loose. Blood hounds they were, and I called them out as if we were going to go coon hunting much like I'd seen Lester do the day before. Once I had them start upon their way I went back into the cabin and grabbed a small handful of leftovers, then I was off. There was no time to pack for a picnic, a trip or anything else, not today there wasn't. I had a very short time to escape the domain of Okefenokee Swamp.

The year was 1863 and I'd been orphaned only a few days before. As soon as my parents had dirt thrown on their caskets

Lester was there to claim me as my long-lost uncle. The town folk didn't question him much as nobody wanted to be saddled with an unwanted orphan child. He seemed to give all the right answers to the few questions they did ask. I learned just yesterday when I found momma's Bible, after he killed them, he had time to go through their things and study what he was going to say. He had even written down some of his answers in her Bible.

No one witnessed the fire and there was little evidence for anyone to make a case for murder, but I was now sure he had killed them both in cold blood. Lester said all the right things and when he was finished, the town folks told him he could take me home to live with him. That was three days ago, and on our first day back at the cabin he made me put on this fancy dress. Then he took my girl clothes and went off in his boat somewhere. When he came back my clothes were no longer in the boat.

Last night after we had eaten and went to bed, I was afraid for my very life. If he could kill my mom and dad, I would be easy to dispose of if he decided I was a danger. He had guns, and always had them handy. Once he was in bed with me, I couldn't stop him from doing the things he wanted.

Today when I found the seven graves I panicked.

Had Lester suspected I discovered he was the killer of my parents the day before, I would already be abused, dead or buried, but thus far I had said nothing, hence he had trusted me well enough to leave me alone.

I said nothing to him about my discovery in the back room of the cabin and had no intention of saying anything until I was safe from harm. I might be only ten years old, but I'd been set upon by others in my life and I understood what it was to be attacked, or forced to do things you wanted no part of. I was getting out now before things went any further.

How long did I have before he returned and found me gone: one hour, two, or had he returned and discovered me missing already? I had to assume the worst. I had to buy time, yet which way should a young girl run? I have been running now for at least an hour. How far? How far away from town was I, and which way was town? Had he killed the others or had they met their death running as I was now doing? Right then I wished to know the answer to that question, yet the answer might only reveal itself in death. I was too young; I had not yet lived!

Would I be better off if I was found naked or wearing this fancy torn and tattered dress? This kind of dress was for a lady of the night. I began to ask myself all kinds of silly questions as I gathered my senses and continued running in the now-chest high water. My breath was coming back, and I was near swimming in deep water. Was I running in the right direction? I stepped on something beneath me which moved so I jumped and started flailing wildly about in the black water swamp. I pushed into deeper water until my feet would no longer touch the bottom and then I began to swim. I wasn't the greatest swimmer, but I was able to. Once I reached ground, I pulled myself up to rest under a big old cypress tree struggling for every breath. Above my head was a big spider.

I lay there listening to the sounds that surrounded me. Then I heard a boat with ore dipping water. Straightway I went silent trying to slow my breath, to be as quiet as possible. Not wanting to be seen by Lester if it was him. I slipped back behind a big cypress and waited with sparse breath.

It was! I watched as he rowed by me headed for home, but unexpectedly he stopped. He was looking at the churned-up water I'd left behind and I could see him growing suspicious. I realized then he could spot a trail, even in water.

"You out here, Sally Anne?"

I held the statue still.

"You left a trail a blind man could follow. Come on out and no harm will come to you."

He was lying. I don't know how I knew it, but he was lying.

"When it gets dark in the swamp all kinds of creatures come out of hiding and start foraging for a meal. Bear, panther, alligators and water moccasin are just a few. You'll be safer if you come on home with me."

I trembled in fear, not of the swamp, but of him. He had lied to everyone in town, he had lied to me and worse, he had killed my parents to get me.

He was scaring me right then, but I was more afraid to go back home with him. I held myself still and tried not to think of the night ahead with wild beasts roaming about freely. The thought was terrifying!

"Suit yourself. I'll leave a lamp on for you so you can find your way home," he said, and he slipped his ores back into the water and began dipping.

I risked a peak around the tree trunk and pulled back. He was moving away yet seemed to be staring right at me. I needed to go out the way he was coming in, but how could I not get turned around once it was dark? Could I get out of the swamp without getting lost? How far away from the cabin was I? What time was it?

In only a few short days I had learned a lot about the Okefenokee Swamp. The swamp covered many square miles of northern Florida and southern Georgia. It was full of Seminole Indians, gators, bears, and cats. There was no doubt about the animals. I was witness to all the skins Lester had tanning back at the cabin. There were two main rivers that got their headwaters in the swamp: the St. Mary's and the Suwannee. Where the rivers were, I had no idea.

I held still not wanting to make a noise, but how long could I remain so? I was wasting precious time trying not to give away my location. Had he seen the wet spot where I crawled out of the water? If he had, the man already knew where I was. How could he be so sure of himself? Simple, he had lived here for a long time from the looks of things; I was an outsider, a tender foot.

To be only ten years old when I needed years of experience behind me seemed a curse. How could I match wits with such a man? He obviously knew the swamp, the tributaries where he lived, yet I knew nothing of them. I was on my own and scared beyond anything a girl my age could conceive of as I had already witnessed some of the animals he conjured up to scare me with. If I wasn't mistaken, I had stepped on an alligator in the black water back there. In my mind it had been a monster, but who knows how big?

When I could no longer hear the boat or Lester moving around, I started out again, only this time back the way he had come when he passed me. Easing back into the water I quietly swam toward the passage he'd used when he went by. I swam slowly and silently, not wanting to attract the attention of Lester or any of the wild animals he'd threatened me with, especially the gators who were sharing the dark swamp water with me.

As the sun went down, I was still dog paddling my way through an open channel. Swimming to the western bank of a wide canal I pulled myself from the water and lay down in a spot of tall grass such as a deer might use, and I went to sleep. I had been running all day and now with darkness looming on the horizon the Okefenokee Swamp began closing in around me, the one with all those wild animals he planted in my imagination, but they'd been there already, only now they loomed much larger.

A spine-tingling screech just after full dark awakened me. A bobcat no doubt, but I couldn't be sure. The screech I just heard could have come from a much bigger cat. I realized with regret I didn't even have a kitchen knife to defend myself. I was in deep, deep danger. I heard water splash nearby which caused me to tense in the darkness holding my breath. Was that an alligator or a bull frog I'd heard? I'd seen Lester's dogs cower at the very same screech I heard a few moments ago. Those dogs would bark up a storm, yet whenever a cat screeched close by in the night, they were the biggest cowards you ever saw. I had learned that much in the last three days. I took note and held very still, afraid to even breathe. I was cold, wet and shivering. It seemed there was no way to get warm. The scant dress was getting torn to shreds, leaving little for cover.

Something jumped right by me and landed in the water. I sat bolt upright looking all around, yet I could see nothing in the pitch-black darkness. Paralyzed by my blindness, my fear of the swamp grew.

The animals of the night which lived in the swamp were now becoming a source of torment for me. I held myself still not knowing what might scare me next. Again, the cat shrieked into the night, only this time it was much closer. If the thing came too close, I would have to swim. If I swam, what about the alligators, wouldn't they be looking for an easy meal?

I struggled with what I should do. The last thing I wanted was to slip back into the water when I could not see where I was going, but if that cat got any closer, I deemed it might be necessary. I saw nothing in the darkness which gave me any comfort. I was blind as a bat, maybe even more so because I had nothing with which to aid my handicap. My hearing was even better though. I heard everything then, the frogs croaking, the fish flopping, mosquitoes buzzing by my ears and the wind in the bows of the trees up above. I heard it all for the symphony it was and wished I knew for certain what to do with so much spine-tingling information. My wits were at their most terrifying end. If I made it till morning, I was going to count myself among the good Lord's blessed.

There would be no more sleep for me on this night. Not that I didn't need it, but I just couldn't let my guard down with so much commotion going on around me. I was in mortal fear for my life, but the thing I seemed to be most afraid of was my fear of the unknown. Most of the sounds I heard went unidentified which meant I was at leisure exaggerating their danger.

Far in the distance I could see the glow of the lantern. It was the cabin! How far had I gone, one mile, two? Maybe I had only gone a few hundred yards? At night I could not tell, and suddenly that seven hundred miles of swamp seemed so intimidating, so insurmountable. What had I done? I had been running all day and I could still see the light of the cabin?

I had no answer for my current situation, all I could do was wait. Elizabeth Ledbetter would have to lay in wait for the sun to break through the grim shifting darkness which for the moment composed my panic-stricken domain, a creepy crawly firmament surrounding me with spellbinding fear. There were ninety-nine unidentified sounds in that liquid forest, all within reach of my ears. They shifted positions as if circling in the darkness, so I knew the varmints were moving in the night, they could see, I couldn't. I waited in terror to be devoured in the darkness by an animal I could not see. At some point, exhaustion overtook me, and I rested, my head on my forearms perched across my knees.

Chapter 2

I awoke again with the realization I had fallen asleep from sheer exhaustion in the middle of the night. Sleeping had been the farthest thought from my mind. The sun was beginning to break through the trees indicating which way was east. I headed north out of the swamp, only that was the worst thing I could have done. Somewhere to my north lay the settlement of Skeleton Creek and I prayed for my salvation. Skeleton Creek was named for the prehistoric man who had been found on the spot the town was built.

I was well aware that Lester did business in that town as I had found receipts in his closet for the charges he made from time to time, but Skeleton Creek would also be the closest place for me to get help. The question was could I get there before he out-guessed me. If he did beat me to town, what then? Might he tell everyone I was crazy and if spotted they should bring me home? There was no ready answer for a ten-year-old girl to make a decision. My circumstances created an unwanted weakness in me simply because of my inexperience in such matters, yet I would be forced to deal with them sooner or later.

How does a ten-year-old daughter of nobody overcome problems when life begins to career down a path of eminent destruction? I needed to know. I had to survive, but what I didn't know then was that there are many things in this life that nothing can prepare you for. I wanted to live, and I wanted my life back. Mother and Father were gone, and it seemed I was next in line to meet the Grim Reaper.

As the sun overhead began to settle on high noon my childhood hunger began to rear its ugly head. What does one eat in a swamp? How was food caught? How would I cook anything I managed to get my hands on? I was still navigating the shallow water of the swamp when I stepped on something in the water, and it snapped shut on my leg. Severe pain shot up through my left leg and I struggled to get myself free to no avail. I was done for. If Lester found me in his trap, I was still done for because I had betrayed a crazy man and set his dogs loose!

I held still then, not wanting to make myself available to every predatory animal in the swamp and suddenly a new fear enveloped me. What if the blood I was no doubt losing attracted alligators? I was in a troublesome predicament. Looking around I could see nothing with which to pry the device open. I was only in about three feet of water, but the water was just deep enough that I couldn't do much of anything to help myself that I could see. What strength I had wouldn't budge the jaws of the underwater trap.

The pain was now becoming numb which meant I was losing circulation to the lower part of my leg. I would lose that leg if I didn't do something. I was an animal caught in a trap and worse, what if no one came this way for several days? I would die right here.

Fishing around below the water's surface I began to feel for how the trap was secured. A chain held it in place, but the thing was heavy. I pulled up on the chain until it gave. I lifted my leg and began to make my way ashore. Once there I found a long tree limb, broke it in two and began to pry from both sides. Just as I got to where the trap was releasing one of my tree limbs broke and I received another dose of unbearable pain. The trap slammed home once again. I was going to need a bigger and stronger limb.

I hunted for about thirty minutes before I found one which would do the job and then I still needed to break it in two somehow, or did I? Placing the trap against a large rock so that one set of teeth were below it I inserted the tree limb and began to pry. More pain came with my attempt and the rock wasn't holding the other side well enough still. Desperately I struggled to get loose, but the thing held fast. Then I passed out.

When I came to, I looked around and my spirit wilted. I was back at Lester's cabin. Although he was nowhere in sight, I knew he would be nearby. My wounds had been dressed, the trap was gone, and I was lying in my own bed (or, rather, that of Sally Ann). How much trouble I was in I had no idea, but I was certain I was in some sort of terrible demise. I had done everything the man had told me not to do and now I was going to pay the price.

I lay there thinking the worst for a while and sometime or another I fell asleep. When I awoke again it was after dark. Lester was asleep with his arm around me, and I just lay there wondering, what now?

I was no longer wearing any clothes. I was completely naked under my blanket except for a bandage and splint upon my left leg. Was my leg broken? It sure felt as though it was, but then I had never experienced a broken bone before. The pain was almost unbearable, but I held quiet not wanting to awaken Lester.

I lay awake for hours then thinking about what my best course of action might be. One thing was certain, I needed to wait for Lester to awaken before I could determine how much damage I had done to our relationship. Would he forgive me, or was he digging grave number eight?

Lester awoke me once more at breakfast and offered me the first food I'd had in almost two days.

"I don't believe your leg is broken, but I put it in a splint just in case. How are you feeling this morning?" he asked.

"My leg hurts and I'm hungry."

"About what I figured. What made you run?" he also asked, as if he didn't know.

I hesitated here, not wanting to seal my fate with the wrong answer. "I found seven graves out back and all of them had the name Sally Anne. You've been calling me Sally Anne," I accused.

I'll give the man credit he was ready with the perfect answer, one which accounted for everything to do with the graves and markers.

"My wife was Sally Anne and I had gone to town one day, much like the other day when I left you here alone. When I came home there were seven big alligators fighting over her remains. I deliberately killed each and every one of them. Then I buried them out back. There are seven graves because there were seven gators. I couldn't think of any other way to bury her."

"Why are you calling me Sally Anne?" I ventured.

"I miss her, and you remind me of her. I'll not find a better replacement. I need you, Sally Anne. I need you here with me. I bought you a new dress in town the other day."

So, I was dealing with a crazy man! That explained everything except why he thought a little girl could replace his dear wife. There is a difference between a girl and a woman. I suddenly felt sorry for him. He had lost his young and no doubt pretty wife to the swamp, but what about me? He had no right to do the things he had been doing to me.

He came over to me then and began to hug me and hold me, which soon led to him kissing me. I pretended my leg was hurting to get him to stop. It worked for now but how long could I fool him? How long could I hold him off?

"I'll do my best for you, Lester," I said. "I didn't know anything about what all you've been through. I'm sorry I ran. I won't do it again," I lied, knowing I might have to endure many nights of humiliation before I would ever be able to try another escape. One thing I was sure of, if I was dead there would be no escape.

When he kissed me, it was like kissing a bear who didn't know how to brush his teeth. His breath was foul, and he smelled of swamp.

He took care of me then and I offered up little of the necessary amount of affection which he asked for in return. I gave him a tidbit here or there to keep him off my back but only as much affection as necessary to buy the time I required to get well.

I looked pretty fetching in the new dress he had bought, but still I was just a girl. My hair continued to grow longer, the dark brown he called auburn. He wanted me to manicure my fingernails, but I had no idea what he meant so he showed me one day.

I was unwittingly creating an unforeseen problem for myself. As things stood, I was slowly but surely becoming the Sally Anne he wanted me to be. His advances were getting harder and harder to head off at the pass.

As the days rolled by, I was growing more confused about my place in his world, yet I knew deep down what I still had to do. The days turned into weeks, and the weeks into months and still I held on. Life for Elizabeth Ledbetter suddenly became a transient spell of misshaped awareness and the vague feeling I was losing my identity. He always called me Sally Anne.

On my eleventh birthday he bought me two new dresses, some makeup and silk stockings with garters. Now I didn't know what his fascination was with such stuff, but he made me put everything on. I was going through all sorts of unanticipated emotions with Lester. He seemed harmless enough most days, but sooner or later he would have a bad one and those bad ones were going to get me killed. Was I beginning to have feelings for him? He was taking care of me in grand fashion. I had to get away, but things had to be just right for that to happen. My hair was now down below my shoulders and looking more and more like a woman's. To date I had managed to stave off his advances, but one of these days that was not going to be the case. I was flirting with disaster, and I well knew it.

He then began to buy me the stuff to fix up my hair. He liked it up, but wanted to take it down himself when we went to bed at night. I was too young to understand that the man was incurably sick and that he was making me so with every passing day. No, he wasn't holding me hostage, but my fear of him and what he might do if I tried to escape again was.

Late in the morning one day when he had gone to town, I came to the inevitable conclusion I was now holding myself hostage. I had recovered from my wound, and it was time to escape before things went too far, but could I get away? What if he caught me again? He would not be so nice the second time around.

After several months my leg was healed up fine, and although I wanted to run, I also felt a longing to stay. Where would I eat? How would I get money? Who would care for me were the questions which held me back. Although Lester wasn't a normal man, he wasn't insane as far as I could tell, and he seemed to care for me more with every passing day. Things had begun to go so smoothly I had forgotten all about the fact he had murdered my parents, a fact which reared its ugly head one day unexpectedly.

I was doing my customary cleaning in the cabin when I came across the items which had belonged to mom and dad. The only way he could have obtained them was if he had been in the house before it burned. I knew this to be true, but now I was in deep, too deep. Should I run, or live life easy? Living life easily seemed to be the answer, but what of my parents? Who would seek justice for them?

It dawned upon me then that if I didn't extract justice, Lester would never pay for his crime. He killed mom and dad because he wanted me, I knew this now, yet I had developed unexpected feelings for the man. What kind of feelings I wasn't sure, but feelings just the same. I felt sorry for him, but why?

These last few months he had been taking care of me as though he really loved me. I was beginning to believe that he did. I didn't even want to hurt the man, but at times I found the only way to keep him at bay was to do so. I was lonely when he left me to go to town, but I still didn't try to run away. Why? Was I now under some kind of spell? Why couldn't I bring myself to run again?

When would be the right time to try and get away? When I was a little older and stronger, but how much older and how much stronger? I was willing to wait, not because I wanted to delay justice, but because I was living well. His affection, however misplaced, was not the answer, not now, not ever.

Those were confusing times for me, but sentimental times, too. I was trying to adjust to a new way of life, yet at the same time gain more independence and find a way to extract justice for my parents' murder. I needed Lester to trust me again if I was ever going to get away. I needed him to trust me like never before.

One day he left for town, and I took the shovel out back and began digging. What I found was not good. I found the remains of three different people in those first three graves, and all of them about my size. He had lied to me, and now I had to cover up my tracks which took a good deal of thought. I sprinkled the dirt back into place and then I began to lay Spanish moss upon them to hide the fact I'd been digging. I also hung some upon the markers so that it would look as if the moss had been falling off the trees during recent storms. Then I got lucky. A late afternoon thunderstorm, which was common in these parts, rolled in and wiped out my tracks. I put the shovel back into the shed after cleaning it and went back into the cabin to fix supper.

That's the kind of things I was learning, how to cook, how to fish, basically how to fend for myself and Lester was seeing to it that I learned. I felt as if I owed him for that, but more for killing mom and dad. He was teaching me how to survive on my own. I wasn't being shown how to set traps for coon or beaver or any other type of animal, but I was regaining his trust with each passing day.

Now, each time he left me to go to town for supplies I got out the items I remembered from my parent's home, studied them, cleaned them up and put them away. I couldn't help but keep their memory alive that way, and those were the hardest days for me because sometimes I would cry for them, for what my life had become. I was living with their killer.

That was my life and the way of things until my twelfth birthday. For two years I had held my tongue, spoke with condemnation when necessary and withheld my mixed feelings, presenting him little opportunity, only now that it was time to leave, I was going to have trouble for I had fallen under his spell.

I really didn't hate Lester for what he had done to my mother and father, but I knew what he was planning for me was wrong! Not only that, but I was also growing into a woman with a woman's desires, and I wanted to pick my own man.

I wasn't a girl anymore, I wasn't Sally Anne, but I was. The real problem lay in the fact I no longer knew who I was. I'd been forced into a lifestyle I would never again be able to return to and the leaving of it pained me. Why? I knew that the days ahead would be the worst of my life. The question was could I survive?

Lester had continued to buy me dresses and the like, but on my twelfth birthday he returned with a corset and told me I would need to start wearing one. I was somewhat put out about the whole matter and suddenly I realized I had been in a sinking ship all along. What would happen when I grew a little bigger? What would he do with me if I began to show signs of becoming a temptress? I was in a life-or-death game, and it was time I took matters into my own hands.

I made up my mind then, the next time Lester went to town I would make my escape. I could wait no longer and there was no need to further subject myself to the man by pretending I was his girl. I was almost five feet tall now, and I could walk out of the swamp, swim when necessary and do whatever was needed to escape. If I didn't leave soon, I had a pretty fair idea what was waiting for me; and when I refused the man, he would take me anyway. I could take my time and escape this time. I knew what I was doing and as a young woman I had it to do.

Chapter 3

No longer could I endure the mind-bending torture of submission to a man. I was almost a woman in my own right now and I was going to prove it. I was not a little girl anymore, but I couldn't let him have me. I had come dangerously close a few times, and the warning bells in my head were going off.

I waited then for the right time to leave. I plotted and planned my adventure daily until I had everything worked out. I had no intention of ending up in another bear trap. I almost lost my leg last time and for weeks I couldn't walk normally. I still had scars on my leg from that mishap.

Then the day came Lester headed for Skeleton Creek. As soon as he was out of sight, I began to gather my incidentals, the things I would need to make the trip to town. I didn't have much, but after wrapping the bear skin up tight I tied it around my shoulder to use for a blanket. I had been building a raft for my journey for some time and today was the day to christen it. I made my way toward my raft and when I arrived my heart sank. It was gone! Lester had found my raft and gotten rid of the contraption. Now what?

"Going somewhere, Sallie Anne?"

I didn't think, I reacted! He had been right behind me, almost whispering in my ear. I spun around so fast all I could do was make a fist and hit him right in the face. It caught him unaware, and he tumbled into the water face down. Not waiting to see how much damage I'd done, I ran.

Returning to the cabin I grabbed a shovel to take with me and I headed off into the woods. If there was another trap out there with my name on it the shovel would find it first. I knew I was in for much slower going than planned, but I had it to do. Lester had a habit of taking the dogs with him since the day I had turned them loose three years ago. Today he would use them well.

As I walked past the seven graves, I said a small prayer for the victims for I knew deep down he was lying to me about the seven gators. I waded out into the swamp away from our hammock. I knew what I was in for. There was no hiding the fact I would be scared half to death, terrified out of my wits after the sun went down, but I had to go. My understanding of manhood was literally being altered daily. The conversation Lester subjected me to was so ingrained, I was no longer certain I could hold him at bay. If I had any intention of holding off his advances to live a normal life, I had to escape now.

With clear purpose I began to move the shovel back and forth in front of me, deep enough in the muddy bottom that it would bump anything in my path, especially a submerged trap. I waded on slowly picking my route carefully. I was going to go one mile west and then head north out of his normal path should Lester get after me right away.

Now that the chase was on, the only question was how much of a head start did I have? I knew better what was needed this time, but the dogs would be with Lester. Old Steamboat was the best tracker of the three, but could he track me through the swamp? Who was I kidding? Any one of the three bloodhounds could follow me anywhere I went. Lester would have no trouble finding what direction I had gone. Joker and Princess were the other two bloodhounds. Three of the best dogs in the country and none of them would have any trouble finding the likes of Sally Ann or Elizabeth Ledbetter!

There had to be a way. Now I remembered Lester telling me that a coon would tap a tree and then jump from limb to limb and come down way out there to throw the dogs off its scent. Could I tap a tree? As I made my way deeper into the swamp, I doubted it. The closest tree limb to the ground was usually twenty to thirty feet high and I had no way to get up that high.

As I walked the filtered sky began to get darker and the evening began to sneak up on me. I struggled on through the darkness below with my shovel making my way toward a hammock I could see in the distance.

At once I heard the dogs. So, he was coming! How hard had I hit him? This time my absence meant life or death. I had to run now, for he would not be hampered by the placement of his traps. I on the other hand would be. I didn't know where any of them were or how he marked them. Was he headed off in a different direction? No, those dogs would be on my trail quicker than a starving catamount, the likes of what roamed these quarters of the Okefenokee.

I studied the map Lester had of the swamp so much it was burned into my memory. Whenever he was out, I studied the places and the interior islands in particular. I was nearing John's Island. As I picked up my pace a bit, I noticed one large tree lying over against another one. It was an old cypress which I could climb to get up into the treetops, and looking about quickly I made up my mind to take to the trees. The dogs might tree me at such a spot if they were closer, but I had the idea I would make my way into other trees by navigating the limbs much as a coon might do.

There were many islands yet to cross, but if I could manage to evade Lester, I might be able to continue on west and escape by Cowhouse Island or Chester's Island. Where that would put me, I had no idea, but I would be out of the swamp soon thereafter and able to run any direction I wanted. I was no longer sure Skeleton Creek was where I needed to go anyway. I needed somewhere he was not known if I was to be believed.

As I began to climb, I realized my shovel was now an undue burden, but I could not let it go. There were still many miles of swamp water ahead of me and I had no idea what direction Lester had a habit of laying his traps. I couldn't take the chance of releasing it.

Making swift work of the tree trunk I soon found myself three trees over from where I started, but then I found myself paralyzed just as I lost the remainder of light in the evening sky. In the next tree over I spotted a cat. (Now I don't know if you know anything about a swamp leopard or not, but just in case you don't, down in the swamps they call them Soldier Cats because they are armed with more weapons than any soldier and they are dangerous wild cats.)

Here I was in a tree next door to one and like I mentioned, paralyzed from having seen it, scared even more because I could no longer see it. I lay back on the big tree limb I was resting on and closed my eyes. Right then I began to say a few prayers. I didn't know if God could hear me or not, but I was fairly trapped between Lester, the dogs, and that cat. I didn't see any way out, so I said a prayer and asked God to deliver me from what I believed was certain death.

My anxiety grew as the dogs drew ever closer. Was the cat hiding from the barking dogs or was he just waiting for breakfast? I wished I knew one way or the other, especially if I was to become his meal before sunup.

I heard the splashing of water then and resolved to make myself invisible from below. Lester was here with the dogs, so I played possum. The question was, could I? My very life hung in the balance. In the dark, even with his lantern, I did not think he could see me up above. Sometimes, being skinny was an advantage.

After a long minute of quiet the dogs began barking up the tree to my left, the one where the cat had been resting idly minding his own business.

"Come on down, Sally, I don't want to be out here all night."

Lester's voice was a terror to me now, yet I held inconspicuously still not wanting to confirm my presence to the bloodhounds below. They could hear and smell, so when were they going to get a whiff of the cat?

Suddenly there was silence from down below. "What's the matter with you dogs? Why aren't you sounding off?" Lester was saying. "You sure whopped me good girl, I almost drowned back there. I'm going to have a black eye for at least two weeks."

In the moment of utter silence which followed we all heard the low purring growl of the cat. I heard it, the uncharacteristically silent dogs heard it, and Lester heard it. The swamp around us grew eerily silent. I was not about to move, not even if that cat walked up and looked me in the eye.

"You stupid dogs, that's not Sallie Anne, that's a cat. Come on, we're getting the hell out of here. I'm not fixing to go up no tree after any kind of cat in the dark, and that was no bobcat," I heard him say.

"I don't know where you lost the girl's trail at, but we'll try again in the morning. Maybe I'm asking too much from you hounds. Maybe, you need to be able to see along with your smelling and hearing." Lester accused.

As the dogs and my captor began to make their way back toward the cabin, a part of me wished I was going with them. At least I would be safe from wild animals back there. For the moment I had a cat to deal with and my only weapon was a long-handled shovel and the kitchen knife I had tied around my hip. I held motionless for a while yet. From time to time the cat would utter a low growl. He knew I was there, and I knew he was there. I had locked eyes with him just before dark. I also knew what his low purr or growl sounded like now. He was there, across from me and after a while he went silent.

I would leave him alone just as long as he kept to himself, and for what it's worth, I suddenly realized this was one night I was not going to get any sleep at all. I had no desire to sleep high up in a tree, for I might roll off and hit the ground, and I didn't care to give that cat or the dogs such an advantage.

When you are a little girl, you have a tendency to fall out of bed, and although those days were far behind me, they weren't *that* far behind me. To make matters worse, I wasn't in any kind of bed. Tonight, I was thirty-five or forty feet up in a Cypress tree. The branch I was laying on made for a stiff bed and I wasn't going back down into the black swamp water until I could see where I was landing.

When I left the cabin, I had taken care to wrap a bear skin up tight and tie it over my shoulder so that I might at least have a covering to sleep under at night. Slipping the skin off over my neck and head I unraveled it and wrapped myself in it down to my knees wishing it was longer. My legs and feet were going to have to suffer, but at least the skin was a comfort to the rest of me. I wrapped myself tighter then and prayed the cat next door would not be curious to smell the bear skin. The last thing I needed up here in the tree was a Saturday night brawl with a wild cat.

I listened intently for I wanted a warning should the cat come my way. If he did, he was going to get a shovel right in his face. If he got any closer, he was going to get a knife. Up in the tree like I was the cat was my only worry, and then I heard him climbing down. He never came my way, but headed off to the west in the direction I had been heading before I took to the trees.

John's Island had to be somewhere close if my calculations were correct and if so, I was going to do some dry walking in the morning. I'd had all of the wet swamp water traveling I wanted for now, yet I knew before I got out of this swamp, I would be in the water many more times.

Now the tree limb I was laying back on was a big one but was nowhere near as comfortable as my own bed. Funny, what I had come to think of as my own bed was nothing of the kind. It had belonged to Lester and my bed had been burned to ashes along with my parents when he burned down our house two years ago. Still, any bed would have been more comfortable than that tree.

The sounds of the night began to pick back up again so I knew the big cat was gone from the area. After a while I heard him squall in the distance. I relaxed a little then and lay back against the tree trunk behind me. Somehow, I fell asleep and when I awoke, I could see I had dropped my shovel and it was resting directly beneath me in the water. The tree the big cat had been in was out of the water and the first in a long line of trees growing out of a small hammock. I made my way on over to his tree and descended that way after wrapping my bear skin back into a tight blanket roll. Then I waded out into the water after my shovel, taking care not to stumble into another one of Lester's traps.

Once I had myself put back together, I began my journey by crossing the hammock before me. No doubt I was heading in the same direction as the cat, but for some reason I was not so afraid of him anymore. If he wanted a piece of me, he could have had it last night.

I might've actually felt safer if the cat was around to scare off the dogs. Without realizing the full breadth of my current situation, I made my way west. As I reached the back side of the hammock it dawned on me that God had answered my prayer the night before. So then, there was still a chance for me. God had answered my terror-stricken prayer the previous evening, even in this lonely corner of the Okefenokee Swamp.

I was back at the water's edge then and looking down I suddenly discovered a turtle nest. Pulling back the sand and leaves I was rewarded with fresh turtle eggs. Gathering up about a half dozen I cracked them open one by one and sucked them dry. Then I rearranged the nest so that the remainder of the eggs would hatch in their intended manner. I then buried my empty eggs to leave no evidence of my passing.

I knew huckleberry season was upon me and one of the reasons I had chosen this time to try and get away. The huckleberry was a mainstay for the black bears of the swamp. If they could live off them, so could I. It was a meal I wouldn't have to pack over my shoulder. The turtle eggs had not been expected, but welcome just the same. I thought about food then and remembered the Wampee root which grew just below the surface of the water. It was a hot and spicy root, but edible just the same. I was not going to starve (that's what I thought).

I headed due west then hoped to reach the next island before noon. If I could make it to Fowl's Roost I would be that much farther away from Lester and his dogs. I traveled then wanting distance between us. What I did not expect was the great wall of forest which loomed foreboding in front of me.

Now the hammock I had crossed earlier had been open and clear for the most part, but the one I was facing now was chock full of various gum trees, bays and oaks. There were also beautiful magnolia trees and cypress of enormous size filtering up through the canopy. Now the bay trees were what I would call overgrown and beneath all this wonderful timber was the thickest bunch of bamboo, ty-ty and willow shrubs trying to push forth that anyone wishing to travel in a northern direction such as I would have to cut a path for each step taken.

I had a shovel, and I had a knife, when what I needed was a machete. I had never seen trees as tall as the cypress I now witnessed, and the other trees were by no means little. Could I navigate them by climbing up and over? They certainly seemed close enough, but was I strong enough? I could manage three to five trees this way, but what if this hammock went on for miles?

One of them did, but which one was it? Thinking back to the map I memorized I found no comfort. This had to be Black Jack's Wall that I'd seen marked on the map and wondered just what was meant by wall. The map Lester had did not indicate its depth and as such I would be taking an awful chance if I went into it not knowing, yet much of what I had to do was based upon little knowledge of my surroundings and more about how to survive in a swamp.

Hitching my bear skintight over my shoulder, I made haste for a likely tree and began to climb. Once I had my footing, I began my tight-walk from tree to tree. Being barefoot I soon learned how quickly tree bark could disfigure someone's feet. These Blackjack oaks were especially rough on me. I was in a bad way by the time I spotted the end of the island. For about three hours I managed to travel cautiously from tree to tree and knew well if Lester and the dogs found my trail, they would never be able to follow me this far into the Black Jack's Wall.

Lester would not pursue me without the aid of his dogs, and they were not tree climbers, so if I made it through, I would be done with them, at least that's what I told myself in my twelve-year-old mind.

As I grumbled to myself about my sore and lacerated feet, I saw the dogs in the distance working back and forth for my trail. Lester was walking behind them with his long rifle, and I was fairly trapped. They were up ahead waiting on me!

He must have gone around knowing he could beat me to the other side. I sat down in the trees and held myself still. There was no need in going any further until he and the dogs had cleared the area and my feet needed rest. I knew I was in trouble after pulling my feet up to look at them. I couldn't walk in swamp water like I'd been doing with my feet in such shape. They would become infected in no time, and I would die. I had a new problem. How was I going to travel now? God was watching over me, I just didn't know it.

I would need a boat of some kind, and a boat was out of the question under the circumstances. How about a log? No, any log I might find would just roll beneath me and dump me in the swamp. I had to think, and I had to come up with an answer and for a while I thought, but in the end I prayed again. It had worked once, maybe prayer would work again.

At nightfall I was still sitting in the same spot, and I decided it would be best if I didn't move for a while. I needed to give my feet a chance to heal, and I thought, *If I didn't move, I would leave no tracks, no scent for the dogs to follow.* For the time being I was better off right where I was. In all likelihood, Lester would give me up for dead, and if he did it wouldn't hurt my feelings anyhow. I was as good as dead where he was concerned, or so I imagined. They were too far away to pick up a trail I had not made yet, so I sat where I was up in that old tree and waited, keeping myself out of sight.

I'd lost my shovel earlier while climbing over all of the bamboo, so when it hit the ground, I knew there was no retrieving it. I could not navigate down there; such thick bamboo would be a death trap for me. I'd never get out.

I rested then, and I knew I would get hungry, but I had no idea how hungry. There was no food up here in the trees, and I couldn't move anyway, my feet were cut and bleeding, and Lester was out there casting back and forth looking for any sign of me. If I move, I will give him just what he was looking for.

Three days, for three days I sat up in that tree giving my feet a chance to recover and waiting for Lester and the dogs to leave. On the fourth day they were somewhere else, no longer up ahead of me. I wished right then I knew where he was at, but all I had to go on was where he wasn't, he wasn't in front of me anymore. He was looking for me in another area now.

I checked my feet and decided that they were good enough to travel. I needed a good pair of shoes, but I had none. That made me think of what my mother had said about our neighbor one time, "That Byron keeps her barefoot and pregnant, she couldn't run if she wanted to." That's what Lester had in store for me, I knew deep down, he would eventually get me pregnant with his child and I'd be his then, nowhere to run, no shoes to run in. Well, I had different ideas.

Chapter 4

I didn't move except to get comfortable. I knew if I moved too soon, I would get caught and if I was caught, I would be buried right along with the others. I was putting the man through a heap of trouble and if he found me, I would pay. I held no illusions; he had abducted and killed other children before me. He had gotten away with the abduction and all his mistreatment of me, but he was never going to get me back. I was going to make certain of that. I would die before I went back. I waited that fourth day, just planning and thinking.

Now that I'd had a few days to ponder and think without him crawling up behind me I knew it was over for good one way or another. Either I lived or died, but any mental abuse from him was over. I would never go back to that cabin as long as I lived. I resolved while sitting there in that tree to go far enough away to allow myself a chance to grow up and in doing so, a chance to return and take revenge. No other children needed to suffer, and I would see to it he never did to anyone else the things he did with the others. Of course, there was the time I needed to grow big enough to handle him, and then I would return to find he had kidnapped others, but I would put a stop to him if someone else didn't beat me to it. I would run a long way if I got away, but I would do a lot of learning, too.

After five days and the fact I hadn't seen Lester or the dogs for the last two I decided it was time to move. My feet felt much better and had healed quite well considering I'd nothing to eat. I used the time to fast and pray and didn't worry about food. Had I thought about food I would have gone crazy. There were many things in the swamp to watch and learn from and I had busied myself with an unusual education. I knew a good deal about the birds, the bears, the alligators and the cats by the time I came down from my canopy. I also knew a good deal more about the snakes, and wild hogs.

I had to cross a pocket of ground outside Black Jack's wall and then I was on another island, Fowl's Roost, and you could tell exactly what it was. There were waterfowl everywhere, and there was a big eagle swooping around overhead looking for an easy meal to be had. My first thought was, I hope I'm not it. The reason my thoughts ran that way was my size, I was still quite small. That eagle seemed much bigger.

A person doesn't realize just how big an eagle is until they are right up next to one. This bird was bigger than me although when I looked up the bird seemed deceivingly smaller. One thing was certain I wasn't going to have any trouble finding eggs around here. I planned to eat my fill today, and that was my mistake.

You don't eat until you are full right after a five day fast. Not if you want to move right anyway. (I did not know this, but I know it now.) I had never been so disabled in my life and if I'd been found by the dogs on that day, I wouldn't have been able to do anything to save myself. My stomach was in so much pain after I ate, I thought I was going to die. There were a few minutes there when I believed death would be a better alternative.

I curled up under a big oak tree and began holding my stomach for want of relief. When it finally came, I was surprised at how much of my food I didn't retain. I began to throw up again and again. After that when I ate my next meal I ate sparingly, and then things went much smoother.

I hung around Fowl's Roost for about three days not seeing the need to make a bunch of tracks when I knew the dogs were out looking for that very thing. I ate well and I rested even better as I was now getting used to the different animal sounds I entertained at night.

My hope was Lester believed I had turned east at the Black Jack's Wall and headed for Skeleton Creek. If he thought I was heading east he would not be back this way any time soon. It made sense for I had left no tracks for him or the dogs while I waited up in the trees. I'd done good and I was proud of myself for what I'd accomplished. I was matching wits with a veteran of the Okefenokee Swamp, and so far, I'd evaded him. No experienced woodsman could have done any better. I thought about how far I had to go and wondered just how far Cow House Island was? If I could make Cow House Island, then where would I be? I wasn't out of the swamp yet, but I now had some confidence I could make it. Cow House Island would be only a few hours from real land; land I could walk on without worrying about sinking in quicksand. Oh, yes, I had done my fair share of worrying about that part of it. Lester had scared me silly with tales of such things which inhabit the swamp, but I hadn't come across any quicksand.

There were snakes and although I had seen a good many of them, so far, I hadn't been bothered by them. Alligators seemed to fit that category, also. I had seen plenty, but we left one another alone. I had only seen two cats, and they made themselves scarce. One bear was all I'd seen up to now and he had been no problem. I was beginning to think that the only thing I had to fear were the images I had concocted in my own head from listening to Lester. None of the mean and rotten animals of the swamp seemed interested in a twelve-year-old girl. Of course, when they looked at me, they would know I was a girl…did animals know the difference? Did they care? Not if they were looking for supper.

Somehow, I had to get out of my torn and shredded dress and into pants and shirt. The way I was headed it could take a good long while before I came across any type of home or settlement, and then I would be in a quandary to explain my condition.

After spending three days resting at Fowl's Roost, I felt a good deal better, I hadn't seen hide nor hair of those dogs, Lester neither. If he was off searching somewhere else or had given up the search completely, then I was as good as free. I began to walk that second week and adjusted my heading toward the west.

I was in no hurry, not now. I had spent the last week all alone in the great Okefenokee Swamp and despite the hot humid conditions and my own wild imagination I had survived.

That morning the weather turned from hot and humid to just plain wet. Then it began to rain, and I was immediately drenched by the downpour. My dress was soaked, the bear skin was wet on the outside but appeared to be shedding some excess water. The rain was making for miserable travel, but it was the perfect way to keep the dogs off my trail. I thought I wasn't making any deep footprints, that I was not leaving a trail I thought could be followed, but I was. When I looked behind me, I could tell where my feet had mashed the grass down, leaving a trail that a blind man could follow.

The rain was not letting up anytime soon. This was to be my plight for a while. My question was how could I start a fire now that everything was wet? I was going to need to get dry because if I stayed wet too long, I would get sick, though it was not cold at all, it was hot and humid. It was then I heard the dogs.

It was well off in the distance, but I could not erase the tracks I just made crossing all that grass in the rain. How long did I have before they got on my trail: an hour, thirty minutes? Lester and those dogs were really starting to get under my skin. He had a gun, three bloodhounds and all the time in the world. When would they give up? For five days Black Jack's Wall had protected me, but now I was once again on the ground, I was fair game, and I was getting mad.

The dogs continued to bark, only now they were onto something; were they were onto my trail? It seemed there was no way out. I'd managed a week on my own in the great Okefenokee Swamp and it seemed as if all was coming to an end. If Lester got his hands on me, the spirited jesting of the last two years would be over. He would take me, and he would take me here, now. He would not wait any longer.

I waded out into the water in front of me, for I'd run out of land. I'd no idea how deep it might be in the middle, but I could swim, and in the rain, the way it was coming down, maybe once I got out far enough, he wouldn't see me. I waded chest deep and knew it was getting deeper. I had to let go of my bear skin, I no longer had a shovel to help me keep it. I could not swim such a distance as this and hang onto it. It was let it go or die, so I let it go way out in the water and began to swim.

I'd seen enough rain in this part of south Georgia and north Florida to know that it could rain steadily for the next two or three weeks with no letup. It seemed that's what I was in for. Looking behind me I could no longer see the shore and I breathed a sigh of relief. If I couldn't see the shore, Lester and the dogs couldn't see me. The rain hitting the water covered any sound I was making while I swam. How far was it to the other side? I didn't remember seeing that far before jumping in. From time to time, I tested to see if I could stand, but the water was too deep. I felt nothing beneath me and continued my journey.

How far could I swim? I was getting better at it, but the truth was, I had no idea: a mile, two or three? I suddenly remembered that I could float on my back, though I would not gain as much ground, it was a way to rest, for my arms were beginning to weaken. I could still paddle with my legs and gain ground.

I alternated back and forth for what seemed like hours and I knew I was crossing the Suwannee River. I was caught in the current! How long would it take me? Was I going in circles? There was no way to tell, the rain hampered my vision. All I could see was water in all directions, but I could feel the current pulling at me. If I drowned, I would be eaten by the alligators. Right now, that was preferable to ever seeing Lester again.

The rain, the river, and the cool water began to sap my strength. I was starting to ache all over. My limbs no longer wanted to do their job. They were beginning to fail me. I was all but done for when I saw a log floating nearby. I managed to reach it and threw both arms over the other side. I knew I couldn't lay on it, but the log gave me a way to rest, and rest was what I needed.

Chapter 5

I had passed out holding onto that log, and the rain had let up. I looked around me and everything was still wet as far as my eyes could see. I was in trouble. I was cold and shivering. When I pulled myself free from the log, most of my body had been in the water. I noticed a big gator was moving toward me slowly, so I climbed over my log and onto the hammock where I'd landed. I was lost. I had no idea where I was now. How long had I been out? Looking down, most of my dress was gone. I was so naked I took off the rest of it and put it in my hand.

What was a twelve-year-old girl to do in such a situation? I was shivering from the cold, only I knew it wasn't really cold, I had a fever coming on and I knew it. I had to get warm, I had to get dry. While the rain had let up, there was no respite from it. I began to walk, not knowing where I was, where I might end up or if anything was here that might help me. I struggled to walk as the fever took hold. I saw a tall bunch of grass up ahead near a tree, but it wasn't shelter. It was, however, all I had. I got to it, looked around and lay down from exhaustion.

I was out of my head then, my fever raging, no shelter and no clothing to keep me warm. I remember looking up into the eyes of someone, a strange someone, but could not fathom that anyone would be here, now. Why would there be anybody in such a place as this? It was a fleeting moment of consciousness.

When I came to, I was in a teepee, and I was covered with furs and pelts. Looking under the covers I was still naked. Someone had found me. The only Indian's I'd ever heard of anywhere near the Okefenokee Swamp were the Seminole. Had they found me? Lester said one time that he had friends among them. Would they tell him? Did they know who I was?

There was a warm fire in the middle of the teepee and, somehow, I felt good. I did not want to get up, and I did not want to move. I wanted to rest some more. I didn't have any clothes anyway.

Just then an Indian woman came in and looked at me. She smiled and then began doing things about the fire. Eventually she turned to me and said something, but I had no idea what she said. I had no way to answer because her language was so different from anything I knew. All I could do was look her in the eyes.

She went back out and came back with a little food, and I knew what to do with that. I was starving! I ate as she watched, and she reached over a time or two to slow me down. Remembering my last bout with starvation I slowed way down. I almost stopped. My stomach began to rumble and shift again, only this time I did not throw up. I'd only eaten about half of my bowl, and I didn't even know what it was, but it was good.

She took the rest of it and ate it herself while watching me, studying me. When she was finished, she left the teepee again. Then I heard drums beating nearby, and I knew this was an entire encampment of Indians. I'd been rescued by the Seminole Indian tribe that lived in the swamp. Now, what was I to do? They were friends with Lester if he was telling the truth. If I knew anything about Lester, I knew he could and often did tell lies. Was he lying to me about knowing the Indians? Only time would tell.

When the Indian woman came back in, she had a leather Indian dress with her, and it was my size! She left it with me and departed. I didn't need anyone to tell me what for, I knew the dress was for me, because I came here naked. Who found me? How long has it been? I was thankful for the dress, and I slid out of my bed of animal pelts and put it on. I was having trouble with a leather tie on the back when the woman came back in and helped me. She said a few things in her native tongue, but I didn't understand a word.

She spun me around and looked me in the eye. She said something and I just shrugged my shoulders. The leather dress felt different to me, but I knew it was what I needed right now. Lester would be looking for me in my old dress, not dressed as an Indian maiden. How long did I have before he showed up?

The woman took me by the hand and led me outside. It was not raining anymore, but the threat of it was still in the air. I wanted nothing more than to be inside that teepee keeping warm, but it wasn't exactly cold. Not this time of year. I looked around as we walked, and people were looking at me suspiciously. At least it seemed that way to me. We walked here and there while she told me of things in her native tongue, things I did not understand.

After about an hour I knew the full breadth of the camp, how big it was, how many Indians were here, how many teepees there were, and I also knew Lester was nowhere around. That was a relief. As it started to sprinkle everyone returned to their teepees, as did we. There were five Indian women in the lodge with me, and they all covered up while talking and cackling in a language I did not understand, so I got back under my coverings and passed out almost instantly.

Awakening again, all was dark except for a few embers still burning in the fire in the middle of our teepee. It was raining outside; I could hear it bouncing off the shelter where we were and the trees above. It was dark, what time of night I had no idea, but I lay there and looked at the fire. I was comfortable, for the first time since losing my parents in the fire I was comfortable. I closed my eyes and rested some more.

Come morning the other women were up before the sun and working to prepare food for the day. I crawled out of my fur surroundings and went outside to see how I could help. I couldn't do much, but they set me up beside another girl my own age. She was crushing wheat in a bowl. We were under a shelter held up by poles stuck in the ground. It was enough to keep the rain off. There was a big iron pot sitting on the fire getting hot while I also helped crush wheat.

There was talking among the women and the men whenever I saw them, but they weren't looking my way. They were talking about something else. Lester? Lord, I hoped not. He's the last human being on the planet that I wanted to see. It occurred to me then, all the monsters that I would meet in this lifetime were human, like Lester. Real monsters were a figment of my imagination. Men, men who kill without a care, they were the real monsters.

I have been here several days now. I had no mirror to look at myself, so I had no idea what I looked like after all I'd been through the last two weeks. In fact, I had no idea how long my journey had taken. Had it been a month or more? How long had I been out? With no idea, I could not estimate my time since leaving the cabin at all. For now, I was safe. I was away from Lester and his dogs.

As the morning went, we all ate in a group at the same time. I found this strange. There were at least fifty Indians here on this Island in the swamp, and they all ate at the same time. No one tried to talk with me for a while, only the woman who tried initially, the one who brought me my dress. I looked at the girl next to me for we were both still crushing wheat and putting it in a pan, and I knew. The dress I was wearing belonged to her. No one told me, but I knew. She was just my size, and of all the children I'd seen, she was the only one my size.

"Thank you, for the dress," I said, looking at her.

She looked at me strangely and then continued her chore. I did likewise. There was plenty of work to do for the day, so I lowered my head and kept up my motion of crushing wheat and dumping it in a larger bowl. I would do my part while here only, I might need somebody to tell me just what my part was. I didn't understand a word that I'd heard so far.

I kept up my job, my contribution until the woman who brought me the dress made me stop. She said something to the girl my age and she took my hand, leading me away. We walked around camp then and she asked me questions. That much was obvious to me, but I could not answer her, I did not understand anything she said. She stopped from time to time and spoke to others as if she were introducing me the best she could, but I didn't know her name and she didn't know mine.

The women back there were now baking, cooking something for everyone to eat. I felt a bit guilty, thinking I should be helping, but then I'd just be in the way. I had no idea how they did their meals. While walking near the water's edge I stopped her, and pointing to myself I said, "Lizzy."

She pointed to herself and said, "Tuwanni."

We smiled at one another then, knowing we understood each other's names. We continued walking but said nothing more until it was time to eat. She said something to me, and we headed back to the area where the women had been cooking for the tribe. She took a plate and handed it to me, so I sat down as if to eat, but she stopped me. She took my hand again and we walked over to where two men were sitting, and she gave her bowl to one of them motioning for me to do the same. I handed my bowl over and we returned. Again, we took food to the men. This happened over and over until all the men were fed. Only then did we get to eat. I'd just learned my first lesson: the Seminole men ate first. This would not be hard for me to remember as experience was my best teacher.

When everyone was finished eating, including the women, several young girls I'd noticed earlier grabbed all the bowls and took them to the water's edge along with one of the older women. She kept an eye on them as they cleaned the bowls. It was odd, but there had been no spoon or fork. Everyone ate with their hands, including me. Did they not know about eating utensils? Their spoons were wooded, but they were big and used to stir the food in the big pot.

I was overcome with weakness then; I collapsed in front of everybody, so one of the women spoke up and an Indian brave came over to scoop me up and put me to bed. He placed me under the covers and then left the teepee. He did this under the watchful eye of the woman who was obviously watching over me. I was ever grateful for the respite and passed into sleep immediately.

I heard men talking, not understanding them, and then I heard a voice that brought terror and fear. "I know she's here, now where is she?"

It was Lester! My spine shivered at his voice; I felt my soul almost leave my body because of the fear he struck in me. The man was answering him, but I could not understand anything he said. I didn't know what was happening, but my body shivered and quaked on its own. If they handed me to him, I was dead.

It seemed that everyone in my Teepee was still out somewhere. I had been left alone. What time was it? How soon will it be dark? Sounds were coming to me from all around the camp, yet it wasn't raining. The rain had stopped for now. I burrowed deep under my covers in an effort to not hear that voice, but it was useless, it still came through.

"Come now, where is she? You are supposed to be my friend."

Again, the Indian responded in a language I did not understand.

"If you don't give her to me, we can no longer be friends."

The Indian spoke in the language of the Seminole Indian. None of it made sense to me, but Lester seemed to understand it, although he was not talking it. Then the voice of the Indian changed to that of broken English.

"The girl must rest, or she die. When she better, we send for you."

"I have your word. That is good enough."

I heard him get up then, and he left the camp, but my fear of him was haunting me. I wanted to leave, I wanted to get away, to run again, but it was no use. I was safe for now. For that reason, I only waited.

When it was dark and the camp was quiet, wearing my old torn dress and leaving the Indian dress on my bed, I snuck out and disappeared into the night…

As I continued upon my journey in another pouring rain, I came to what was marked on Lester's map as Roasting Ear Island. I had asked him about that one for how anyone could ignore such a place. He had said there were some Yankee soldiers down south in sixty-two who had brought with them a bunch of seed corn for planting. Having settled in upon the island they planted their wares thinking they might be there for several seasons. Within weeks they had come down with fever and died from their sickness leaving a huge corn crop behind for the taking, of course with no one around the corn began to grow wild and to this day anyone who wanted corn could go to the island and have their fill.

Some folks said that the soldiers deserted the swamp after a few weeks because no bodies were ever found, but some stuck to their story of fever. As Lester put it, one thing you don't find in a swamp is dead bodies. The swamp critters just naturally have their fill when a dead body shows up, which made plenty of sense to me. I just didn't want to end up one of them. A swamp was nowhere to try and grow up, not for a little girl.

So it was that I took shelter on Roasting Ear Island and had sweet corn with every meal while I waited for the rain to subside. It didn't! I ate rabbit the first day and turtle the next. Then I noticed that the water began to rise and would soon engulf my little camp. I had used a shovel I took from the camp to cut bamboo and make myself shelter under a big old oak tree my first day there, and my feet were all healed up now.

As I stood and watched I realized the water was now coming at me from a different direction. I was soon going to drown if I didn't move my shelter to higher ground. Looking around I decided it might be best to take to the trees once again, so I began looking for a suitable perch. There in the distance I saw what I was looking for, a tree of such magnificent size I could lay down and rest out of the rain if I could create some shelter over me.

I set out then to get the job done, I had little time to make my nest. It was a unique and convenient fork in the big tree which gave me my home, and for the first few days I was alright. But a few days passed, and the water rose, and the corn disappeared, and the forest began to float beneath me. Every once in a while, I would see an animal floating by on a log, but for the most part they all just disappeared which made eating impossible.

For two solid weeks it rained and then when the rain stopped, the water below kept rising. Eventually the entire island disappeared below me, and the next day I began to see signs of the corn reappearing. The water was dropping. Where it was going, I had no idea, but that it was going down I was certain. In two years of living in the Okefenokee swamp I had never seen the water get this high.

My thought was the cabin would be flooded or destroyed by water such as this, because the cabin was only a few feet above normal water level. This flood was ten or fifteen feet and would completely submerge the cabin if my guess was right. If so, Lester would have no reason to return home because there would be no home to return to. If that was the case, I might find my traveling a much more challenging thing. Just when I thought I was through with Lester, Mother Nature had seen fit to set him free. In my mind I was struggling with a new dynamic, I had not prayed for him to be set free to come after me.

If as I suspected, the cabin was done for, Lester would have no home and would be free to pursue me. How far would he go? Just how far would Lester be able to reach in order to take care of me? Would he forget about me? No, he wasn't the type. He would want any loose ends wrapped up. I could not be allowed to go free because I knew about the bodies.

I had some thinking to do, and with the water so high I had nowhere to go, so I did my thinking. If Lester was flooded out, where would he go? To Skeleton Creek! He had a boat and could go anywhere he wanted; dogs included. At Skeleton Creek he would be out of the swamp and safe from the flood waters so going to the settlement was out of the question.

As I thought about it, I wasn't going in that direction anyway. I was heading west. Would Lester figure me out and follow? Was he that industrious? Was he like his blood hounds, relentless in his search? I didn't even have to ask myself. He was very intent until he had what he wanted, weren't my own parents dead because of him? He could leave nothing to chance.

I rested in my cradle for three more days waiting for the water to recede enough to allow travel. I was once again unwillingly fasting. I say unwillingly because I had not planned to fast at all. I was a growing youngster and needed nourishment on a regular basis. I was not in need of losing weight, there wasn't much on my bones to begin with. The last several days had given me an advantage though, any trail or trace of me was wiped out!

Now my mother had taught me before she died that to have fought against any man or woman was to put a limit on my own happiness. What she meant was that carrying a grudge was harmful only to me.

I understood her now, Lester had killed my mother and father and I would like to see justice done. My disadvantage was clearly the fact that he had stirred emotions in me which were unexplainable. I had no want or desire to see him hanged. Were my feelings simply childish and simplistic emotions which I could not control? Was I wrong? Mother had always said, "Let God do your fighting for you," especially when the chips are down and to never take revenge yourself because revenge was the lowest form of human behavior on the planet.

Well, I was listening to my mother on this account because I lacked enough experience on my own to make such a judgment call. Mother had a much better shot at being correct with such observations. I hadn't actually been able to develop any of my own ideals yet. That part of my life was still to come. For the last two years the only schooling I got was swamp survival and the twisted instruction Lester had given me to make me his.

Why didn't I hate the man? This was something I didn't quite understand. He had kidnapped me from a town of folks who didn't know who he was, he'd killed my parents, and yet I had trouble being mad at him. Maybe it was because I thought him crazy, maybe it's because he had slept close with me, maybe I was just scared, whatever the reason I didn't quite understand my own position.

I had a problem to deal with, and the problem was quickly becoming me. I found that I missed Lester. Somehow, I had to put my past behind me, but I had never expected that I would find myself at times wishing I was back in the cabin waiting for him to come home. After two years of him taking care of me I found myself with a problem.

It's alright to ask yourself a question from time to time, it's even okay to respond, but if you happen to catch yourself saying, "hum," to the answer you might just have a problem. Well, I caught myself with a problem. I didn't hate the man. I should have hated him, but I didn't. Now what exactly did that mean? The longer I was away the more it seemed I wanted to go home to be with him, but that was crazy, I was in mortal fear of the man.

There was no chance of returning to him now. He could never trust me again, and the cabin probably wasn't there anyway. I had to get away and I had to grow up. Where could a twelve-year-old girl with no parents do such a thing? I had some years to put on and they needed to be normal years. The war was just over and now the reconstruction was beginning, but what about the orphans? Where would they go? How would they live? I needed to do some checking around and find out where my best chances were.

Chapter 5

One of the things my mother had taught me through example was to never start a fight or an argument, "they would come often enough without you helping to start one," she used to say, so I had developed her habit of not starting anything. Sometimes I think that in itself was cause for me to be picked on more than other girls. I was not an instigator, and I never pushed the envelope, this more than all else made me appear weak, but when a girl has to grow up, every time a new kid decides he needs somebody to rile, that girl will naturally learn how to defend herself. I had done so in school, and now in life.

Now the swamp was deep under water and much of the outlying fields along with it. Southeast Georgia and North Florida were still quite waterlogged when I made my appearance on Cow House Island. The first thing I saw was a small cabin and I stepped back behind a tree to watch. There was someone here but whoever it was still lurked inside the structure. It had taken me nigh onto three weeks to get out of the swamp and I wasn't quite out yet, but

I was close. My first thought was, if this cabin had survived, maybe Lester's had.

I took stock of the cabin and saw the clothesline at the back corner of the house. There appeared to be some clothing hanging back there, but I could not see it very well from the angle at which I was trying to look. Could I make my way around back without being detected? No, there were dogs about and if they caught a whiff of me the game would be up. I had to stay put and watch for now.

Presently a girl of about eight or nine came out through the cabin door followed by a girl about my age. They went around back and began to take clothes down from the clothesline. The dogs followed, jumping up and down as if they were helping.

Then the lady of the house came out and if I hadn't known better, I'd say she looked right at me. Then she, too, went around the back of the cabin, picked up her laundry basket, and disappeared from sight. This was a family and no doubt the father was at work for the day. Where I had no idea, but if I wasn't mistaken, they would have food to offer. I was on a three-week diet. I was also getting weaker by the day.

I noticed several furs stretched out for tanning. No doubt this cabin belonged to a fur trapper. There were a few cows roaming the grounds nearby and they seemed content. The cabin sat on a high ridge in the middle of the meadow, high enough that the recent floods had not bothered the family at all. Even the cattle had been safe from the looks of things.

Still, I saw no chance to gather the clothes I would need to resume my journey. What I had on was pretty well shredded and I must have looked a fright. I heard a twig snap behind me then and I turned abruptly. The man I locked eyes with had a look of puzzlement on his face, but he spoke first.

"Are you alright, young lady?" he asked.

"Sir, I am a victim of the recent floods, and this dress was all of the clothes I could find," I said, hoping he wouldn't ask me anything further.

"If you'll wait here, I think Jean has an extra dress. I'll bring it out to you, then you can come on up to the cabin. We're just about to eat."

"Thank you, sir, I could sure use a new dress."

"How did you come to be in this here swamp?" he asked.

"Sir, I won't mind discussing how I got here, but I would rather do so with my dignity."

"Of course, I'll be right back."

"Please, sir, don't send anyone else," I begged.

"I wouldn't think of it, young lady. Hold tight and I'll bring you something to wear."

I stayed behind the tree then and waited for the longest time it seemed, although it was only a couple of minutes. The man returned with a nice blue dress which made me cry. It was so nice.

"We tend to go barefoot in the summer months. Hope you don't mind, but this is all we have at the moment," he said, looking away from me.

"This will do just fine," I told him, and he turned back toward his cabin. I stayed behind and got myself dressed. The dress was just right. I took the old tattered and worn-out dress and buried it right there with my shovel deep under the mud in the black water part of the swamp. That dress was something I never wanted to see again.

Taking my shovel and bear skin blanket, I walked out from behind the tree and felt terribly odd. It had been two years since I had been able to put on a normal dress that didn't have some kind of goofy frills on it.

Still, I made my way up to the cabin and knocked on the open door. There was a lot of moving around and commotion coming from inside, but I stepped up anyway.

"Come on in young lady, we're just setting the table for dinner. There's a towel out back next to the water barrel if you'd like to wash up. Jean, take the girl out back and show her where to wash up for supper."

"Come on," Jean said, and she motioned to me, and I followed her around the house to a wash basin next to a rain barrel.

She dipped me up some water, pointed to the soap and said, "The towel is hanging right here."

She stood watching me which made me nervous. This was my only contact with anyone but Lester in the last two years. I had almost forgotten how to act. I thanked her and said, "I'm ready."

"After supper, we can wash your hair and do it up if you like," she said.

At that point I realized my hair must look a fright.

"What's your name?" she asked without moving.

"Elizabeth Ledbetter."

"Well Elizabeth, my name is Jean."

We ate then and I'm ashamed to say I ate very little. I had the memory of what it was like to eat one's fill after a three-day drought and I wanted no reaction of that kind in mixed company, or any company for that matter. I had eaten little in the last three weeks and my ribs were beginning to show.

"Eat up girl, don't let it go to waste," the man's wife said.

"Ma'am, I can't. My stomach is shrunk. I'll have to eat a little at a time until I get used to food again."

"Well, you'll not starve in our home. You make do here for a couple of weeks until we get you back to eating normal."

"Yes, ma'am," I said gratefully.

"My name is Obediah Barber," the man said then. This is my wife Abigail and my daughter Jean. The young lady sitting next to you is our daughter Morgan. Have you got a name?"

"Yes, sir, Elizabeth Ledbetter."

"Well Elizabeth it looks like you've had yourself a time. How long have you been in the swamp?"

"Two years sir."

"Two ye..." the man almost dropped his spoon. "I'll not ask you anything more, young lady if you don't want me to," he promised.

"I would rather forget about it, sir."

"Then that's what we'll do, but if you ever want to talk you can talk to me or my wife. Anything you tell us will be held in strict confidence."

"Yes, sir, but like I said I'd rather forget about it."

"And forget about it we will," he said, staring his family down.

Nothing more was said after that, and I didn't have to repeat myself either. When Obediah Barber said something to his family it was the law from that moment forward.

I stayed with them for about two weeks and became good friends with Jean. Now I could have stayed longer, and maybe I should have, but the feeling was upon me that Lester would be searching the surrounding communities trying to see if I had gotten out alive. If he was searching, I needed to be making some tracks.

What I knew of the country was local only. I had heard of a place called St Louis where men had been gathering for years to travel west. It was upon me to go there and see about going west now that the Civil War was over.

I didn't exactly get my chance. One day I was sitting in the cabin when I heard someone talking outside. It was Lester! He was here! I didn't wait to see what for, I grabbed the pistol out of the drawer and made sure it was fully loaded. When he stepped into the cabin he stepped into hell! I didn't wait for him to speak, to try and make me feel guilty or anything else, I just pulled the trigger! He took a step back and whoever had been coming in the door behind him scattered. He stood in the doorway looking down at the hole I had just opened up in him and then he looked at me. I squeezed the trigger again. This time he staggered outside and fell to his rear looking up at me. I stepped into the doorway and shot him one more time for good measure. He rolled over dead, and I dropped to the front step and began bawling. I had just killed my first man at the age of twelve. Revenge, the lowest form of behavior on planet earth, but suddenly I was free. They could lock me in a cell forever, but I would remain forever free!

No one came to lock me up. Once I told Mr. Barber what happened, once I told him my story, he looked at his family, looked at me and said, "It's over. From this day forward you are free to live your life. No one will ever ask you about this again."

He stared his family down hard to warn them against ever bringing the subject up in conversation.

I stayed on then, not going to St. Louis at all. Not after learning the town was overrun with orphans from the Civil War. I stayed and became part of the Barber family, I never left that liquid forest and never felt the need to. I became one with the swamp and inherited three of the best hound dogs to ever track a coon or anything else.

RATTLESNAKE PASS

Chapter 1

The stage rounded the bend leading to Rattlesnake Station. For three hours the coach pitched this way and that, passengers tossed from side to side until they just wanted out. In the ninety-degree heat of the desert, it was even more miserable inside the stagecoach. Not one of them cared if there were rattlesnakes waiting for them at the station, to the man and the lone woman simply wanted out of the coach.

Dooley, the stage driver, informed the passengers about the state of the station ahead. A few years ago, old Morgan had been robbed late at night while he slept in the back room. Vowing it would never happen again, he brought in two six-foot-long rattlesnakes and placed them in cages on the counter so anyone who entered could see them plain as day.

After the first visitor asked him about the snakes, the rumors began. He couldn't have planned better, but his answer was a simple one. "I let them out at night so they can hunt rats and mice what get into my goods, then when I get up in the morning, I put them back in their cages so that they can't bite me or anyone else unexpected."

"What if you can't find them?" the fellow asked.

"Oh, they can't get out of this dugout. I find them. Sometimes they get ingenious, but I find them."

No more was said, but the rumors started immediately. They were simple at first, "He's just a crazy old man." Then someone said he wasn't crazy, but the smartest old buzzard they ever met. Such reckonings did nothing to squelch the rumors; all it did was stir up more conversation.

As the months passed, those snakes grew! They weren't going hungry, which had people wondering the obvious—if he was feeding them or if they were eating on their own when they were let out at night. No one in the territory had the gumption to ask old man Morgan one way or the other, so it was a topic of conversation round about campfires.

Dooley was thorough in his description, if nothing else, and he was wild behind the reins. His passengers knew all this, because he was thorough, but they were tired of being tossed to and fro. They wanted out of Dooley's stagecoach, and they wanted out bad.

The stage was on time. At eleven in the morning the passengers had endured enough when it rolled into Rattlesnake Station. Dooley started to hop down when old man Morgan came up the steps out of his dugout.

"Be careful when y'all climb down from yon coach," he admonished. "I hain't found neither one of them no good rattlesnakes this morning. Dey's still on the loose!"

The door to the stage swung open to let the passengers out, but as if on cue it swung shut again from inside someone said, "You have got to be kidding me!"

"Nope, I wish I was, but them sidewinders outsmarted me this morning. Hain't found neither one of them hiding anywhere."

"But we've got to get out of this coach, we're dying in here!"

"Nobody's stopping you, mister."

"What about those snakes?"

"They're in the station. Long as you stay out here, you'll be fine."

"How can you possibly know where they are, you haven't seen them this morning," the passenger argued.

"They never go too far. I'll find them," Morgan said.

"Mister, we're not coming out of this coach until you do!"

"Suit your own self, but I hain't bringing your food to you out here. You want to eat; you'll have to get out and go inside. I've got horses to change out."

Silence overcame the passengers. No one said anything for a while, then one of the passengers, a Mr. Brady said, "I've had enough. I'm going to get out and stretch my legs."

He reached over to open the door and then carefully looked at the ground below. Slowly he stepped down from the stage. He didn't see anything out of the ordinary. As his right boot hit the ground, he heard a rattle and instantly dove back into the coach with the others, landing in a heap on the stage floor.

When Morgan slapped his knee in laughter the rest of the passengers began to laugh, realizing the two men had played a whopper of a joke on Bradley.

It could have been any one of them, but Bradley insisted that he stretch his legs. Bradley wasn't laughing. He was mad as a skinned cat. He wasn't used to being the brunt of anyone's joke.

Slowly he pushed himself off the coach floor and eased onto the ground. When he looked over at the Morgan the station manager, he saw the man produce three rattlesnake tails which he began to shake back and forth in his right hand.

"Ha, I hain't seen anybody jump that far or that quick in a long time," he said, still laughing.

"Where are the snakes?" Bradley wanted to know.

"They's inside yonder locked up in their cage," Morgan choked between laughs.

"Well, doggie, that was a fine example of skin fright," Dooley said.

"Now that you two have had your fun, how about feeding some hungry passengers?"

Dooley climbed down from the driver's seat and held the stage door open for the young lady while Morgan was doing his best to catch his breath. Neither man moved to unharness the horses.

The young lady in the bunch was Miss Janette Yarbrough. She'd just graduated from Princeton University back east. She was heading west to take up residence as the head school mistress in Grants Pass, Oregon. She still had about twelve hundred miles to go.

The next passenger on the ground was Bev Johnston. He was a gun maker from Ohio. He learned during the Civil War how to mass produce weapons and was heading west looking for new markets to which he could sell. He had no idea how sparsely populated the west really was until now.

Charles Dover was a businessman as well, but he made his living buying distressed farms, then selling them to folks back east who wanted to try farming out west. He was good at his job, though he was always on the road to somewhere. He survived seven stagecoach wrecks, two holdups and several other catastrophes in the last five years, which had him considering a change of career.

Finally, Bradley Teeter was from Florida. He read about the gold rush in Alaska, in California, and even in Nevada. He was convinced he was just as lucky as the next bloke. All he had to do was get to the land where gold was being found and he would be able to find some of his own. He wanted to try Nevada first, then California, and if he hadn't found the mother lode by then he would head up to Alaska.

It was Bradley who got down first, and he was the first to the door of the dugout where he looked in and saw that the snakes were safely in their cages. He took a deep breath, let it out, then stepped inside. He walked over to the closest cage and took a closer look at the venomous snake. It drew back, curled up in a circle and began to shake its rattle.

He eased back from the cage at that point and took a seat at the table. The stage station wasn't much, just a little two room cabin built into the side of a hill on the road to Denver. Old man Morgan had a few things for sale, but mostly he was a fur trapper. Furs of every description could be seen hanging from the walls.

Bradley looked back at the snake in the corner and then looked the other way to see the other one. Those were some big snakes. They were apparently eating well, and they didn't like being disturbed.

The others came cautiously through the door once they saw Bradley had taken a seat. Inside was stifling from the fire in the fireplace and the smell from the furs made sitting inside almost impossible .

There was a curtain on the back wall which covered the entrance to another room, and Bradley, being the inquisitive type, pulled the curtain back to reveal a small cave with a cot in one corner. "So that's where the old man sleeps."

"Close the curtain, Teeter, the man does have a right to his privacy," Bev said.

"After what he did to me out there?"

"After what he did to you out there. Now close it."

Bradley Teeter closed the curtain and looked around the table at his traveling companions. They were good folks, and he didn't want to stir any trouble, so he let the curtain go. Just as he did something caught his eye and he pulled the curtain back once again.

"Close the curtain Teeter."

"I'll close it in just a second."

Suddenly, a rattlesnake landed on the front step of the dugout barring the exit of the front door. Then another one landed just a few inches from the first. Both snakes were of good size, about four feet in length, and both were mad.

Where had they come from? Bradley jumped up, letting go of the curtain. In an instant he was standing on the tabletop leaning over to give his head some room. The others followed suit. As they helped Miss Yarbrough onto the tabletop, the front door closed with a thud. There was some laughing outside, and then the door was barred shut. The four traveling companions were effectively trapped.

Janette screamed, "What are you doing?"

Bev Johnston put his arm around her and said, "Calm down, miss. They probably didn't get enough laughs with their first joke."

"I wish I could believe you, Bev, but what I saw behind that curtain isn't any joke," Bradley said.

"What did you see?"

"Human body parts!"

Janette screamed again, then began to sob uncontrollably. Searching the cabin for a way out, the men weren't laughing, either. There was one small window in each room, but both were too small for a man to crawl out of. Besides that, they were barred on the outside.

With the door closed, little light reached inside. Once again Bradley pulled back the curtain which hid the back room. It was a large cave on the back of the dugout. There were several human legs and arms hanging from the top of the cave. Then he saw the cage. Another rattlesnake cage, and the door was wide open!

Reaching up he pushed on the ceiling to see if he could get it to move, but it was solid. The other men tried their luck against the plank roof with no results.

"I knew something was up the moment we turned down that old road several miles back. Did you notice it? The road that leads to this place is almost grown over with grass. It doesn't get used very often," Bev said.

Charles Dover looked around and said, "What I want to know is, how do we get out of here?"

"You don't," Morgan laughed from the window and a bullet from Dover's gun clipped the frame just beside Morgan's head. He ducked a bit late and took a few splinters in the face, but he laughed anyway.

A snake dropped through the other window while no one was looking, but the thud of it landing on the dirt floor was unmistakable. Janette let out another shrill scream and Bev shook her by the arms. "Get a hold of yourself, miss."

"I can't," she cried, "we're all going to die."

One thing the men noticed was how quickly the cabin was heating up with the front door closed. Near the ceiling like they were, it was even hotter.

"We've got to put that fire out," Bradley said.

"And just how are we supposed to do that?" Charles asked.

In the darkness of the room one thing was obvious, the floor was moving beneath their feet. Bradley took a match from his vest pocket and lit it. There on the floor below them were rattlesnakes of every size, making their way in from the cave where they had been held captive.

He glanced over to the cages sitting on the counter. The snakes were gone!

"Oh, hell," Bradley said in disgust.

"What?" Bev asked.

"The big ones are loose."

Janette screamed again and Bev slapped her. "Get a hold of yourself, woman. All this screaming isn't going to help us any."

From outside they could hear the two men laughing. They were in quiet conversation at times, but then they laughed again at their victims—four unsuspecting souls who walked right into a trap.

"I could put a few holes into that pot that's sitting over the fire," Bev suggested. "That might douse the flame enough to put the fire out."

"That's all the food we have for several days. You sure you want to waste it?" Charles Dover asked.

"Do you think that food is any good? I'll bet ten to one it's poisoned," Bev argued.

Miss Yarbrough continued to sob, resting her head in Bev Johnson's arms. She was terrified of snakes, yet she had never seen one this close. Now that her life depended on their knowledge of reptiles, she couldn't think straight. Her world was consumed with fear.

"Go ahead and shoot the pot, Bev. Maybe we can get the fire put out."

Bev handed the girl off to Dover, who was closest, and took aim with his pistol. The bucket was an old wooden affair with oak staves and iron hoops holding it together tight. The trick to using a bucket like that was not to get it into the flame. However, a bullet would shatter it, spilling the contents all over the fireplace, they hoped.

As Bev squeezed the trigger, the bucket exploded. As the contents spilled from the pail, the fire sizzled, dying a slow death. Only a small flame was left after just a few seconds.

"What's going on in there? You aren't killing my snakes, are you?"

"No, but that isn't a half bad idea," Bev said.

Smoke rolled from the fireplace and soon the fellows outside knew what the passengers were up to.

"You shot my bucket!" Morgan shouted, "Why there was no cause for that, I've had that bucket half my life. Our mother cooked in that in the old country."

"What country was that?"

"Romania," Morgan answered.

"You'll have to order a new one!"

"I don't want a new one, I want Mother's!"

"It's in a hundred pieces. Maybe you can put it back together after you let us go."

"Ohhh, you're going to pay for that," Morgan said.

"Oh, yeah, show me how," Bev replied.

"We ain't letting you go," Dooley said from the other window. The stage driver was a little too close and Bev put a shot through the window before the man could react. It hit him right between the eyes. He collapsed on the hard earth with a thud.

Suddenly a yell went up from outside. "You killed my brother!"

"You're next."

There was quiet for several moments, then they heard the bar being removed from the front door.

"He's not stupid enough to open that door and show himself," Bradley whispered to the other passengers.

The front door swung open, and a shadowy figure stood silhouetted against the daylight, shotgun in hand. Through a smoke-filled haze the three men on the table didn't wait for him to get the gun into play. As one, they unloaded everything they had into the dark figure gracing the doorway.

Janette screamed at the suddenness of it. Helpless and unarmed, she watched the men on the table kill the man. If this was what it was like to go west, she was going to have to reconsider her decision to teach in the western schools.

The blackened silhouette fell backward onto the hard-packed earth, dead before he hit the ground. Sunlight unveiled his features. He had been a hard man, an evil man, and he died suddenly at the hands of men who wanted to live.

As the smoke began to clear from the room the men realized most of the snakes had returned to the cave to escape the smoke-filled room. Climbing down from the table, Bev took Janette in his arms and carried her outside.

It was then the real killing began. All three men emptied their guns into the rattlesnakes that chose outside rather than the cave. With empty guns, they turned to shovels, picks and knives to cut heads off, stacking the carcasses in an empty rain barrel, laying the heads in a pile knee deep. When they were finished, the men reloaded their weapons.

"All right, Bev, you keep an eye on the miss, and we'll go in and see what happened here."

In a few minutes the men returned with wallets, purses, and other documents which amounted to twenty-seven people who died at the hands of the two brothers from Romania.

"I guess we better give all of this stuff to the U.S. Marshal at Denver. He'll want to notify relatives if there are any."

"What do we do with those two?" Bev asked.

"Let the dead bury the dead!"

The passengers headed for the coach.

"I'll drive," Bradley Teeter insisted.

As Bev swung open the door to the stagecoach two rather large rattlesnakes hissed their displeasure at being disturbed. They were the two biggest snakes the brothers owned. As they hissed and slithered, Bev pulled his pistol and shot at them, but the snakes moved with precision as if they could actually see the bullets coming, dodging the projectiles with uncanny ability.

It took another two hours to get the snakes out of the coach. With a shovel and gunny sack they pushed them out, but even for seasoned western men, the day was overloaded with death. They let the creatures go and the passengers headed for Denver. It was a lonely, solemn ride, and looking back they wondered how so many could die at the hands of the two brothers, yet only they had escaped.

Suddenly a scream came from inside the coach and Bradley's reaction was a simple one. "Oh, hell," he said as he slapped the horses one more time with the whip to start them up the steep grade.

YELLOW BOY

No weapon in American History has had quite the impact of the Winchester Arms model 1873. The Winchester .73 was unique in our history at a time when new weapons were the order of the day. When our nation had come full circle out of the Civil War the rifle manufacturer had been working on a repeating rifle which would mow down the enemy in short order. Twelve rounds could be loaded into the chamber and the rifle fired repeatedly until those rounds were spent. However, the war was over.

With no other front available Winchester began shipping large quantities of the rifle west to the new frontier. The result was inevitable. With so many orphans from the Civil War now living out west, young men who no longer had families, these weapons in the hands of so many orphans, (cowboys as we have come to know them today), created what we now celebrate as the Wild West. What did they think was going to happen? Truth be told, gun manufacturers didn't care, they just needed a new market and they found one in the untamed lands of the west.

"A gun is neither good nor evil, but a human being makes it so."
~John T. Wayne

Chapter 1

Irene Kennedy shielded her hazel blue eyes against the bright unforgiving sun to witness the lone rider ambling through the fort gate. Familiar with the routine of men who rode long distances in the barren desert wasteland surrounding Fort Union, she unceremoniously noted the exhausted blue roan on which the man rode, then she noticed the man.

The sunbaked rider had not shaved in several days and his short, almost military haircut hinted a slight gray around his ears, although the man seemed much too young for graying hair. Then she realized the gray was dust. His dust-covered shirt and vest spoke of a great deal of elegance had it been clean. As anticipated, the horse and man ambled over to the water trough where the man dismounted, nearly falling to the ground before gathering his balance. He wore two guns tied low on his thighs, thighs of a very muscular variety she noted, not those of a horseback riding cowhand. His guns were clean when nothing else appeared to be. She noted his narrow hips and broad shoulders then shuddered for this was a man who appeared to have seen and done much, yet he was young, much too young.

He allowed the animal to drink, but not too much. Then he walked the horse out of reach of the trough and tied the animal to the hitch post. It was then she saw the bandage around his right knee and the hole that gleamed sunlight through his hat brim. He walked with a slight limp and picked up the gourd dipper, drinking the same water as his horse. Removing his trail soiled shirt and handkerchief from around his neck, he began to bathe what appeared to be an open wound in his side, his tan rippled torso a rare sight even for the likes of Irene Kennedy, who out of habit, ever searching for her beloved, watched all men arrive and leave the fort.

Turning, the man put on his shirt and started in her direction. Irene knew she was the only person outside now, but not likely the only one watching the trail branded stranger as he covered the distance from the army stables to the colonel's front porch. She stood stock still as the man weaved about while he limped her direction.

When the muscular young man was only a few steps shy of the boardwalk, she noticed the fresh blood stains on his shirt and pants. His square jawbone was chiseled and firmly set beneath a high cheekbone and penetrating dark eyes. He seemed as though he was about to speak when his knees buckled, and he tumbled face first into the dust before the steps.

"Uncle Winston," Irene called toward the colonel's office.

At her beckoning, a perfectly dressed soldier blanketed the doorway and looked down on the man lying in the dust at his feet. Two other soldiers scattered around the colonel to flank him, looking on in surprise.

"Who is he?" the colonel asked.

"I don't know. He just rode in on that blue roan over by the corral," Irene said.

"Sergeant Daniels, get some men and carry this man over to Doc Curry. He seems to be suffering from heat stroke."

"Yes, sir," said the one enlisted man on the front porch.

Irene stepped down and took the man's hat from the ground where it had fallen and stuck her right index finger through the hole in the brim. "This was done by an Indian arrow."

"Let me see that," her uncle ordered.

He took the hat from Irene and examined the brim with caution born of experience. The hole had been a recent development as it hadn't had time to wear. With his jaw set in a grim line, he stared off into the distance.

"Captain McGavin, get those gates closed. I want sentries posted at the openings and in the towers. This man was attacked only this morning."

"Sir?"

"I know we haven't got a fort wall on any side, captain, but we'll need to form a line of defense in all directions. It will have to be made of soldiers until we can get walls built. Now, post the men."

"Yes, sir," the captain replied with a salute.

By the time Sergeant Daniels returned with help, the incomplete fort was locked down and guards were posted. Four men gathered the stranger onto a gurney and carried him over to Doc Curry's place with Colonel Winston Scott and his curious niece in tow. The girl noted the man smelled strongly of stale sweat and trail dust.

One of his guns fell out of its holster and landed at Colonel Scott's feet, who responded by picking up the empty weapon. Duly noting the condition of the weapon, he slipped the other gun free of its holster only to see it was empty as well. Two

Navy colts and both empty! Hastily examining the man's gun belt, he noted there were no cartridges left to refill them.

"Irene, see to this detail and give Doc any help he needs. I need this man alive."

Colonel Winston Scott marched to the man's horse. Pulling the rifle from its scabbard he noted its empty status and then searched the man's saddle bags for ammunition, an army dispatch, anything that might hint as to why the young man was here. He found nothing. Something seemed familiar in the man's face, yet Scott could not immediately place him.

He shoved the two pistols into his waistband and took the saddle bags along with the rifle back to his office. There were too many unanswered questions and Winston Scott did not like unanswered questions, not when he had soldiers in the field.

E Troop was supposed to be riding to a rendezvous with a shipment of three hundred crates of rifles en route to the fort from Winchester Arms Company out of St. Louis. Winchester Yellow Boys. Now was not the time for Indian trouble.

The new Winchester rifle was supposed to be the best ever produced and would be needed on the frontier to help ward off Indian incursions into army strongholds, which had been happening too much of late.

Had the Civil war not ended in 1865 with Lee's surrender, it would have ended anyway less than a year later with the introduction of the Winchester model 1866 and the Henry repeating rifle. Both manufacturers insisted their weapons could be fired at a pace of sixty rounds per minute, an unheard-of fantasy in the minds of some, but it wasn't a fantasy.

Once again seated at his desk, Colonel Scott dumped all the contents from the man's saddlebags onto his desk and began to catalog the items. A small gun cleaning kit, some leather string, a pair of moccasins, a fixed handle knife, some food stuff and a small bar of soap wrapped in a white washcloth.

Just then Sergeant Daniels returned holding a folded banner. "Sir, I think you should see this."

Colonel Scott unfolded the flag, which he discovered denoted E troop. It was torn, burned and full of both bullet and arrow holes! He stared in disbelief. Had he lost an entire troop? It seemed the only credible answer, but it simply couldn't be. E troop consisted of forty-three men, some of the best under his command. *They couldn't be dead!* "Sergeant, I want to know as soon as that man is awake and able to talk."

"Yes, sir," Daniels saluted, snapped his heels, did an about-face and left the room. Captain McGavin filled the void almost immediately.

"What is it sir?"

"E Troop seems to have been wiped out."

"That doesn't make any sense, sir."

"Do you know any other way to acquire their company standard?"

Captain McGavin looked down at the flag as if seeing it for the first time. His heart sank as the truth of the statement sunk in. There was only one way to wrench a banner from a troop of Calvary, to be defeated to the last man. If one man remained, he would carry the banner home. Fear struck at the heart of the captain for he could not conceive any way possible to defeat such a well-armed detachment of veteran soldiers and veterans they had been.

"It seems we have lost Captain Johnston and his men. Get me the rest of my commanders immediately. I want to see them now."

"Yes, sir," said the captain as he saluted, clicking his heels in the same manner as Daniels as he left the room.

For Colonel Winston Scott, what had been a beautiful routine day suddenly became a nightmare. Men were dead, his men! Reports would have to be written and sent, but an answer must be prepared, but an answer to what? So far, the colonel knew nothing. If the men were dead, where had they died? His lack of information meant sending another troop into unknown circumstances on a fact-finding mission. A burial detail would have to be assembled at once leaving the fort at one third strength.

In Doctor Curry's office the man opened his eyes and looked at the young lady tending to him. She was a rare beauty he noted, and no doubt spoken for. No such beauty was likely to go very long without an engagement ring. She was mixing something and leaning over a table with a bowl in hand when the doctor spoke. "Well, young man, you're no worse off for the wear, although I did need to put a few stitches in you," he said.

The girl raised upright at the doctor's statement and looked at him with curious eyes, then replaced the damp cloth resting on the rider's now-cool forehead. He noted with calculating eyes there was no ring on her finger and his heart suddenly felt strange.

"Who's in charge?" the young man inquired.

"Colonel Winston Scott is in command. He'll want to see you now that you're awake," the doctor said.

A sudden look of shock appeared on the patient's face. "You don't mean the same Winston Scott from the battle at Crossroads, Virginia!"

"Why, young man, that's exactly who I mean? What's the matter?"

"My father rode for him in Virginia. He'll not believe anything I say, yet he must."

"If you don't think he knows about E troop being wiped out, he does."

The young man felt around for the banner which he'd tucked into his trousers and realized the banner must already be in the hands of the colonel.

"He was informed as soon as I discovered the banner. He knows he's lost men and he is preparing to ride as we speak."

"He mustn't ride out. That's exactly what the Indians want. They're after the fort and the armory. They know about the rifle shipment, and they want the ammunition stored here. The rifles won't be any good to them without ammunition. If they get their hands on the fort, every settler in five hundred miles will be wiped out."

"How do you know all of this?"

"It isn't hard to figure. Someone's been feeding information to the Indians," the young man claimed.

"An officer?"

"I don't know who, but somehow they know what every man among you is doing at any given time."

"I see. Well, the colonel's the one you need to explain things to, he's the fort commander. I'm just an army doctor."

The patient looked at the girl, wondering about her part in all of this. Of course, she would have no part except to assist the doctor.

"I'll get your shirt for you. You might want to be dressed when you report to the colonel," she said.

Just then the door burst open, and Sergeant Daniels stepped in.

"The colonel wants to see him if he's able."

"He's able," Doc Curry said as Irene Kennedy helped the young man into his shirt. Once he was dressed, he stood erect and tested his movements. For a moment he seemed all right. He took a few steps and then turned to face the girl.

"Thank you for your help," he said as he retrieved his hat from a nearby table.

"You're quite welcome." *And a gentleman to boot,* she thought.

Doc Curry looked on in disbelief as the young man gathered his strength, yet he never acknowledged the surgeon, having eyes for the girl only. "Well, how do you like that!"

Falling in step behind the sergeant, the young man left Doc Curry's quarters and headed for the office of the post commander. Although the walk was a short one, he noted his guns were not in their holsters. *Who had removed them, and why?*

Ike Gastineau eyed the post as he walked. It would do well to know where everything was when the Indians hit. Boot heels sounded out their cadence on the hollow boardwalk along the row of headquarter buildings. Ike knew the commander would have serious doubts when receiving his account of things, simply because his father had been in a similar position several years earlier and had advised then Major Winston Scott of impending trouble. The result being his company was attacked by ambush at Crossroads, Virginia and the Colonel would not soon forget the name Gastineau. He had lost nearly his entire command but managed to escape with the few remaining men.

"My God, of all people it has to be Colonel Scott!"

"What was that?"

"I'm just talking to myself."

Young Ike Gastineau Junior gathered himself with great effort. Though he was exhausted, he walked upright and straight to put forth his best image. As the two men neared the headquarters building, Ike paused as if noticing the compound for the first time. Shading his eyes from the imposing glare of the brutal sun, he glanced around the unfinished compound and studied the layout of buildings. There were the officer's quarters, enlisted quarters, a few personal quarters, the armory, the stockyard, parade grounds, and a small store, all evidence of the army's presence. While there was a gate, there weren't any walls but for a short section which had been started on the southeast corner. So, why was the front gate closed? It was then he saw the men posted to cover the wall which wasn't there.

Everywhere the sun blanketed their efforts. Men were beginning to move about although at the high point of heat during the day most wanted to stay in the cool shade offered by the barracks.

"Good grief," Ike said as he stepped into the headquarters building and removed his hat.

Irene Kennedy was in the army. She was the colonel's niece and had lived in army posts all over the country. Her father was killed just after the first salvos of the Civil War at Bull Run. Her mother died in 1865 at the close of the war. At such time, the only place left for the youngster was with Uncle Winston and he wasn't a married man. He didn't balk at the prospect of having to rear the young girl at an army garrison, and as such, she knew the army well. She had grown up traveling under the army's umbrella, learning to move at a moment's notice. She knew army regulations and if she saw the man she wanted, she would have been married already, but her man had never stepped forward, until today.

Irene was quite humbled by the prospects of men or lack of them, but today she saw a civilian man who could fill any two army uniforms. He was considerate of others, a rare and lacking trait in most army personnel. Surprised and caught off guard, she was totally unprepared for such an out-of-place character. The young man was more southern gentleman than the rough western type. The way he carried himself even when injured spoke of a quiet inner strength and good staying quality.

Since the incident at Crossroads, Virginia, promotion for her uncle had been slow. Finally in the last year he had been sent to a new fort, a fort which was not yet finished. Her heart felt for her uncle when she first saw the place, for this would be the nail in the coffin which had become his career. Watching from the doctor's office, her curiosity was aroused as the two men entered the headquarters building. Unhappy with any man in the fort, or any man she had seen anywhere else, she was inflamed by the muscle-bound limbs of this man, a man who might ride out at any moment to never be seen or heard from again. She didn't even know his name. This was an error she must correct as quickly as possible.

Colonel Winston Scott was the consummate professional soldier even if his recent years didn't reflect as such in his army record. One of seven officers who hadn't taken a reduction in rank at the end of the Civil War, he had been duped at Crossroads, Virginia, but he would never be duped again. Ike Gastineau, the man who had tricked him, had long since been taken care of.

Although many years ago, the scars of that battle remained on the career of Colonel Scott. It was the only engagement he ever lost, and it almost cost him his life. Ike Gastineau, a Confederate spy, an implant in Colonel Scott's command, had a mission to give false information to the Yankee troops preparing to attack. At the time of the battle of the

Crossroads, the colonel hadn't known this. He did his job well, and Major Scott, at the time, acted in haste. The information provided meant he could route the Confederates and quite possibly get another promotion, but it had all been a trap. The young major found himself quite literally fighting for his very life. He had been lucky to escape, but in his escape, he came across Ike Gastineau in a Confederate uniform. "So, this is how it's done in the south," Major Scott had said then.

"I'm sorry, major, but war is war."

Without any further hesitation, Winston Scott drew his pistol and fired three times into the man who had cost him his command. Ike Gastineau Senior would never again cause the deaths of any troops. "War is war," he repeated.

This was the man Ike Gastineau, Junior, was reporting to when he entered the colonel's office and Ike Gastineau, Junior had been told the story by friends of his father. He knew Winston Scott, the post commander, was the man who'd killed his old man.

"So, young man, what news is it you bring me?"

"It is no good news, sir. I found E Troop wiped out. No one was left alive."

"May I ask what you are doing in the area and what your name is?"

"I was riding across country to meet with a group of fur trappers in the Rocky Mountains."

"And your name, young man," the colonel ordered, demanding an answer.

Shuffling his feet, he tried to avoid this part, "Ike Gastineau, Junior."

Colonel Winston Scott was speechless. He killed this young man's father ten years ago and now he was facing the spitting image. To make matters worse, he had to rely on information the young man gave him, and he wanted to do anything but. Silence enveloped the room as the colonel absorbed the impact of what the young man's presence meant. Slowly the colonel's right hand came to rest on his hip gun.

"Your father once brought me information, son. I shot him for the traitor he was. I should hope I won't have to repeat myself with you."

"Sir, I know the story, but I've never heard it from the horse's mouth. If we manage to live through this, I should like to hear it directly from you."

The colonel's eyes widened in surprise, "Well-spoken, young man. Now what the devil's going on?"

"Sir, putting all past feelings aside, I believe the fort is about to be attacked by Indians, a lot of Indians. They've gone after your rifle shipment, and they want the ammunition stored in your armory."

"How many of them would you say there were?"

"My guess is about two hundred of them wiped out E Troop. Otherwise, I'd say about four to five hundred all together."

"Are you telling me my boys ran into two hundred Apache Indians?"

"No, sir, they were ambushed. Once they rode into the canyon they were surrounded, and the battle was over. They never had a chance."

"How do you know all this?"

"I can read sign, colonel, and I listen. I can scout for troops, if need be, but I'm no army scout."

"How did you get the E Troop Company banner?"

"I rode in after the fight was over. When I saw the banner on the ground, I figured the army might want it back, so I came straight here."

The room filled up with officers.

"Could you lead us to where this happened?"

"I could, sir, but I will not. They are planning to attack here at the fort."

"How do you know this?"

"Everyone in town knows it."

"By town you mean Benton's saloon and store down by dry creek?"

"Yes, sir."

"Somehow that doesn't surprise me. That man seems to know everything that goes on here."

"I believe he's trading with the Indians, sir."

"Well, now, how would he do that? We can see everything he does from right here at the fort."

"I don't know just yet. I don't live around here, but I believe he's doing so."

"Sergeant Major Ivy, get C Troop ready to ride. I want them ready within the hour."

"Yes, sir," the sergeant major answered, saluted and left the room.

"The rest of you men look at what you might have to do to defend the fort and make the necessary improvements. I want this fort defended and I want it done right."

Everyone left the office, everyone but the colonel and young Ike Gastineau.

"Young man, I would like for you to lead us where you found E Troop, if you don't mind. It would be best if you stayed with me until we got to know one another better."

"Sir, I'll draw out a map for you, but I won't go with you."

"Then you're lying to me just like your father did," the colonel accused.

"No, sir, I'm not."

"If you thought the fort was going to be attacked by Indians, you wouldn't want to remain here in the shelter of it."

"May I speak freely, sir?"

"I insist," said the colonel waving his hand.

"I see you have my guns, and if you look at them, you'll have noticed that they're completely empty. Every last bullet was fired in my escape from a small band of Apache warriors. I want to reload my weapons and I never want to be without ammunition again. You, sir, have an armory full of ammunition. If I survive it will be because I have an unlimited supply of ammunition, not because I rode out with you."

"There's a pen and paper on my desk. Would you be kind enough to draw me the map?"

"Sir, the moment you ride out, the Indians will know it."

"How?"

"When I rode out the other night it was because I overheard a fellow at Benton's. I've never been to the fort, sir. He whispered to Benton the Indians would take care of Johnston. I didn't know who Johnston was at the time and I didn't arrive in time to warn him."

"You rode to warn him? Why, that's army business."

"Yes, sir, I was just passing through. I had no intentions of staying, but like you said it was army business and those men down to Benton's seemed to know more than the army about what was going on. Had there been a soldier present or even a local they wouldn't have talked so freely. I overheard too much to just walk away, sir. I also knew if I came to the fort, they would know about that, too. If I did anything but ride on, I would have been a marked man, so I let them think I rode on. In doing so, I circled around and went straight for E Troop, but failed to reach them in time."

"Just draw me the map, son."

Chapter 2

There were two problems confronting Colonel Scott: one was personal and the other military. The young man in his office was the son of the man who'd derailed his army career. *Was he of the same dastardly character as his father, or was he different? What was the old saying: the apple never falls far from the tree; and then, what about the blood?* Blood was not to be taken lightly. Many things are passed down through the blood. A child receives his mother's flesh, but the father provides the blood.

"Why did you ride after E Troop?"

"I told you, sir, if you sent someone from the fort, they would know everything."

"Where are you from, Ike Gastineau?"

"You mean my home?"

"I don't mean anything else."

"I hale from Big Bone Lick, Kentucky, sir."

"Why are you traveling?"

"I'm old enough to have seen all the reconstruction I want to see. I figured the west was the land for a young man like me. Out here is where I'll make my mark in life."

"You wouldn't be the first young man to go west to get away from the reconstruction," the colonel said.

"No, sir, and I won't be the last, either."

"What about your mother, is she still alive?"

"She died at the end of the war, never really lived after the death of my father."

"I regret having to kill him, son, but it was war."

"I know that sir, otherwise I should be looking for revenge."

"Revenge has caused more problems than it ever solved, it's the devil's own weapon, the best in his arsenal. You'd be smart to stay away from such temptation because I've found revenge has a habit of backfiring and," he paused for effect, "revenge is the lowest form of human behavior on the planet."

"Are you saying that because you want to live or because it's true?"

"I'm starting to like you, son, although I'm not sure why. So, anything I tell you will come directly from my heart or my gut. You didn't get to learn a man's ways with your father's help. I shall do my best to make up for any loss you've suffered in that department. I owe you that much."

"Sir, I've drawn the map to the best of my ability. I hope you find the spot with no trouble. And, sir, I don't need a father."

Colonel Scott, looking out his window, watched the movements as the fort began to bustle with life. He walked over to the young man and took up the paper.

"Why, that's Choate Canyon!"

"I don't know the name of it, sir, but that's the best I can draw a map."

"I've got to ride out with C Troop and recover what I can and bury my men. I would take it as a personal favor if you would make certain nothing happens to my niece. She was in the doctor's office with you. Her name is Irene."

"Sir, if you ride out now, the Indians will attack us before morning."

"I'm aware of that possibility, son, but I have a job to do."

"Sir, it's not a possibility. We'll be attacked by dawn. The Indians will know as soon as you leave the fort. Once they attack, they will likely have ammunition and they'll be able to wipe out C Troop."

"I don't need to be told what can happen. I know very well what is possible. That's why I am asking you to keep an eye on Irene for me."

"All right, sir, but I can only do so much. May I go now?"

"Yes, you may go."

"May I take my guns with me?"

"They're your guns," the colonel gestured with his hands.

"Thank you, sir."

Stepping around the colonel's desk, Ike dropped his Navy revolvers back into their holsters then picked up his rifle and saddle bags. He turned to walk out the door, stopping to settle his hat back on his head. Looking about, he wondered where they had taken his horse. He saw the girl, Irene, sitting in a rocking chair in front of Doc Curry's office.

With a new purpose in mind, he headed in her direction. When he was halfway there, he stopped and turned toward the fort commissary. He felt naked without loaded guns and he needed ammunition. Entering the store, he dropped his saddlebag on the counter and ordered four hundred rounds of ammo. Immediately he shoved bullets into waiting cylinders.

"Are you planning on fighting a war, son?"

"Yes, I am, before sunup tomorrow. If you're smart, you'll do likewise. When the Indians strike, they'll want your store and the armory first," he said as he stuffed his saddlebags and headed out the door for Doc Curry's. He never looked up to see the man's cigar dangling farther from his lips in a state of shock.

The girl was still sitting in the rocker as he approached.

"I see you're feeling better," she smiled at him.

"I'd feel a lot better if I were somewhere else. Your uncle is making a mistake."

"Whatever do you mean?"

"He's riding out. I believe we'll be attacked by the same Indians who attacked E Troop. They'll hit just before sunrise."

"But this is an army fort!"

"Yes ma'am, an incomplete fort which will be less than half-staffed, completely vulnerable."

"What are you going to do?"

"I would like somewhere to rest, ma'am. At least until dark, then I have got to be awake and able to move."

"Come with me," she said, getting up from her chair. "I won't need my bed for I'll not be able to sleep a wink until Uncle Winston returns."

"Ma'am, I don't want to get your bed soiled. I'm in no shape for sleeping in elegance."

"You're in no shape for sleeping at all, but you need sleep. I bathed most of you already while you were lying in the doctor's office. You may not be as dirty as you think."

Surprised, Ike followed the girl through the front door to the colonel's quarters. Several officers watched as the two young people disappeared from prying eyes.

"You can put your things over by the fireplace. I'll get you some water if you still want to clean up."

"Thank you, I'd like that."

Irene hustled to and fro for a few minutes and then appeared with a large water bowl. "If this isn't enough, I can get more."

"That will do just fine, ma'am."

As she left the small room, she pulled the curtains and left Ike alone. He did what he could to bathe then lay down on the soft bed and pillows. With his guns within reach, he was asleep almost instantly.

All was silent when he opened his eyes. C Troop was gone, and the fort was still. *It was late, but how late?* The girl rested in the corner in a rocking chair sound asleep. Slowly he raised himself up in the bed and froze. A silhouette of human form was trying to see into the window, straining to see into the depths of the colonel's quarters.

Slipping from beneath the blankets he eased one of his pistols from its holster and slithered to the window under the cover of darkness offered by the room's interior. *Had the girl put out all the lights or had she been instructed to douse them?* There was a slight scratching sound at the window as the Indian tried to pry it open with his knife. Easing his navy colt up into position, Ike squeezed off a round directly into the Indian's face. Suddenly, the night exploded, and gunfire was heard from all over the fort. Irene screamed and dropped to the floor instantly.

"Shhh. Are you alright?" he asked the girl.

"No, I'm not alright, why didn't you warn me?"

"There wasn't time."

"Did you kill him?"

"I think so, but his body will be gone before sunup," he whispered.

"Are you sure it was an Indian?"

"Yes, I'm sure I shot an Indian. Grab my saddlebags and I'll get my rifle. We've got to get out of here."

"Now?"

"Yes, now! We're all by ourselves here and they'll get us sure if we stay."

"They'll get us if we set foot outside," the girl said.

The gunfire outside subsided and the night once again became still and quiet. Others had been firing and Indians had fallen. What of the soldiers? The compound could not afford to lose even one. How many Indians were down was anybody's guess. They wouldn't try again before dawn. The Indians wanted ammunition, not dead bodies.

"Indians don't like dying after dark. Considering what just happened I don't believe they're anywhere around," Ike said.

"We're in the safest building in the fort. If they got us here, they would have gotten us anyway."

"How are your living quarters the safest building?"

"Simple. The back windows aren't large enough for anyone to get through, the side windows have latched shutters no man could possibly pry loose, and the front windows and door are the same. When others begin to think of where to hide out, they will naturally want to come here. It's the safest building save for the armory, and if the Indians want the armory, they'll get it."

"The armory can be covered from three different buildings. I hope that's what the sergeant major has done."

"Sergeant Major Ivy insisted on reinforcing those buildings with soldiers and he is reinforcing those troops with cover from sharpshooters in hidden locations throughout the fort."

"What time did your uncle ride out?"

"He left within an hour of you going to sleep. He did his best to make certain he set a trap for the Indians."

"It was the Indians who set the trap and he took the bait. I just hope he knows what he's up against. Several hundred Indians may be a bit on the overwhelming side of things. They won't all be here at the fort. Some went after the rifle shipment coming out from St. Louis. Likely some of them will be following your uncle."

"You're scaring me with all of this talk about hundreds of Indians. Why there aren't that many of them in the whole west!"

"Ma'am,—"

"My name is Irene, please call me Irene."

"Okay, Irene, I don't know where you got your education but there are hundreds of thousands of Indians all over the plains and in the mountains. There used to be more, but over the last hundred years as many as two thirds of them died from cholera, the black plague, and countless diseases that we brought over from England. They died mostly because their immune systems have never been exposed to such a malady of illnesses. They're out there, Irene, and I hope for our sake the soldiers here understand what we're up against. If they don't, we'll go down in history as the men who failed a nation."

"You make it sound like the Alamo."

"Just like the Alamo."

"You'd better reload your gun. You're one round short."

"You may not have seen me do it, but I reloaded as soon as I fired through the bedroom window."

"I didn't notice."

"This is going to be a three-day siege in the short term. I don't see them pulling out before your uncle gets back, providing he gets back."

"I'm used to thinking in a more heartening manner. What's your name anyway?"

"Gastineau, the name is Ike Gastineau."

"I believe the best will happen and so the best usually does. When something else develops, I make adjustments and carry on."

"Yes, ma'am, providing you aren't dead."

"I shall go absolutely insane if I have to listen to your negative dribble for the next three days," Irene said.

"I'll try not to speak when my mind is making calculations. I, too, like to hope for the best, but my mind has a way of cataloging all possibilities prior to an event so whatever happens I'm ready for whatever comes next."

Silence overtook them and Irene Kennedy realized she had been viewing the man's statements incorrectly. *Of course, he was cataloging what might happen just as Uncle Winston was known to do. You couldn't plan for every eventuality he often said, but you could eliminate most of them on the basis of practical thinking. Usually only one answer was needed to eliminate several prospects if one thought the subject through well enough.*

If Ike Gastineau was capable of thinking in such a tactical manner, he was well advanced mentally for his years. For want of no other man she had ever seen, Irene Kennedy began developing a plan in her own mind, a plan which had nothing to do with Indians waiting for daybreak to resume their attack. If she was going to die right here and right now, she wanted to die in the arms of the man she loved!

"I'm frightened, Ike Gastineau," she said in the dark as she eyed the silhouette of her man from across the room.

"It will be alright," he assured her without moving.

There's a time for observation and for Irene Kennedy that time was past. There was also a time for action and the time was now. With her mind made up she got up from the floor where she had dropped into a fetal position at the sound of Ike's shot. Ever so carefully she made her way to Ike and stretched out her hand.

"Let's rest on the bed for now. It's softer and we have a few hours of darkness before we need to worry about Indians."

Ike looked up in abject fear. He knew about horses, he knew about cattle and a little about prospecting, but women? Not wanting to insult Irene he put out his hand and she helped him up from the floor. Well, she didn't really help him up at all; she did, however, hold his hand during the process. Then she led him over to her bed and sat on the mattress, urging Ike to do the same.

"You can use the pillows to lean back against the wall if you want. I'll make out just fine," she said as she rearranged the pillows for him.

He lay back and placed his head against the solid log wall where he could eye the now-broken window. Irene Kennedy took advantage of the familiarity of her own room and nestled in the bed beside him, placing her head on his shoulder. He melted instantly. Here was a girl he could love, and she was the niece of the man who killed his father. *How on earth could a relationship such as this even start?* he wondered as Irene snuggled closer to her aim.

With a long-drawn-out breath, Ike realized somehow the relationship had already commenced. Yielding to the awkward situation he placed his left arm around the girl as she burrowed herself deeper against his muscular frame. Finally at rest, Irene's left hand was on his chest just below her head. If he died right here, he would die a satisfied man. Neither of them spoke another word for the remainder of the night. All was dark and quiet outside, but inside two young bodies could hear each other breathing and Irene could hear Ike Gastineau's heartbeat, which was all she wanted.

Several things were happening as the two slept in quiet accord. Troop C was moving at night. Not willing to risk three days' absence from the fort, Colonel Scott was pushing his men and their horses beyond all endurance. They would arrive back at the fort in two days, tired maybe, but they would be alive. He hadn't thought about the possibility of another ambush in the same spot with dead troops lying all about, not until Sergeant Daniels brought up the idea.

"Sir, what's to stop the Indians from wiping us all out if we ride into the same canyon as Captain Johnston?"

"The difference, Sergeant, is we know what to expect."

"I beg your pardon, sir, but who's to say that Johnston didn't know what to expect. Captain Johnston was one of the best tacticians the army had to offer, and he rode right into a slaughter."

"Sergeant, sometimes you get under my skin, but that's why I like having you around. I suppose the situation bears greater study."

"I hope so. sir, because if we don't study this thing out proper, it's our own carcasses which will be feeding the buzzards before another day is gone."

"I haven't seen one Indian, sergeant. What do you make of that?"

"With all due respect, sir, I've seen several. If they don't want to be seen, you won't see them. When they're ready, you'll see plenty. They've been paralleling us all night."

"Do you believe Ike Gastineau's estimation of several hundred or more Indians?"

"I do, sir."

"Then God help us!"

Just before sunup, in the wee hours of dawn, the Indians began their attack at the fort. It was expected and the soldiers were ready. Two hours into the attack the Indians broke and ran.

C Troop rode in from the east and within minutes there was no sign of any hostiles. Colonel Scott looked around at the blood spots on the grounds, but the bodies of the Indians who spilled that blood were gone.

"Captain, secure the fort, get me an accurate count of troops, dead and wounded. I want to know what we have to work with."

"Yes, sir." Captain McGavin saluted and was gone.

"Sergeant, secure the horses and check the stock. I want to know what we've lost, and what we still have."

"Yes, sir."

As the colonel finished giving orders to the men, he stepped down from his mount to see Ike Gastineau, Junior standing in the doorway of his quarters with his arm around his niece. He looked on in disbelief, then pulled his rifle from the scabbard.

The colonel looked again with measured eyes. This was going to be one hell of a day. He had Indians to fight, and these two youngsters were making googly eyes at one another.

"Young man, I want to see you in my office, now!"

Ike took his hand from around Irene and started down the boardwalk between the buildings. He walked step by step to meet the colonel at his office the moment he reached the front door.

Colonel Scott paused just before opening the door to his office. "Love, is it?"

"It wasn't a planned thing, sir."

"No, I suspect not."

The colonel pushed open the door to his office and stepped in. He hung his cavalry hat on the rack just inside his door, then placed his weapons on a table near the entrance. Walking over to his desk, he unstrapped his cartridge belt and laid his pistol aside.

"You want to tell me about it?"

"About what, sir?"

"About your love affair with my niece!"

"Sir, don't you want to hear about the Indian attack?"

"I'll get that report directly from my men, now what's going on?"

"We're in love, sir."

"Love? You met less than twenty-four hours ago!"

"I am aware of that sir, but we're in love."

Colonel Scott placed his head in his hands and shook it from side to side. He knew how to handle men, he knew how to handle horses, but how did he go about handling two youngsters in heat? Of all the people for Irene to fall in love with!

"I'm going to have to hear from her before I'll ever believe the two of you are in love."

"I wasn't looking for it, sir."

"I just bet you weren't."

Irene appeared in the doorway and Colonel Scott ordered her into the room. "Come in here, young lady. What have you got to say about this?"

"Uncle Winston, we spent the night together last night. I love him. We didn't do anything but fight Indians, but we do love one another."

"One Indian fight and you're in love! My God, child, what do you think love is?"

"Whatever it is, I choose this man."

"Man? He isn't even dry behind the ears yet."

Ike interrupted. "May I say something, sir?"

"Please do; as post commander, it's my duty to know what's going on in that head of yours."

"We want to get married right away."

Colonel Scott stared in disbelief. "Married? I absolutely forbid it."

"But, Uncle Winston, it's what we want."

"Young lady, one of these days you're going to learn you don't get everything in life that you want. As post commander, I would have to do the honors, and that I will not do. Now, if you two love birds will excuse me, I have a fort to run."

Chapter 3

Colonel Scott readied his men for another attack. From the reports he received, he understood the young Ike Gastineau to be very good with his weapons. To a man, his troops insisted it had been his sharp shooting abilities that kept the Indians at bay long enough for C Troop to return.

They lost only one man: Private Dunsford, a young recruit of eighteen. He stuck his head up at the wrong time. The burial detail was preparing for the funeral as the colonel ascertained his troops strength and ability. He found he couldn't discount the ability of one young man, one stranger in his midst, the one who wanted to marry his niece.

By all accounts the young Gastineau had killed between ten and seventeen Indians on his own. *That's a lot of killing in any book.* What pained the colonel was the fact he had to note such a thing in his daily log. He made the notation then set about to prepare his men for the next attack, the one he knew would come at dawn, this time with many more Indians in the force. He had drawn some of them off with his ride the night before, but the Indians would join forces now.

There was strength in numbers, but what he had to remember was the fact that the Indians would really outnumber them now. They had gotten lucky defending the fort against the last attack. The question was how much of their luck remained? What about the rifle shipment? If Ike Gastineau's information was correct, the Indians would have sent a party after the new rifles coming into the fort. He could only pray they didn't get their hands on them.

Getting up from his desk, he stepped outside to survey the fort, looking for the weak spots which would need defending. They had gotten lucky the night before, but they couldn't count on luck again. This evening would require a great deal more than luck. On the other hand, they didn't need to worry about an attack until morning. The Indians had lost enough men the night before to be cautious of any night-time assault.

There were no real walls up yet, only the towers which indicated the four corners of the fort. He thought about the post and its completion, it should have had the walls up by now, but he'd had other pressing matters to attend to. If they survived this attack, he would not wait any longer. Those walls could mean the difference between life and death, and right now they were not in place.

Grabbing the sergeant, he gave instructions as to where he wanted each troop, and the number of men at each location. He also gave orders for a certain amount of ammunition at those locations. There could be no mistakes, no shortages of men or ammo at any given spot.

Just after lunch he gathered the entire fort together on the parade ground and gave them a quick talk. "Men, I can't afford to lose even one of you, so stay alert, keep your head down and make every shot count. No warning shot, if you have to give a warning shot, you had better be killing an Indian, understood?"

They all answered in the affirmative, and he continued. "We are going to be outnumbered nearly four to one, but we have the better weapons. We need to make sure we kill an Indian every time we pull the trigger. If you are wounded, patch the wound and keep fighting.

"We have new weapons headed our way, but we can't go after them. We can only hope they arrive in spite of the efforts by our enemies to get their hands on them. No one knows the outcome of this evening or tomorrow, but I want each of you to know, I am proud to serve with you. Now, A Company, you eat first. We'll be eating in shifts until further notice.

"Sergeant, you may dismiss the men."

The fort was quiet as dusk turned to night. There was no longer any movement. Like the evening before, no one would be out and about, but all would be held up in a predetermined location with plenty of ammunition. The fort was on lockdown. If someone needed to go to the bathroom, they would have to improvise. Even the ladies of the fort were on lock down.

It was nearing sunrise before the first Indian was spotted and he didn't live long. As he moved along the ground one of the soldiers in the south tower squeezed off a shot and the Indian fell face down into the dirt. Then, there was nothing to shoot at, but the entire fort was alerted.

For nearly an hour there was no movement from either side. The Indians were just out of shooting range making dust out in the desert, moving to and fro at will. The Indians were too far away to hit if shot at, so all the soldiers could do was watch in curiosity. This was not a preferred strategy, but there was nothing anyone could do.

About noon the Indians drew a little closer, but still they were out of range. Soldiers were watching all sides of Fort Union. Many of the buildings had been built eighteen inches off the desert floor, meaning anyone could get up under them if they wanted. This was something everyone had to watch for: an Indian under a fort building would not be a good thing.

When the main attack came it was late in the afternoon, during the hottest part of the day. The heat was stifling, making uniformed men strip their blouses. Even the colonel had stripped down to stay cool. Little did he know it, but this one move had saved his life. The Indians were head hunting, and the colonel was the head they wanted.

Without wearing his military blouse, they could not identify the colonel and the attack broke quickly. The Indians had been much closer than expected, but they had paid a dear price once they made their presence known. Moving targets were quickly eliminated in all directions and heavy casualties were taken by the rogue Indians.

Colonel Scott asked for an accounting of men and found he had lost none. He was pleased with the result so far, but there was still a long fight ahead. Until he or the Indians got those rifles, there would be a standoff at the fort.

Scott wondered just how many Indians were out there. Hundreds was a good guess, but how many hundreds? Three, six, eight, he needed to know. He could not stand a siege if there were fifteen hundred Indians waiting for them to make a mistake.

So far, he had identified Sioux and Apache, but what other tribes were involved? What about the Comanche, Cheyenne, and Kiowa? They were all in this part of the country as well, not to mention Pima, Yuma, and Ute.

Had the chiefs come together to facilitate one last giant raid on a Federal Post? If that was the case, Fort Union was in serious trouble. He had already lost C Troop; he could not afford to lose any more men.

Suddenly Ike Gastineau Jr. was beside him. "Colonel, how far out is that wagon?"

It took a moment to register in the colonel's mind. "My guess would be two, maybe three days from here, and it isn't one wagon, it's no less than seven."

"Colonel, we've got to warn them."

"Son, we are completely surrounded by Indians. You want to tell me just how I am supposed to do that?"

Silence filled the air for a few minutes then Ike spoke up. "I can try to sneak out in the middle of the night. If I can warn them, maybe we can make it back to the fort in the dark."

"I can't let you do that. My niece would hate me if something happened to you. If you go, I risk our entire relationship."

"Sir, I beg your pardon, but if the Indians get their hands on all those guns and ammunition, Fort Union will be wiped out. Everyone here will die, including Irene. We don't have a choice."

"Do you really think you can get through?" Colonel Scott studied the young man as never before, and then remembered his father.

"I have a good chance if I go late enough."

"Alright, but If anything happens to you, I'll never hear the end of it."

"I'll be careful, Colonel, and you keep an eye on that niece of yours. She has a mind of her own."

"You're not telling me anything I don't already know."

Chapter 4

At two in the morning, Ike Gastineau Jr. slipped off his boots, slipped into his moccasins, gave Irene a swift kiss on the cheek and started out of the fort. He carried no weapon but a knife. Any combat he might have on this evening would be hand to hand. If he made the wrong step, he would find himself among Indians up to his neck.

His side was bandaged up, and he had stripped down to his pants. His footprints must look like that of an Indian brave come morning if he was able to get through the lines. If he failed, everyone at the fort would be at risk of dying, and he did not want to see such a thing happen to be his one true love. Funny, they had just met, but it seemed as though they had known one another for eternity. No one needed to tell him how important it was that he got through, and if he did, the next question was, how did he get home with the wagons in tow?

He knew the Indians for the most part would be sleeping, but there were always one or two light sleepers. It was the light sleepers he had to keep shy of. Some would be up because they were worked up. He also had to avoid stumbling upon an encampment blindly in the dark.

A short way out from the fort he heard running steps in the sand behind him. Palming his knife, he turned just in time to thrust it into the chest of a young Indian brave. He fell the man flat on his back and drove the knife into his heart while holding his left hand over the Indian's mouth. It was a muffled cry; in the dark of night, it fell on deaf ears.

He scalped the young Indian brave, then slid the scalp over his own head and continued to walk his way to the east, braids dangling. If spotted now, he would look more like an Indian and no one would likely bother him, but he still needed to keep shy of any encampments as he didn't speak their language.

He walked until sunup and continued to walk. Late in the morning he spotted a stray Indian pony and ran it down. He got upon its back and began to ride, still wearing the scalp and moccasins. His skin was sun tanned, but not near so dark as the usual Indian, so he wasn't fully confident in his measures, but he was doing all he could to look and act like one of them. He only hoped that they were convinced.

Bumping the pony with his heels he lost his moccasin off his left foot. Within ten minutes the other fell off as well. He didn't bother to stop and retrieve them but kept riding to warn the wagons of the impending attack. It would be a miracle if he found them, but he had to. The fort needed those guns, and they needed the ammo.

He rode alone as the sun came up in front of him. For several minutes he was blinded by the light which seemed relentless. During those minutes he rode very slowly, continued to check his back trail and both sides. When a man rides alone, he is always riding point, picking up the drag and watching everything in between if he planned to survive.

Ike was not ready to die. He had no intention of dying, but the odds were stacked against him. It would take a miracle to get those wagons through to the fort. It would take a miracle for them to not be in the hands of the Indians already, yet he pressed onward. Chances were slim that the Indians had not yet attacked, or that the wagons had managed to get this far, but like the outcome or not, he had to know. Lives depended on it.

With so many Indians in the area, he was surprised that he had not seen any since sunup.

Wide open desert surrounded Fort Union, and the Indians would be thick as prickly pear in the sand for miles surrounding the fort. Truth be known, he never expected to get through them without much of a fight. He had expected all sorts of trouble, but he had slipped through.

Then he saw the wagons in the distance. He was directly in their path. He also saw the Indians flanking them in the hills both north and south. They were ready to attack, just waiting for a signal from their leader. *Were the men inside ready? Did they have some rifles loaded ready to shoot? If not, they were about to die,* he thought to himself.

He continued to walk the pony toward the head of the column of wagons. The distance was closing, but it seemed not fast enough. At one hundred yards Ike threw the scalp from his head and spurred the pony forward with all he had. He was immediately recognized as a traitor by the Indians, yet a fellow white man by the wagon drivers.

As he reached the first wagons the canvas dropped on all of them, and each wagon had a driver and a sharpshooter. Leaping from his pony he joined the boys in the first wagon; and boys they were: not quite so old as he himself. It shocked him at first and he started to say something, but when the first bullet spat wood into his face, he grabbed a Winchester and began firing. Suddenly he stopped. They weren't going to hit anything until the Indians got closer.

"Save your ammo," he yelled over the gunfire.

The guns settled down as the wagons picked up more speed.

"Hold your fire until you have them point blank!"

"How far is it to the fort?" the driver of the first wagon yelled.

"Four, maybe five miles, and it's surrounded by Indians."

"Keep the wagons in line until we get close, then spread them out," Ike yelled to the wagons bringing up the drag.

Each wagon had an eight-mule team, because guns and ammunition are a heavy burden, not to mention any food or water along for the ride. There was one outrider, and he had tied his horse to the last wagon before jumping in. They were making about twenty-five miles an hour, flying by the standards of those wagons as heavy-laden as they were. The boys could only hope they stayed together.

Shots were fired randomly by the Indians, but nothing such as an accurate shot was coming through. Occasionally one got close, but it was becoming clear no one had instructed them as to how one actually can take aim and hit the target with a white man's rifle. When they figured that out, all hell would break loose.

The Indians closed in but didn't get too close. They were not making themselves readily available as targets.

"Why aren't they attacking?"

The lead driver looked over his shoulder. "We had a shootout with them a couple of days ago. They know better than to get close."

"You've been fighting Indians for two days?"

"No, just one, they've been riding our flank ever since."

All the young men could do was watch the Indians ride beside them at a distance. They knew what was waiting up ahead, they knew the wagons were about to ride headlong into several hundred warriors.

"Okay, drivers, get down behind your seats and spread out the wagons!"

To a man the drivers did as told, not wanting to offer up a fresh target for the Indians they could see up ahead. In less than a minute, seven wagons were spread out heading at breakneck speed for Fort Union. One building was on fire, and so was one corner of the post, the south lookout tower, but the Indians had not yet taken the fort.

As the wagons began to tear through the Indian stronghold, the boys with rifles took out any targets closest to them. One Indian jumped over the rail siding of one wagon, but he was dispatched before he could scramble up to his knees in the moving wagon. He fell out of the back, dead.

Another Indian grabbed at the tailgate of the wagon Ike was riding in and he never took another step, thanks to a soldier in the bed firing immediately. Suddenly the wagons were pulling in tight to one another, the only way they could fit seven eight mule teams onto the parade grounds of Fort Union.

As the mules outran the Indians, the drivers brought them to stops within the fort; the men jumped down and began filling the hands of every soldier with a Winchester model .73. The rifles were already loaded. The Indians took so many casualties in all directions those first few minutes they pulled back more than a mile. More loaded rifles were placed in the watchtowers and the fires extinguished.

As the soldiers began to unload the wagons an old Indian chief came riding up on his horse, displaying a signal for parlay. Colonel Scott walked out to meet him and gave a sign of peace.

The chief spoke solemnly but with great strength. "We gather our dead in peace, we go now."

Colonel Scott saluted the Indian and watched him ride away. As he turned back to face Ike, Irene was already in his arms looking at the dried blood all over his head, searching for the wound which was not there.

"It's okay, honey."

"I've never been so happy to see anyone in my whole life," Colonel Scott admitted.

"Me, neither," said Sergeant Major Ivy.

Ike leaned down and kissed Irene on the lips, then looked into her eyes. "Youuuuuu had better be worth it," he said with the biggest smile Irene had ever seen.

Cyndi Williams-Barnier

I grew up in what was once the small town of Beaufort, S.C., with a population of approximately 6,300 in the early 1960s. Our small town now has a grandiose population of nearly 13,000, and the county 191,000! Things sure have changed!

After graduating from Beaufort High School, I went on to the University of S.C.-Beaufort studying Advanced Composition. From there I worked for S.C. Probation, Parole, and Pardons. After a 20-year career with the Beaufort County Emergency Management Division, I entered retirement. About the same time, we moved to our retirement house in Ridgeland, S.C.

In retirement I caught up with my dear friend Jack Gannon from Beaufort High School, where we often talked about writing books and were even planning out our storyline and characters for a book that we wanted to write. As fate would have it, we lost touch with each other after graduation. Fast forward some 32 years, we reconnected and finally began writing the book we talked about so long ago. To date we've written nine books in total with more to come!

In 2016, Jack and I formed an LLC called YBR Publishing. Not long after, my husband Bill signed on as our Chief Editor and Staff Manager. To date, we have published 29 books for clients (including the one in your hands now), with many more to come.

When not working on client's books, I can be found with my "lap warmer" cat, "Scooter".

MOTHER'S COFFIN

We've all heard the phrase "humor in real life". This is one perfect instance: a day many years ago when Cyndi's mother decided she wanted to shop for her own coffin. As she told Jack, it was a killer day!...

Mother insists on driving to the funeral home today, no matter that I always do the driving for her. This is her day, I suppose; she wants to pick out a coffin and begin the morbid closure to her seventy-five years.

She seems happy, almost giddy about the trip. Shopping always cheers her up; I don't know why I thought this day would be any different, but this isn't the kind of shopping I had in mind when she said she wanted to go out. I mean, look at her: she dressed up, put on powder, lipstick, and mascara. She's wearing her good knee-highs, the ones without runs in them. She put on that tacky silk blouse: the one with the yellow toucans and their big green bills.

Oh, God, I just saw her put her teeth in while she was driving! Just the uppers; she quit wearing the lowers years ago, she says they just aren't comfortable anymore. *"Hey, Mom, you wanna talk about uncomfortable?"* I'd like to say. *"I'm uncomfortable beyond all uncomfortableness! After all, why can't we die and let some other poor guys worry about picking out our coffin? Let them figure out how to pay for the expensive funeral (that no one wants to come to)."*

My nerves are on edge, as I've never had the pleasure of coffin shopping before, and I don't quite know what to expect. Where's a coffin expert when you need one?

Thoughts race through my mind as I stare out the car window; momentarily I recede to a hidden place in my mind; a darkened room lined with black pine boxes—I see vampires lying in repose, hiding from the sun. My shoes echo loudly with each click of my heel, walking slowly on the cold concrete floor—

Dracula's already here, he lies in wait, ready to push open the coffin lid and jump out with fangs bared—

Horns blare loudly as we whiz through an intersection, wrenching me from thoughts of bloodsuckers and back to the reality at hand. "Mother, you ran a red light again," I say with no emotion, but I really want to yell, *"Mother, you nearly got us killed again!"* I can't do that though. Hunched over the steering wheel, she squints at the rear-view mirror, mouth half open, and shrugs her shoulders as she usually does. This is the reason I always drive. I'm not ready to pick out my own coffin just yet, thank you.

We pull into the driveway of the funeral home, gravel crunching beneath the tires as we travel down the long tree-lined road. Spanish moss billows in the gentle wind, giving a come-hither appeal to the place.

My stomach does a little flip, acknowledging the fact that some sort of end is near. This funeral home looks like any other in the south: long porches with white columns out front, beckoning with that "Gone With The Wind" motif. Was this supposed to put us at ease? Looking around, I wonder at the expense of keeping up a place like this, mowing all the grass, paying the high electric bill to keep it heated and cooled—especially for the dead folks, they gotta stay cool. No wonder we pay so much for a funeral!

We park the car and walk slowly up the steps to the front door. I hold my mother's frail arm in my arm, silently leading her to some unspoken finality. If I wasn't uncomfortable before now...

A gold-plated sign attached to the exterior greets us, reminding us to enter quietly and reverently. Really, ya think? I was actually thinking about popping a Bud-Light and screeching "howdy y'all" when I got inside. It was just a moment of irony and morbidity screaming through this ridiculous reality, perhaps.

I open the door, guiding my mother behind me. She attempts to charge past me, not allowing the door to latch fully. I want to ask, *"What's the hurry, Mother? Not like there's a Kmart*

Blue Light special here." My eyes search the foyer, half expecting to be greeted by Lurch from the Addams Family, with his black coat-and-tails, and sunken hollow eyes. "You rang?" Lurch would say, with his deep, gravelly voice.

Instead, a tiny, older man shuffles in, looking much like Tim Conway's comic "Old Man" character, with the quick little steps and crazy white hair. He extends his hand and cocks his head sideways in a surreal postulation of sympathy. "Welcome to the Sweet Rivers Funeral Home," says the small man, smiling.

I'm thinking, *Sweet Rivers—What river? There's no river anywhere near here.* Mother blurts out the reason for our appointment, and the man says he will show us to the viewing room where we can view the wide selection of beautiful custom-made caskets. Slowly we proceed down the long hallway. Old wooden floors creak beneath our feet. More white ornate columns and crafted molding stand out and greet us as we proceed forward. It smells old and musty, with a hint of mothballs.

The sign beside the door reads "Caskets". *Caskets? Not coffins?* Then it hits me; the proper term is "caskets". It must be the southerner contained within that provides the reason.

We follow the man to the viewing room, and I'm staring at the expansive balding spot on the back of his head. I'm suddenly reminded of the growing bald spots on my mother's head, and how the chemotherapy eats away at her, poisoning everything from the inside out.

The man takes his leave, giving us free reign to run around the multiple aisles of coffins—I mean caskets—lie in 'em, take them for a test drive, whatever. Suddenly there's a desire to kick a tire or two, but there's not a tire in sight.

"Ohhhh, this one looks nice," I hear mother say from across the room. She gazes happily at me and says, "It looks soft inside." Really? "Soft"? Is coffin softness supposed to be a deciding factor for your eternal rest? As if you can roll over if it's not soft enough.

Mother walks down all the aisles of coffins, inspecting each for the qualities she finds appealing. According to her, the coffin needs to be "comfy", not too masculine but not too feminine, either. She doesn't like the ones with ruffles and frills, nor does she like the ones with dark wood and heavy-looking; she says the pallbearers will have a hard time carrying her as it is.

I roll my eyes as my head falls backwards in a gesture of impatience. Images of men straining, knees buckling under her 90-pound weight comes to mind, and I almost laugh aloud.

I hate this room, and all that it stands for. I look around at menacing death boxes, open and taunting, waiting to ingest its occupant like a Venus Fly Trap closing in on its prey. I don't want to be here, but I must be here. Honor Thy Mother and Thy Father. It's what I do; like it or not. In the past, I was so impatient with her—if only I could go back in time and change the ugly things I said. If only she could have been a better mother.

The reality is as comedic as the purple velvet coffin she's just found. "This is it!" she shouts. "Look at the beautiful purple velvet!" My eyebrows raise involuntarily as I look around, thinking Elvis might be close by. In a high-pitched voice I say, "Mother, it's purple, and it's velvet—don't you think it's kind of tacky?"

Her eyes lock onto my eyes and the word "incredulous" resonates on her face, signaling me to stand tall, smile wistfully and amend what I just said. "Just kidding! The light oak wood is really pretty," I say, trying to take back the previous words.

The purple velvet coffin with the light oak wood is selected and placed on a short payment plan. The man wants a down payment, just like one you would put on a car. Now I really want to kick a tire. Put wheels on it and we can hook it up to the back of the car and wheel it home—set it up in the living room for the next few months and mother's little-old-lady friends can "ooooh and aaaah" over it. Mother can polish its wooden exterior with Pledge and spray Scotch Guard on the velvet, just in case they spill iced tea on it. What a great conversation piece it will be.

Ten thousand dollars later, give or take, we're out the door and heading back home. Mother is still excited about our little shopping excursion and her head is buzzing with thoughts of spending more money. "When we get home, we need to talk about hiring an attorney, and writing up a will, and have him write up a 'Do Not Resuscitate Order' for the hospital, and—" she goes on and on as we whiz through another red light.

"Sure, Mother. Whatever you want." I just close my eyes at each intersection.

She's actually happy to be at the end of her life's journey, making plans for now and the hereafter. "—and I want you to make sure my grass is kept cut and don't let anyone cut down my tulip tree, and don't sell that house, that was your father's house, you know. Oh, and we have to go clothes shopping, I need a new outfit for the funeral. Let's stop at Belk on the way home."

I hang my head in resignation, and wonder how long she really has left…
`

INTRUDER

This was a little suspense story Jack and I wrote several years ago and submitted to a publisher who was producing a noir-style suspense short story anthology, "Amazing Adventures", which was published in late 2014. This story is based on a true event.

Sleep came as it always did: slowly, accompanied by continual turns and kicks as I strove for some semblance of the ever-elusive comfort of the bed. My mind waited for the chemical assistance to kick in. I've always been puzzled as to why I stayed in this house, after that incident. Eventually, my bed won out as it did every night, and I finally drifted off to a restless sleep.

# # #

The noise was loud, jarring. It had to be loud and jarring, as I'd been snoozing deeply with the welcome help of several sleeping pills and a tall glass of red wine—I'd needed extra reinforcements to help push myself, once again, into slumberland—to drive me over the edge for a while, so I could forget, at least for a few hours.

I woke from the unnerving sound to the black abyss of the bedroom; shades closed, door locked, the way I needed it, the way it had to be. That thunderous noise I'd heard sounded like, well, distant cannon fire.

The pills and wine left me groggy, not knowing where I was or what was going on. My mind battled for sudden, needed clarity. My body surged with electricity, anticipating the worst, just like with every sudden sound anymore. I sat up, now cognizant that I was in my own bed, and listened. My hearing was attuned to every noise.

Sounds of distant footsteps and muffled voices permeated the bedroom door. Adrenalin-fueled fear forced blood to course into my brain, pound into the arteries, echo in my ears.

Unlike my father, I'd chosen not to think about or look at people's race, the color of their skin, pre-judging them—even though it's the South, and even though I'd been taught otherwise during the 70s, I suppose I was the family rebel. Why did someone's skin color matter, anyway?

My mind races back to that long-ago terrifying night when others broke in: *the sounds thrashing around in my head, remembering the men, the guns, them yelling, "On the floor!" I remember their dark skin, nappy hair, black eyes, and sweat.* I think for the zillionth time it didn't have to happen. Yet they ruined me, my life. All had been so peaceable twenty years ago. Within minutes, they'd destroyed everything. Nothing was the same afterward. Walking through stores, driving down the road, even a stroll down a sidewalk; all these years I've felt the fear, feeling their eyes following me everywhere.

The evil ones in my shadowy nightmares, the haunting demons that show up, make sleep fail me night after night. The memories of that night so long ago; they grabbed me from behind, creating the sounds of ripping cloth. I'll never forget the feel of that icy gun barrel on my neck, of strange people's hands on my body, touching, penetrating, the screaming, demands, humiliation. Every night since, I wake in a sweat to the recurring nightmare, my heart pounding like it's ready to explode from my chest—but no one's there in the silent darkness.

I quietly push aside the covers and slide out of bed, feeling my way through the darkness. My hands shake as I check to make sure that the door's still locked, just like I do throughout the day anyway—a long-standing ritual, rehearsed to perfection over the years, because of *them*.

Soundlessly I step toward the dresser bureau, hoping the socks I wore muffled my slow steps.

My fingers find Father's old service revolver in the dresser's top drawer, the one he'd used before he retired from law enforcement; the one I inherited when he died. The one he should have used on those men, long ago. It was an old .38-special six-shooter, still in its original black weave leather holster, sleeping in the same place for years. All six bullets nested snuggly inside the chamber—they waited, just like me.

Those voices—they're men's voices—came closer to the bedroom door. Again, my mind races back twenty years, anticipating the worst. The telephone sits atop the dresser, as does my cell phone, and I briefly consider that I should call for help, but I—don't—want—to. The thought is quickly lost in time, as fully rehearsed over the years.

I can always say I didn't have time or couldn't find the phone in the dark. They couldn't arrest me, they wouldn't. It's self-defense after all. I'm the innocent one.

Once the men find the locked bedroom door, they'll instantly know that someone's hiding inside. They'll crash through just as they did the front door only moments ago.

The time's ultimately here. I wondered how many years it'd taken them to get here. Could it be the same men? Had they come back again, all these years later? My brain flies into panic overload. I'd planned, rehearsed, schemed, dreamed—not knowing when it would happen. So many nights I'd lie in bed, thinking of how to get back, to get even.

When alone, I'd yell aloud at the invisible enemies. "You son-of-a-bitch," I'd scream at them, tears rolling down my face. I ruminated on what weapon I'd use: a knife, or a gun, and somehow torture them the way they tortured me.

I longed to see the fear in their eyes, wanting them to feel, hear, smell, and experience the entire event of terror, just as I had. For so long I've wanted them to know helplessness, feel how the world closes in, the panic, the inability to breathe in the throes of horror. Now, as it's happening, I wish I could go back and plan more for this long-awaited event.

It seems it came too soon, with no warning, in fast motion, without time to think each reaction through to its end. My hands still shake uncontrollably, my heart pounds loud in my ears, and my throat's dry. Desperately focusing on the door, my pupils dilate, and I wait for any light that might possibly stream through when it dissolves into splinters at the hands of the intruders.

Crashing noises come from the dining area, just outside the bedroom door; instinctively I jump at the sound. Their fumbling in the near dark resulted in the mishap of knocking over China and decorative vases that rested on the buffet.

Sounds of cursing from the intruders gave knowledge to the fact that they were in the house and obviously heard by those slumbering nearby.

I wonder what could be going through their minds, the adrenaline rushing through their veins. Are they just as afraid? Who are these men, how had their lives lead them to this one event that would predict to be the last day of their lives?

Do they have any inkling of what's behind this bedroom door, awaiting them, their "unsuspecting" victim within hoping they'd crash in to meet their end? Do they have families, children, wives who would miss them when they're gone? Did they just happen by the neighborhood, or was this planned, nice and tidy?

These intruders could be capable of raping, torturing, killing anyone that might cross their path. It's a likely possibility, because that's the caliber of person pilfering my house at this very moment.

The band on the holster is snapped open, exposing the hammer, ready to fire at will. Old leather groans and stretches as the gun is removed. The faithful revolver waits patiently in my hand, to ease someone into their final fate. It lets me glide the hammer back with such simplicity. The metallic sound of the hammer almost echoes in the dark room—click, click, click, rotating the cylinder once to the left. The gun feels as if it were yawning, *"I'm here to help you, let's get it over with so I can go back to sleep."*

Its wooden handle is smooth and worn from years of target practice. The steel on the Smith & Wesson's barrel is cold, cold like the souls of the men who have broken into the house. All six bullets are in place, unemotional, menacing. Silver-colored casings with lead tips are baby bombs, made to obliterate someone's life.

Kneeling on the floor beside the bed, I wait and listen, anticipating what'll happen next. Somehow, I thought I'd be braver than this, steadier than this, angrier than this. Yet, I've longed for this moment for years.

Ah, finally—a rush of expectation and excitement hits at once. I shake off my trepidation, reverting to the position of the aggressor. I'm finally ready, ready for the thrill of being "the victim", having to shoot someone for self-preservation, of course. I await the pleasure of hearing their screams while I fire the weapon, once, twice, maybe three times, however many times it takes. I would watch them fall to the floor in the near darkness as their blood splattered on the walls, on the carpet, and on me. Hearing them gasp that final breath, the one that won't come soon enough to end the pain and suffering that I alone have inflicted, is the perfect sound of a debt paid.

This all runs through my mind like a reel-to-reel film in just moments, skipping and crackling through my brain, as I sit waiting for them to kick in the door—how long could it take them to figure out that the prize is behind door number one?

However, all I hear is silence. Dead silence. Could it be they got what they wanted, and left? Did they steal what they needed, and moved on as quickly as they entered? Did they hear me in the bedroom and flee?

No, they can't! What about my nightmares? They'll never end now! I agonize in the sudden fear that my tortuous nights will haunt me for uncounted more years to come. I may never get to do that one forbidden thing that all of us think about doing: killing another human.

I argue with myself, wondering if I should go look for them, look for that fight. This couldn't happen! It can't be all for nothing.

The minutes pass and fade. I can't wait any longer.

I step to the door, unlock it, open it, and face my fate as it stands there waiting for me, as much as I've waited for it. Our eyes lock in mutual surprise! We raise our guns toward each other in unison in combined offense and defense. But only one gunshot thunders in the night.

In a moment the silence was broken by the sound of one…body…dropping…

YBR PUBLISHING, LLC

YBR was created just to publish a Christmas memoir. But as other authors saw the book on our display shelf at book signings or conventions, we began receiving inquiries about helping other authors get their books into print. Thus, in 2016 was born, and in 2017 it went public with its first client's book "Emerald" by Ridgeland, SC author Garry Richardson. At this writing (March 2023), YBR Publishing has produced 31 published books for authors in the United States and England, including this edition in your hands; 23 are 5-star award winners, as reviewed by Readers' Favorite, LLC.

The mission of YBR Publishing is to help writers of most any genre get their stories into print with professional editing and production comparable to larger publishing houses in shorter turnaround times.

Please visit our website www.ybrpub.com to learn more about us, and perhaps submit your own manuscript for free review and even potential publishing!

YBR Publishing is now accepting submissions for:

Tales On The Yellow Brick Road 2024

Submissions are due by December 31, 2023. Please send all short stories, poems, etc., to contact@ybrpub.com with the subject line "2024 Anthology". Include an introduction about yourself and your submission.

Acceptance is not a guarantee for inclusion. All submissions will be reviewed according to normal publishing standards for determination of inclusion in the next anthology.

www.ingramcontent.com/pod-product-compliance
Lightning Source LLC
Chambersburg PA
CBHW070452300726
48975CB00007B/2134